Laughter's Echo

Cyberworld Publishing

www.cyberworldpublishing.com

ISBN 978-0-9808011-2-5

Cyberworld Publishing is an imprint of
Puppy Care Education *publisher*
Jindalee St, Toronto, Asutralia

Koniotis Mysteries Series

Each book in this series stands alone, but they are also all connected in various ways and form the different parts of one story.

Laughter's

Echo

Koniotis Mysteries - Book One

by Gina Drew

Caitlyn's map of sites visited in this book

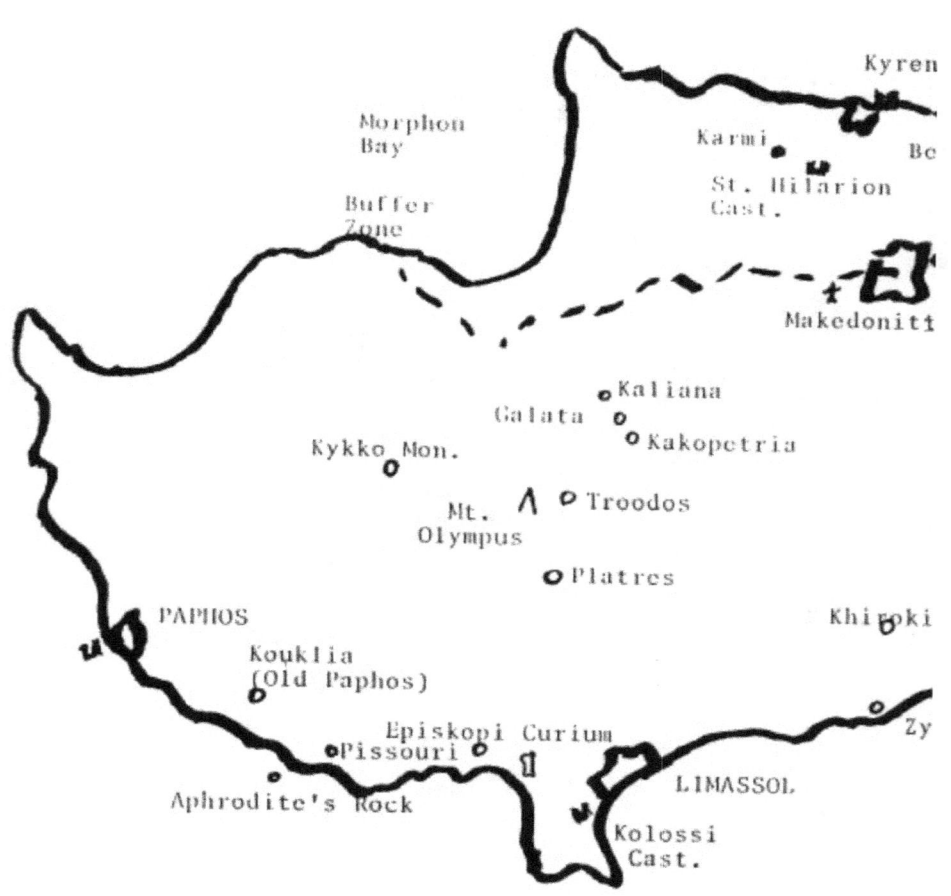

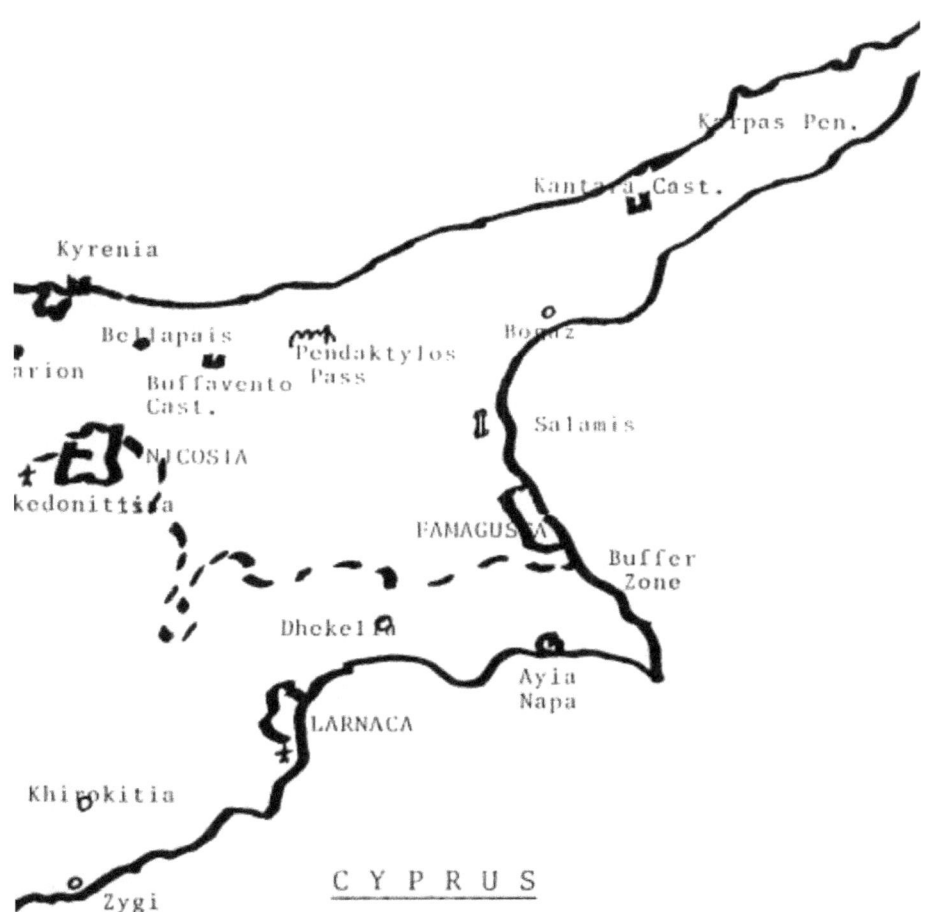

Karpas Pen.

Kantara Cast.

Kyrenia

Bellapais

Pendaktylos
Pass

Boğaz

arion

Buffavento
Cast.

Salamis

NICOSIA

kedonitti:a

FAMAGUSTA

Buffer
Zone

Dhekelia

Ayia
Napa

LARNACA

Khirokitia

C Y P R U S

Zygi

Primary Characters:

Paul Conte—American Embassy political officer

Viktor Gorodov—Russian; deputy UN coordinator for Cyprus

Takis Koniotis—Chief of Cypriot police department International Investigations Unit

Bob Murray—American; Pharmaceutical distributor; husband of Jill Murray

Jill Murray—American Embassy economic officer; wife of Bob Murray

Nicos Petrou—Former Cypriot president; deceased husband of Nora Petrou and father of Vassos Petrou

Nora Petrou—Cypriot Bank and travel agency CEO; wife of deceased Nicos Petrou and stepmother of Vassos Petrou

Vassos Petrou—Cypriot MP and newspaper publisher; son of deceased Nicos Petrou and stepson of Nora Petrou

Eleni Piccard—Cypriot; Shipping and handicraft industry CEO; wife of missing Guy Piccard, mother of missing Pierre Piccard, and aunt of Jacques Piccard

Guy Piccard—French; Missing husband of Eleni Piccard, father of missing Pierre Piccard, and uncle of Jacques Piccard

Jacques Piccard—French Ambassador to Cyprus; nephew of Eleni Piccard and of missing Guy Piccard

Pierre Piccard—Missing son of Eleni and Guy Piccard

Kurt Schwin—German; Missing fiancé of Caitlyn Spencer

Caitlyn Spencer—American archaeologist in Cyprus on Fulbright project

Maria Solonos—Assistant to Takis Koniotis at Cypriot police department International Investigations Unit

Alec Stuart—British High Commission political officer

Andriko Visiliou—Chief archaeologist at Kaliana dig

St Hilarion Fortress

Chapter One

The most unnerving part of the experience was the echoing laughter. The laughter, more a sense of hysteria wafting in and out of the breezes rising up the mountain off the Mediterranean below than a real sound that others around her could hear, was calling forth the most disturbing memories. Or maybe it was not laughter at all. Maybe it was just the way the wind whistled in the pine trees. Caitlyn was shaking uncontrollably. This did not help her in the least to maneuver the steep and rocky trail rising from the lower to the middle ward of the St. Hilarion crusader castle. It also did not help that Paul Conte, her somewhat irritating escort from the American embassy, was already at the gate of the middle ward, grinning down at her and asking if she was all right. Did she need him to come back down and help her up?

All right? Help her up? Caitlyn's irritation momentarily wiped out the inexplicable sense of foreboding that had set in as soon as their car had climbed to the dell at the foot of the St. Hilarion peak. Paul had been showing off his manliness and signaling his interest ever since they had left Cyprus's capital, Nicosia, that morning and cleared through the checkpoint to this excursion into the Turkish zone. But Caitlyn wasn't remotely interested in playing the admiring cheerleader. She was an experienced American archaeologist, on the Mediterranean island of Cyprus to work on a major excavation project. She had been roughing it for years. Hiking a simple mountain pathway was a piece of cake.

But, then she reached the stone terrace in front of the gate into the middle ward. She involuntarily looked up at the tower of the high ward rising out of the rock cliff immediately above her head and was immediately overwhelmed by the vision.

She had been unwillingly cramped up in this alternately drafty and smoky hall of the castle's middle ward for the better part of a week of evenings. Worse, for the entire time she had been forced to endure both the narcissistic droning of the young royal representative and the openly assessing ogling of the Bulgarian mercenaries. She had somehow displeased Queen Eleanor. Perhaps she had too insistently queried why they had come by choice to this castle, under siege by the Genoese. Eleanor of Aragon had held her husband's brother, Prince John, responsible for her husband's death and the abandonment of her son, Peter, into the hands of the Genoese. Only the Bulgarian mercenaries remained loyal to Prince John. Why had the queen willingly entered the besieged mountain fortress and submitted herself to his control?

She was shocked back into full consciousness as the door to the hall opened. A gust of icy wind swept in and swirled about the room. The tattered wall tapestries flapped against the stone walls, raising billows of dust. She felt, but did not hear, herself sneeze, as a page beckoned with an almost languid motion at yet another one of the Bulgarians. She realized that the Bulgarians, one by one, had been disappearing from the hall all evening. As the door shut in a swirl of light snow on the last of the Bulgarians, she heard the faint cry. It was just the suggestion of a cry. It sounded more frightened and frightening than either the

6

drunken bantering that had echoed in the hall earlier or anything that could be construed as a battle cry or the typical taunting that rose from the siege camps below the walls. She was trying to locate and identify the sounds. She found herself outside, having slipped past the young diplomat who had been boring her to tears.

She was desperately moving around the middle-ward level of the mountain peak. Now she was staring up at the upper ward. A single beacon defined the arched door in the rock wall between St. Hilarion's twin caps, the doorway that marked the entrance to the royal apartments located in the dell between the two peaks. The sounds were muffled from here, almost as if they were coming through the mountain peak itself. The light began to move. It seemed to be climbing the steep stairs of one of the peaks, toward the high tower, the apartments of Prince John himself. As the light began to wind up and toward the east, she herself also seemed to be moving around the peak toward the fortified gate at the top of the wide, stone stairs that descended to the lower ward.

She pushed open the large cedar wood doors of the gate, emerged onto the wide terrace at the top of the stairs down to the lower ward, and looked almost straight up toward the dizzying high tower. As she looked up, the terrifying cry enveloped her, merged with her own horrified scream, and shook her like a rag doll. She recoiled from a crash in the thicket at the base of the cliff, almost at her feet. Then her senses were consumed by the jarring sound of a woman's triumphant laughter—laughter that assaulted her ears with increasingly jarring waves of volume and hysteria; eerie laughter rolling down the mountain from the high tower battlements.

"Caity . . . Cait! Yo, Miss Caitlyn!"

Caitlyn Spencer hauled her attention back from the haze of time and turned, not too affably, toward the irritating young man who was squeezing her arm a bit too possessively. The two were teetering at the edge of the stone terrace at the entrance to St. Hilarion's middle ward gate.

Caitlyn extracted her arm from her companion's grip and physically withdrew onto the somewhat firmer ground of the broken-stone terrace. At the same time, she also attempted to withdraw mentally, at least for the moment, from Paul's hovering presence. It didn't help that this character insisted on calling her Caity, a name that only her family—and Kurt, of course—had used. She found the nickname grating and presumptuous coming from someone outside the family, especially someone she hadn't even met until the previous day.

The young American diplomat didn't seem to notice the effect he was having on Caitlyn.

"As I was asking, how do you think this castle came to be located here?" This obviously was a quiz, as Paul was holding a guidebook open.

"A religious hermit first. His hut right about here. A monastery developing from there, eventually coming to the notice of the Cypriot court as favorable both for defense from invasion by sea and as a cool retreat in the summer." Caitlyn's answer poured forth in almost distracted, straightforward tones, as her attention became fixated on the sheer rise of the cliff directly above her to the ruins of a tower high on the peak above. She was confused and a bit frightened. She was doubly perplexed that the mere sight of the tower remains was making chills run up her spine.

"Hey, neat!" Paul exclaimed with admiration. "That's just about what it says in this guidebook. You must be a whizbang archaeologist. Can you tell all that just from looking at these ruins?"

Caitlyn, her gaze still transfixed on the tower above, did not respond. Her silence, however, quite evidently was taken by Paul as a signal that she was enjoying the guessing game and wanted it to continue.

"You seem to be fascinated with that tower. So, bet you didn't know that it has a grizzly story all its own. The one about the Romanian mercenaries and the decline of the Lusignan crusader dynasty on the island."

Once again Paul didn't notice Caitlyn wrap herself tightly in her arms and give a shudder—all without being able to tear her eyes from the battlements above her.

He continued, consulting the guidebook. "It was in the late fourteenth century, and some Italian invaders—not the Venetians. They came later. Ah, yes, it says here they were from Genoa. Seems like everyone from Cleopatra to the British have invaded this island. Anyway, these Italians were laying siege to St. Hilarion. The island's ruler was holed up here and was so unpopular with his own people that the only force loyal to him was a group of Romanian mercenaries he was paying as bodyguards. Well, he somehow went mad one night and called his mercenaries up to that high tower up there, one by one. As each one reached the tower, it was a jab by the madman and a pitch out over the walls down into this ravine here."

Once again Paul didn't pick up on the distress his blunt discourse was having on Caitlyn.

"They were Bulgarians," Caitlyn muttered under her breath and then looked startled at what she had said. Paul didn't notice her interjection and continued gaily on with his recitation.

"It wasn't until he got to the last Romanians that the prince realized he had just done away with his own protection. The Italians just waltzed into the castle and carted him off. It doesn't say here what they did with him—or why he had killed the Romanians."

"It was Queen Eleanor," Caitlyn whispered.

"Huh?" Paul moved closer to Caitlyn, as he hadn't been able to pick out what she had said.

"She tricked him. She got his confidence and then convinced him the Bulgarians were plotting against him. Of course! *That's* what she was up to. That's why she sent me away. Prince John might have heard my questioning of . . ." Caitlyn went rigid. What was she thinking? This didn't have anything to do with her. Was this another one of her spells? She could already feel the headache coming on.

"What?" Paul muttered. "I didn't see that here. Where did you read that? Have you already read up on St. Hilarion? What's this about Bulgarians?" He was paging frantically through the guidebook, trying to find the explanation she had provided. Mercifully, he hadn't heard the last part of what Caitlyn had been saying.

"It was for revenge. And for love." Caitlyn shook her head violently at what she had involuntarily uttered and tore her eyes away from the high tower. She couldn't let these moods get the best of her.

Paul was still sputtering and flipping through the guidebook as Caitlyn brushed past him and started trotting down the broken stone steps, through the castle's lower ward, and toward the parking lot just outside the main gate.

"I feel a headache coming on. And all this dust being swept up by these mountain breezes has my throat parched. I thought you promised me a cool drink."

10

"Of course," Paul sputtered. "I told you there were drinks waiting for us down in Kyrenia Harbor. We're already behind schedule. You seemed so fascinated by St. Hilarion that we've been here longer than intended. I'd planned to do Kyrenia Castle and the abbey at Bellapais today as well."

Caitlyn made a great effort to respond with jaunty good humor. She wasn't at all happy to be taking her history at a gallop. But she felt a sudden need to put St. Hilarion Castle behind her, and there wasn't anything she needed more now than that good cool drink. This had been the most troublesome spell she had had yet. She had thought that coming to Cyprus would cure these inexplicable forays into a much too vivid "other time." But this time the experience had been all too graphic. Paul's chilling, insensitive review of the legend had only made the horror of the vision worse.

Caitlyn normally could have spent the entire week exploring just St. Hilarion Castle alone. Her American father, a university history professor, had instilled in her the love of painstaking research and careful examination and categorization of every fact and find. This had been so successfully drummed into her that she had taken up archaeology and, at the rather young age of twenty-eight, was meeting with a good deal of success in the field.

She had thought that colonial America was to be her specialty. Up until a few short weeks ago, she had been deeply engaged in an internationally noted dig at a seventeenth century Virginia plantation on the James River near Jamestown, one of the earliest permanent European settlements in the New World. She had gone there to help with a newly constructed and innovative project to trace settlement at this site back several centuries to uncover evidence of the earliest civilization in the area. The project had quickly excavated to a period far preceding that of the American Indians, the earliest habitation Caitlyn had been exposed to in her prior studies.

The sudden realization that all meaningful history didn't start with either the European colonization of the Americas or with the American Indians had hit Caitlyn hard. She, of course, realized this had been naïve of her. She knew she certainly would have intellectualized the shallowness of archaeological opportunities in the United States had she bothered to think much about the issue.

Caitlyn could, in fact, remember and appreciate the old joke she occasionally shared with her Canadian mother, a collector of and dealer in ancient artifacts, when shopping the antique stores in Georgetown, the posh precursor town to the capital city of Washington. Wherever Caitlyn's interest had been drawn to a particularly old-looking potential treasure and the salesclerk ventured to date it to the early days of the Republic, Caitlyn's mother would just sniff and declare that an antique in Washington was just yesterday's used junk in London. Then she'd majestically sail on down the aisle.

The amusing way in which Caitlyn's mother had always been able to put world history into proper perspective for Caitlyn, along with the exciting expansion of archaeological interest at the Jamestown plantation dig, had contributed to a redirection of her professional horizons.

And when she was being truthful with herself, she also had to admit that the loss of Kurt had thrown her so out of kilter that she had been thinking for some time that she needed at least a temporary change of pace, direction, and locale to regain her balance.

A couple of Caitlyn's colleagues from the university now lived and worked in Cyprus. Thus, when a brochure presenting international opportunities for archaeological projects had been circulated at the Jamestown dig the previous autumn, she was immediately attracted to the chance to participate in an entirely different project. The Fulbright program was sponsoring a short-term study project to open up a newly discovered Neolithic site in the foothills of the Troodos Mountains on the Mediterranean island of Cyprus.

Caitlyn's mother had been instrumental in this focusing on Cyprus as well. Caitlyn had never been to Cyprus. Indeed she had never previously been to the Mediterranean area. But her mother had shared with her an old family claim that one of her ancestors had joined up with Richard the Lionhearted's crusade in the twelfth century. The English ships of the fleet headed for the Holy Land crusades had been caught in a storm off Cyprus. Fatefully for the Cypriots, the storm blew the ship of Richard's intended, the Princess Berengaria of Navarre, into the southern harbor of Limassol—and straight into the waiting arms of the local "emperor," Isaac Comenus. Richard and his troops apparently didn't appreciate Comenus's rough notion of hospitality for Berengaria. Within days, the Cypriots had once again lost their independence, and the era of crusader rule on the island had begun.

Caitlyn had been delighted when she had been accepted for the Troodos dig under a six-month Fulbright Program grant. Upon arriving in Cyprus, Caitlyn had been both enchanted and appalled at the extent of history and of the archaeological treasures offered by this strategically located island. She had been enchanted because she

13

had had no idea that so much history could be both openly available and crying out to be discovered within such a small geographic space. But she had also been appalled, because she had very little time in which to discover it all. What she had not counted on was the strange familiarity about the island and, in particular, of any and all of the sites dating to the Medieval period and earlier that she was encountering.

It was on her third day on the island, while still recovering from jet lag, that Caitlyn had accepted Paul Conte's invitation to visit the most accessible crusader period sites on the northern coast. At that time she had not yet decided whether the American embassy diplomat was charmingly outgoing or boringly aggressive. After spending only a few hours with him today, she was strongly leaning toward the latter assessment. Paul had quickly claimed the role of her guide on the basis of his membership on the Cypriot board of the sponsoring Fulbright Commission. His position with her sponsoring organization was itself a reason for Caitlyn to try to remain as diplomatically polite to him as possible.

* * * *

A few minutes later, when they were sitting in the shade of the umbrella at Kyrenia's harbor-side Chimera Café, directly below the massive harbor castle's walls, Caitlyn's irritation was mellowing. The slightly oily, but still deep-blue water of the harbor was lapping against the sides of boats bobbing up and down just below the railing at the side of the table. The Bixie Cola—Turkey's answer to Coke— that Caitlyn held in her hand had gone a long way toward both making her threatened headache recede and renewing her humor and sense of well-being. She was also becoming more comfortable with Paul. For some unknown reason, he seemed to be enjoying the sludge-like Turkish coffee he had ordered that had been ceremoniously delivered in a cup the size of a thimble.

The harbor was exquisite. Composed of a wide flagstone avenue encircling a small harbor and, in turn, being encircled by three- and four-story stone or stuccoed buildings, the one-time fishing and commercial center had been changed into a tourist's delight. Thankfully, Caitlyn noted, this had been done without losing the harbor's charm. The street had been closed to traffic and the ground floors of most of the buildings fronting directly on the harbor had been turned into restaurants whose umbrella-shaded tables spilled out onto the street and directly up to the edge of the water of the inner harbor.

The hovering castle, Venetian on the outside and Byzantine on the inside, presided over the harbor above Caitlyn and Paul's table. Just to the west and on the street behind the harbor buildings, a slender pencil-shaped minaret peeked up just in front of the imposing Ottoman Turk-period governor's mansion that also straddled a rise overlooking the harbor. Further to the west, in a break between the buildings, stood the corner tower of the original city wall. On the western side of the harbor, directly opposite where Caitlyn and Paul sat, stood the customs house—to the right the original Ottoman Turk building and to the left the distinctly British colonial addition. Rising above the buildings at this end was the white tower of the forlorn Greek Orthodox church that had been in disuse since the 1974 Turkish invasion that split the island between a Greek zone in the south and a Turkish zone in the north.

Floating over the entire landward expanse of the harbor was the Kyrenia Mountain range, whose jagged peaks proudly thrust upward not more than five miles from the coast. From where Caitlyn sat, she looked directly up to the twin peaks in which St. Hilarion was nestled, and the profile of the crumbling walls and towers could clearly be discerned. She shivered, finding the brooding presence of the mountain castle both compelling and foreboding.

On the seaward side, the harbor was protected by a wide sea wall that was crowned with a wide stone promenade. The inlet to the harbor passed between the sea wall and several hundred feet of the broad side of the castle, creating a long battery. This required ships to negotiate a lengthy approach under the guns of the fortress before entering the harbor.

Inside the harbor were two lighthouses. They both were ancient rock columns, where illumination had been provided by building open fires on top of a conical tower. The oldest of the two, marking the original inner harbor and dating from the Roman period, was almost within touch of Caitlyn and Paul's table. The newer, but still ancient, lighthouse was located about a third of the way down the sea wall. Caitlyn was particularly happy to see that the harbor was filled with boats of all kinds. As many working fishing boats were tied up to the walls just below the tables as were luxury sailboats and small motor yachts. This was a working, living harbor, not just the reconstructed fantasy that she was often accustomed to seeing in the United States. As she sipped her cola, it also occurred to Caitlyn that much of Cyprus's history was reflected in the architecture laid out in front of her.

In the mellow mood brought on by the beauty and leisurely pace of the harbor, Caitlyn made an attempt to draw Paul out. Heretofore she had been afraid to ask him anything about himself.

She had feared that, once he had been unstoppered, she'd never be able to stem his apparent natural Yankee effervescence, and that he, in turn, would pump her to reveal aspects of her own life that she would just as soon bury ever deeper.

Upon more objective observation, Caitlyn had to admit that, on the surface, at least, Paul seemed to be quite personable. He had the build and springy step of an athlete. In fact, he had the somewhat off-center nose of a boxer who hadn't managed to win all of his fights. This was an adjustment that, in Paul's case, seemed to complement a boyish charm, set off by engaging watery, gray-blue eyes. Perversely, now that Caitlyn was attempting to find out more about her companion for the day, Paul was being reticent.

"I'm just a junior political officer. You know, nothing too interesting. Entertain the people no one important wants to bother with and do the reports and paperwork that are too mundane for the seniors."

"Oh, just somewhere in the Middle West; nowhere to be proud enough of to talk about. Yes, the name's Italian, but the family's been in America for several generations."

This clampdown in Paul's normally bubbly demeanor suddenly made Caitlyn suspect that he was more than he seemed to be and that she was perhaps being un-American to pry. She therefore quickly looked for another topic.

Fortunately, Paul was much more willing to provide her with a foundation on the political situation on the troubled island than he had been in sharing with her the details of his duties at the American embassy. For the next half hour Caitlyn was treated to a concise and comprehensive, if dismaying, thumbnail sketch of recent Cypriot history, while she sipped through her second cola and Paul chased off the effects of his Turkish coffee with a glass of water.

Paul told her how the growing ethnic trouble on the island, the population of which was three-quarters Orthodox Greek and one-quarters Muslim Turk, came to a head during the British colonial period. The British had assumed power following the somewhat benign Ottoman Turk era in the late nineteenth century. Their own turn at control had ended with the island's grasp at independence in 1960. A subsequent attempt at shared power in a republican system that provided for a Greek president and a Turkish vice president collapsed into chaos and partition in 1974. This sad state of affairs had been the result of a mainland Greece-led coup attempt and a resultant occupation of the northern third of the island by mainland Turkish troops.

"So, what you now have, in a nutshell," Paul concluded, "is a polarization of communities—Greeks in the south and Turks in the north—that were once intermingled. An ever-decreasing, largely symbolic contingent of United Nations troops for decades maintained a buffer zone between these two forces."

"All of which is why we had to get you a day pass to come from the Greek side to the Turkish side. As a diplomat, I can come and go as long as the border isn't closed by a demonstration. You would have found it difficult to go the other way, incidentally, because the Turkish Cypriots are trying to establish their presence over here into a separate political state. The Greeks refuse to recognize this and, even though they claim the border is open more now than it was before, it is virtually impossible for anyone who entered the island by way of the Turkish zone to get into the Greek zone. And they will carefully check your passport for evidence you've been on the Turkish side if you try to enter by air or ship on the Greek side. The border has become more open in recent years, but it's frequently closed by demonstrations and caprice of both sides, so it's always safest to have an official pass."

"This is also why we'll have to hurry up now and see all we've set out to see over here today. We have to get back before the pass expires." Paul had accelerated his speech in delivering the last two thoughts, as he waved at the waiter and pulled out his billfold.

Caitlyn had wondered at Paul's sudden mobilization. He had seemed as content to sit and watch the harbor activity as she had been up until just a few moments previously. In fact, it was just a brief time ago, while he was outlining the UN's role in Cyprus to Caitlyn, that she had noticed him taking a few furtive looks along the curve of the harbor and upward. As he became distracted by trying to catch the eye of the waiter, Caitlyn looked up in the direction in which Paul had been repeatedly glancing. She had plenty of time to check where Paul's attention had strayed, because the waiter, who had been very attentive during the serving process now, at the close of the chase, seemed unwilling to acknowledge that this was his table—or even his restaurant. Paul's efforts were completely taken up with this typically Mediterranean duel of wanting to serve but not wanting to acknowledge the role of servant.

Checking the direction of Paul's gaze, Caitlyn noted that just to the west of the Chimera Café, occupying a corner position slightly behind the other harbor-side buildings, perched a white stucco building with a red-tiled roof. The sign on the building said "The

Harbor Club," and the only persons visible were a couple sitting on an upper floor balcony.

The man sported attention-demanding flaming-red hair and a ruddy, sunburned complexion to match. The woman had straight, nearly waist-length platinum blonde hair. Caitlyn could see that the two were closely engrossed in conversation, and to all appearances they were completely engrossed in each other as well.

The waiter finally was captured. As Paul settled the bill, he noticed Caitlyn's scrutiny of the couple and quickly stood, with his body placed between Caitlyn's line of sight and the Harbor Club.

"We'd really best be tackling the castle if we're going to be able to see Kyrenia and still get to Bellapais in time for lunch," Paul said with a seemingly feigned brightness. His ugly American speedy tourist guide demeanor seemed to be getting the better of him again.

With that, he nearly lifted Caitlyn out of her chair, conveniently keeping himself between her and the Harbor Club balcony. He then practically dragged her in the opposite direction, toward the stairs that led to the bridge crossing the dry moat to the Kyrenia Castle gate.

As Caitlyn came up from her chair, she was pulled slightly off balance by Paul, who was continuing to tow her toward his sightseeing schedule. Caitlyn tripped slightly against someone. The someone proved to be one of two dark-complexioned, very serious acting men who had previously been sitting at a nearby table and to Paul's back. As Paul built up speed and pulled her along by the elbow, Caitlyn turned toward the men to voice an apology.

But neither man acknowledged that she was there at all. Both were gazing with fixed stares and nearly palpable hatred at the retreating back of the American diplomat.

Chapter Two

As Paul was bustling her across the stone bridge and toward the awaiting Kyrenia Castle gate, Caitlyn suddenly dug in her heels and swung him around.

"Please, Paul, stop. I am not going to rush through this. I've got five months to see it all, and I just can't be flipped through history like this. I'm an archaeologist, not a fast-food restaurant."

"Sorry," responded Paul. He was staring past her toward the castle stairs that led down to the harbor.

"What is it? What are you looking for?" Caitlyn asked, as she too looked around at the stairs. "And who were those men in the café? They both gave you such hard stares that I expected you to melt on the spot. And who was that man and woman on balcony? The ones you didn't seem to want me to notice. Are they friends of yours?"

"What men? I don't know what you're talking about," Paul answered after a brief pause. For some reason he didn't look at all happy, and it didn't escape Caitlyn's notice that he hadn't responded to her question about the couple. But she decided to leave that issue in suspension for the moment.

Caitlyn let out an exasperated sigh. "The two men who came up to the café just as we were sitting down. The two men who seemed to be trying to huddle as far under their umbrella as possible and who didn't seem nearly as interested in the harbor activity as they were in us. I realize it must just have been my vanity, especially since they were so rude just now. But their interest in us made me think they were planning to make a pass at me if you showed any signs of leaving the table."

"Well, if you had walked all over *my* feet, I'd probably be pretty rude to you as well," smirked Paul.

"Ah, ha!" exclaimed Caitlyn. "So, you admit you *did* see them."

"Yes, I saw them," Paul acknowledged grudgingly.

"So, why did they give you such dirty looks?" Caitlyn bore in behind Paul's admission. The two were still standing on the stone bridge spanning the dry moat. A busload of German tourists gave them the evil eye as they jostled past them to enter the castle. "And wasn't that the real reason we made a fast exit?"

"Oh, I've gotten used to those looks and to being hated by Cypriots from both sides. It's so easy to blame the Americans for everything that isn't going right in Cypriot politics. And we diplomats, who continually have to pass on bad news, get to bear the critical looks quite a bit."

"Something's fishy here, Paul. On the one hand you tell me you're a meaningless drudge imprisoned in the bowels of the embassy, and on the other hand you indicate that everyone in Cyprus recognizes you as an official responsible for making their lives miserable."

"Maddening, isn't it?" Paul grinned.

Caitlyn shook her ash-blonde curls in frustration, started to say something, and then changed her choice of retort.

"Well, you can just keep your secrets. I've got a castle to attack." And, with that, she resolutely trudged toward and through the castle gate—and into her medieval fantasies.

* * * *

Caitlyn had always been prone to attempting to reconstruct in her imagination the purpose all the archaeological finds she encountered had served when they originally were in use. And, as she had experienced at St. Hilarion in the shadow of the high tower earlier in the morning, she was easily swept up into earlier eras in her imagination—or, at least what she thought was her imagination. She had also seen several castles along the Rhine several years earlier—with Kurt. So, she strode through Kyrenia's gate with full expectations of what she would find and of how the fortification would be laid out. Immediately inside the gate, however, she was brought up short, and she was struck with a feeling of déjà vu that had not been present before they had entered the castle. Now that she was inside the fortification her mind was conjuring up a confusing array of flashing images. She was receiving the sensation that she had been here before, but the images of "here" would not stand still. There seemed to be several visions of what "here" represented. Caitlyn was thoroughly confused, and she felt the headache that had plagued her earlier in the morning fighting to reemerge.

They had entered into a dark, rather narrow, open-air passage, the floor of which was rising slightly, twisting toward the left and further into the darkness. As Caitlyn looked down at the dank cobblestones of the passage, an inexplicable feeling of distress and dread started to rise from within her.

Paul mistook Caitlyn's drawing in of breath as mere surprise that the entrance gate did not open directly into the castle proper.

Chuckling, he said, "Sort of surprising, isn't it? You expected to enter into some sort of courtyard, I'll bet. Probably a large courtyard because of the massiveness of the castle as seen from the outside. Instead, you arrive at what appears to be the forecourt of another castle gate. Come with me and let me show you a *real* surprise. Here, take my hand until you've become adjusted to the darkness."

Still distracted by the sensations she was having, Caitlyn did as she was asked without objection, and the two entered a passage opening just inside the outer gate. Her mind was already racing. She was trying to force thoughts about what this or that was used for and why the castle entrance was constructed this way to the front of her mind, while trying to submerge the unreasonable sense of helplessness and of being trapped that fought her for control.

After a short walk through the cobblestone passageway and just beyond where it started to bend, the two came upon a dirt-floored side passage off to the left, which they entered. This passageway was quite narrow, and Caitlyn, who was well above average height for a woman, found that she was ducking her head to escape the illusion that she might bump it against the uneven stone ceiling. She automatically clicked into a professional estimate of probable height, weight—and even diet—of those who had first fashioned and used this construction. And, for some reason, she seemed surprised that the ceiling seemed so low.

"Funny, these passageways never felt this cramped before." She was astounded that she had muttered such nonsense out loud, not to mention that the phrase had entered her mind at all. Her gaze darted to Paul, who was tramping well ahead of her in the passage, but, thankfully, he apparently had not heard her speak.

In a short time, the passage opened up abruptly into the sunlight—but a restrictive sunlight resulting from a very narrow area between high walls. They were in some sort of well, which, as it turned out, fully enclosed a small, domed stone building. A soft chanting started to intrude upon Caitlyn's consciousness, and there was something awfully familiar about the domed structure. But for some reason she associated it with an open, grassy knoll rather than in this rock-clad well. After a brief inspection, she looked quizzically at Paul.

"OK, I give up. If you know what the purpose of *this* is, please don't keep me in suspense."

"This," Paul explained with a twinkle in his eye, "provides the key to this unusual castle. Kyrenia Castle is just like Cyprus itself. Civilization upon civilization has come and conquered and settled and, in turn, been conquered and disappeared. All have occupied essentially the same space and have refashioned what they have found, never totally destroying what went before. And the evidence of their own occupation has only rarely been totally obliterated in their wake."

"The Kyrenia Castle you saw from the harbor was built by the Venetians, starting in the late fifteenth century. It was the Venetians who replaced the Genoese, whom, as the guidebook passage we read this morning up at St. Hilarion noted, replaced the

26

French Lusignans. No one really has been able to trace the origin of this castle back to the earliest fortification, however. This harbor has surely enjoyed its strategic location back to the dawn of civilization on the island. We do know that fortifications existed here at least as early as the Greek and Roman periods."

Caitlyn was struck with the urge to interject that the Greeks and Romans were veritable latecomers to this stretch of the coast, but she managed to bite off the remark, while Paul continued his discourse.

"Here," Paul said, leading Caitlyn over to one side of the well. "Look there. What do you see in the wall, just above eye level?"

"Why, it looks like the base of a marble column," exclaimed Caitlyn.

"That's exactly what it is," declared Paul. "You'll see this all over the castle and in the construction at ancient sites all over the island. Many of the civilizations that came and went from here were helped in their 'going' by earthquakes. The island is right on the edge of the gigantic plates that underlie the meeting of the European and African continents. In fact, the island owes it very existence to this positioning. The jagged Kyrenia Range is the result of where the two plates have rubbed together and the edge of one of the plates has been thrust up to form this range, bringing the rest of the island up out of the water in the process."

"Fascinating," intoned Caitlyn. "But you were telling me about this column . . ."

"Yes," continued Paul. "All of this geological activity makes the whole region very unstable. In other words, this is a very active earthquake area. Cyprus has not had a serious quake for several centuries, but it's ripe for one. And what one civilization lost in one of the many devastating quakes, the next civilization considered free game for construction material. Environmentally sound, of course, even though it has tended to mess with the calculations of you archaeological types."

"So, this column is Venetian salvage from the Romans and Greeks," said Caitlyn, "and this little domed building . . .?"

"Ah, yes, before the lecture I had been saying this domed building illustrated the unique character of this castle. This is a Byzantine-era chapel. It originally stood outside the walls of the Byzantine version of the castle, which was constructed here in the seventh century on whatever foundations then existed from an earlier fortress."

"That column is not salvage for the Venetian castle we see today, but for the Lusignans' thirteenth-century expansion of the structure. Instead of tearing down this chapel in their additions to the fortress, the Lusignans built their walls around it. They left it in its own enclosure, and, no doubt, continued to use it as one of the castle churches. The main passageway . . ."

. . . *The Lord Jean d'Ibelin looked so strong and handsome, as Frederick's marshal, Richard Filangeri, entered the chapel to proffer his sword in long-last surrender of the Holy Roman Emperor's invaders to the Cypriots. Linnette was bursting with pride at the victory of her lover, one of the most popular and respected Christian lords in the eastern Mediterranean, over Frederick's attempt to crush the d'Ibelins in Syria and Cyprus. Jean had won battle after battle across the island, and the old marshal had retreated to the castle enshadowing this ancient chapel near Christmastide in 1232. D'Ibelin had*

invested Kyrenia Castle for more than a year. And, not being able to be parted
from him any longer, Linnette had slipped into the harbor town and into Jean's
bed the following summer. Just as Jean grasped the sword and raised it so that it
shimmered in the torch light across the chapel dome, the child in her womb gave a
mighty kick, and Linnette was barely able to contain her laughter . . .

". . . we originally entered served the purpose of taking us through the fifteenth-century Venetian walls that were built to encase the earlier, less substantial Byzantine and Lusignan walls, specifically to counter the introduction into warfare of cannon and . . ."

Paul's discourse abruptly stopped, as he flashed Caitlyn a very peculiar look. His face turned a bit red, and he started to work his way back down the passage. Caitlyn found she was standing, entranced, with both hands spread over her abdomen. The embarrassment that flooded her face when she realized how she was standing more than rivaled the embarrassment Paul had shown. She turned and followed him back down the narrow passageway. She was not at all sure she had wanted to hear any more of Paul's lecture on the Cypriot continuum, as it seemed to fuel her involuntary reveries. One thing she did know, however—and perhaps if she concentrated on this line of thought, she could stave off thinking about the other issues. She was developing a new respect for the diplomat.

"Perhaps he isn't as shallow as he seems—or wants to seem—to be," she mused.

Having gained the main tunnel, Paul pulled Caitlyn off again, this time into a small chamber off the right side of the passageway.

"This is said to have been the gatekeeper's quarters," said Paul, as he led her into yet another small chamber located beyond the first.

"I'm not sure anyone knows anymore to what extent these walls are solid or whether passages and chambers honeycomb this portion of the castle," he continued. "Most of the interior of the castle, especially on this older side, has been closed off for as long as anyone can remember."

Caitlyn drew into the small chamber only to be pulled back immediately by Paul.

"Do mind your footing wherever you walk around here" he admonished.

Caitlyn looked down, and her heart went to her throat. Paul had brought her back from the brink of an opening in the floor that was small, but certainly not too small for her to have fallen through.

"Thank you," she shuddered, as a now-distressingly familiar sensation of foreboding began to grip at her nerve endings. "Where does that lead, and why isn't it covered?" No sooner had she voiced the question, then it occurred to her that she needn't have asked what lay below.

"Very sorry," Paul answered. In the darkness he could not tell that Caitlyn had turned pale. "History has so much breadth and so many layers here that the Cypriots can't package their historical sites in pristine theme park style as we tend to do in the States." Then he laughed at the imagery that had occurred to him. "First off, if they tried to preserve everything of significant historical value, they couldn't walk or breathe between the ruins. And then we also need to appreciate that Cyprus is one of the world's smaller countries. It simply doesn't have the money to explore and preserve all of its antiquities. There isn't enough wood in all of Cyprus to cover all of the holes in ruins such as this one."

"I take your point," said Caitlyn, not sure at all she deserved the lecture and unable to shake the apprehensive feeling that had enveloped her. Both to change the thrust of the conversation and because she couldn't help herself, she repeated, "I wonder what's down there?"

"Well, there is some light down there, enough to see that it's some sort of chamber. But I can't see to the bottom. From what I've been told, we may be standing over an area originally used as a dungeon by the Genoans. I have heard that the Turkish Cypriot Antiquities Department, which, interestingly enough, is housed in the Kyrenia Castle proper, is going to open up some of this area in the coming weeks. So, maybe we'll know more about this part of the castle before you have to return to the States."

Caitlyn was barely conscious of this last discourse, as she was standing at the threshold to the rear chamber and gazing fixedly at the hole in the floor. For yet another time that day she found herself being dragged deeply into a time-travel reverie by her vivid imagination. Without having any inkling why it was having this affect, she started to feel suffocated. An uncanny sense of deprivation and despair began to sweep over her. She gave out a low moan and staggered almost imperceptibly.

She was hurriedly packing Queen Charlotte's trunks. This normally would have been Lani's duty, but the principal lady in waiting was in such a state from the news that she couldn't function. Thus Sybilla was bustling around her sobbing friend—she herself hardly able to stifle her own tears—trying to guess what a queen would need for a long sea voyage. After four years of being besieged in the castle by the queen's "brother," the illegitimate usurper of the granddaughter of King Janus, the queen was being permitted to flee—but only if she left on the day's tide and only if she and her entourage agreed to the permanent banishment in Rome that James had arranged.

This in itself did not disturb the Lady Sybilla. As one of Queen Charlotte's poorer cousins whose family had intermarried with an old Cypriot family, Sybilla had long known that her future prosperity was forever dependent on her powerful patron. But the news of the impending move from Cyprus had been devastating to her dearest friend, Lady Lani, whose husband and young son had gone missing shortly after Lani had asked leave of the queen to live with her family. Lani's family had allied with the usurper, and the queen's favorite attendant had borne the struggle of divided loyalties for as long as she could before choosing to return to her husband and son. Now the royal household had only a few brief hours to embark on their ship, and Queen Charlotte had left no doubt that Lani would be departing with the rest of her entourage, since Lani had apparently been forsaken by her husband.

As they were being bustled down the castle passageway toward the ship, Sybilla's sharp ears picked up faint sounds of lament that rose over, yet were much deeper than, those still pouring out of Lani. She stopped short just before leaving the postern gate by the ancient chapel. She looked around wildly, trying to locate the sounds. No one else appeared to hear them. Lani turned and looked sharply at Sybilla, whose powers of observation were well known. Sybilla started to speak, but the queen's men also now turned, bundled up both of the women and rushed them toward the waiting ship. Lani's wails rose once again, and Sybilla blacked out.

Paul steadied Caitlyn as she staggered against him. For the first time he picked up on the change in her demeanor and rapidly guided her back into the entry tunnel.

"Sorry," Caitlyn smiled wanly as she quickly regained her composure. The heaviness in her limbs and mind was rapidly dissipating. "I guess the combination of the close air, the early start, and lingering jet lag got to me." She didn't feel all that confident, though, as they resumed their walk down the entry tunnel. She took a swift glance back toward the gatekeeper's rooms, sure that in some way she had connected with one of the many unresolved—and, in this case, terrifying—mysteries of the castle's long and violent history.

She also felt very uneasy about the state of her mental well-being. She had withdrawn into reveries such as this much too often since Kurt had disappeared from her life. She was beginning to fear that this was a sign that she could easily go mad if she did not pull herself together and cut her losses in that particular aspect of her life.

* * * *

Almost as soon as Paul and Caitlyn had resumed their journey deeper into the castle, they came out into the strong Cyprus sunshine. In front of them and to their right was a wide, flagstone ramp that rose between and to the top of what Paul told her were the outer Venetian and inner Lusignan walls. Before them and to the right was a slight down ramp that turned to the left at the bottom and thence into the central Byzantine castle courtyard via the original outer gate of the Lusignan structure. Having cleared the Lusignan gate, Caitlyn let out an involuntary gasp. After all of the close tunnels and narrow courtyards, they had quite unexpectedly entered a central area as big as a football stadium.

"Why, this could hold and sustain an army for months!" she exclaimed.

"Actually, for years," Paul responded with amusement, "which has been proven over and over again through the ages. The castle withstood many a siege during the years of convoluted fighting over the spoils of the Crusader Lusignans by the Genoans and Venetians. Even the British used this as a prison for Cypriot dissidents earlier in this century," he added.

"In the mid 1960s, Greek soldiers were housed in the castle and, after 1974 and until just a few years ago, the castle was occupied by Turkish troops. Now the place has been given over to the tourists and, although most of the interior of the castle is still closed to modern exploration, at least now you can walk on top of all the walls. With Cyprus's history, however, there's no telling when the castle will again be occupied and used for its intended purpose. It has, in fact, gotten little rest from war over the centuries."

Caitlyn shuddered in sudden remembrance of the creepy feeling that had gripped her in the darkness within the castle walls, and she started climbing a stone staircase that rose just to her left in an effort to get closer to the sun. Paul followed in silence.

The two found themselves at the top of the circular northwest tower—which an oxygen-taxed Paul managed to gasp out was called the Venetian Tower—that jutted into Kyrenia's tiny yacht basin at the point at which the ship channel linked up with the old harbor. It had been a steep climb to the top and both arrived winded. But the climb was, Caitlyn reasoned, a cinch compared with her early-morning climb to St. Hilarion's upper ward.

The first sight that accosted Caitlyn at the top of the Venetian Tower was, in fact, that of the twin peaks of St. Hilarion's upper ward, glowering down on the harbor. The view was breathtaking, and Caitlyn felt she probably would have immediately floated off into another one of her daydreams of life "back then" if the center of the top of the large, circular tower had not been dominated by the rusting hulk of some sort of twentieth-century gun emplacement.

"Sorry," Paul said apologetically, somehow sensing the magnitude of the violation Caitlyn felt concerning this modern intrusion into the castle's aura. "No doubt placed here by the Greeks in the 1960s and kept here for use by the Turks after 1974."

Directing her attention to the view seaward beyond the rusting metal, Paul pointed out a new artificial harbor that had been constructed to the east of the castle. "That's called the new harbor. It's where the Turkish gunboats and the ferries to mainland Turkey dock. Most of the cargo vessels still operate out of the Famagusta harbor on the east coast and, of course, only Turkish vessels are permitted to dock on this side of the buffer zone. It is embargoed to all other nations."

"Hello," he said and gave a low whistle. Paul's speech had slowed as he completed this last thought. "Very interesting. Very interesting, indeed. That doesn't look like a Turkish vessel down there now. Romanian. No, I think that's a Bulgarian flag. And is that who I think it is? And what's being loaded in that vehicle he's pacing around? And who's that big blond guy he's talking to? Don't think I've seen him around anywhere."

Not being greatly interest in the new harbor, Caitlyn had already tuned Paul out and had moved to the landward side of the tower and cast her eyes downward and into the old harbor. "How utterly charming," she exclaimed. And charming it certainly was. As fascinating as the harbor and its activity had been at the street level of the Café Chimera, it was twice as enchanting when viewed from above.

"Oh, look," Caitlyn said, "The Café Chimera is just below us. There's our table. There's the table where those two unpleasant men are sitting. Or were sitting," Caitlyn corrected herself. The men were no longer there. Caitlyn's gaze went up to the balcony of the Harbor Club, where the couple Paul had too obviously ignored had been sitting. Caitlyn could see that only the red-haired man was still there. He was apparently finishing a cigarette and staring out toward the customs house. Following his gaze, Caitlyn was just in time to see the long platinum blonde hair of his companion disappear along the promenade and beyond the customs house. Her attention was held there long enough to see one of "the disagreeable" men from the café also pass beyond the customs house in an apparent parallel journey to that of the balcony blonde.

"Hm, this is getting curiouser and curiouser," thought Caitlyn. "Paul, come look at this . . ."

But Paul wasn't looking in that direction. Nor was he mulling over the activity in the new harbor any more. Paul, in fact, was fully occupied in looking down from the tower to her left, down into the dry moat at the castle entrance. Drawn by the tension she could feel in Paul's total absorption in his own vigil, Caitlyn glided to his side and looked down into the moat. A few cars, Paul's BMW among them, could be seen parked at the curb of the road that now ran along the moat bed and to the side of the harbor. What had drawn Paul's attention was a man giving Paul's car a very close inspection and the alarm that was being sounded by his car as a result. Now Caitlyn knew what had happened to the second of the unpleasant men from the café.

In an expulsion of breath that probably had been building up in Paul over the previous several seconds, Paul blurted out "See you at the car," and raced for the stairs.

Knowing she was no marathon competitor and having already almost fallen into one abyss in this castle, Caitlyn made a considerably slower and more dignified descent through the castle and into the moat. When she reached the car, which she was very happy to note was still parked at the curb, Caitlyn found Paul alone, standing in front of the BMW's raised hood and scrutinizing the engine's inner workings. The car's doors and trunk were also open, and the alarm had been disengaged. The suspicious man was nowhere in evidence.

"Everything still here and accounted for?" she asked as breezily as she could muster in an attempt to clear the tension in the air.

"I suppose so," Paul answered with an attempt at bravado that was gilt-edged with nerves. "Well, hop in," he said, gaining control. "We might as well be off to lunch in Bellapais while we still have wheels."

As they drove off, Caitlyn ventured a question. "Looking for anything in particular under the hood?"

"Bombs," Paul quietly answered, tossing a lopsided grin in her direction.

A choked "Thrilling" was the best Caitlyn could manage in return.

Which, she later thought, wasn't bad under the circumstances. "I may be starting to get the hang of this diplomatic racket. But think I'll stick with archaeology. Much safer."

Which was to prove to be not exactly correct either.

Chapter Three

Both Caitlyn and Paul were absorbed in their own separate, somewhat troubled thoughts as the little convertible powered up the steep hill from the Kyrenia Castle moat. The BMW neatly negotiated the blind intersection between the police station and a small Anglican church and entered the central square of the newer town. In this case, "newer" represented construction dating from the eighteenth rather than the fourteenth century.

Paul carefully turned east from the square at the bus station, where baskets of fruit and cackling chickens spilled color, chaos, and confusion into the street. Once out of the congestion, Paul once more showed that he was aware of his attractive passenger by starting to review his plans for the remainder of the day's sightseeing in the Turkish sector.

"I thought we'd have lunch at the artists' village of Bellapais half way up that mountain there on the other side of the Kyrenia pass from St. Hilarion Castle."

Caitlyn looked above the red-tiled roofs of the Turkish quarter of Kyrenia and up the slope in the direction Paul's hand gesture had indicated. The atmosphere was heavy with haze and the sun was strong. But, as the stuccoed walls of the village started to thin out to a more rural setting as the BMW sped along between sea and slope, Caitlyn became able, barely, to make out a brownish outcropping set into the scrubby hillside about two-thirds of the way up the curtain of mountains.

"Where's the village?" she asked. "Is it near that distinctive rock outcropping?"

"No, not that far over. Oh, do you mean just over there? That's not rock, that's the ruins of the Lusignan-period abbey that occupies the center of the village."

"Do we really have time to go all the way up there for lunch?" Caitlyn asked with obvious doubt. She was thinking of the open-air reception she had to attend that evening. Today's outing had already been somewhat grueling, given Caitlyn's jet lag, and most of the Cypriots were already quite sensibly taking their mid-afternoon break from their daily activities. It didn't seem to Caitlyn that they had time to be traipsing all over the island for the rest of the day.

"Oh, nothing's as far away from anything else in Cyprus as it appears to be," Paul laughed breezily. "We'll be up there in a jiff."

Caitlyn wearily sank deeper into the well-cushion seat. She didn't really have the energy to argue. It had been well past noon when the BMW pulled out of Kyrenia, and the late spring day was beginning to turn sweltering. This seemed especially so for Caitlyn, who had not yet adjusted to the heat of Cyprus—particularly that of the humid northern coastal strip. The heat on the central plain where the capital city, Nicosia, was located had been quite tolerable in relation to the humid weather of Virginia's southern peninsula.

"God, why is it *so* hot here?" moaned Caitlyn. "You told me it was hotter in Nicosia."

"That's right," Paul grinned, as he suddenly turned from the coast. He shifted gears, and the BMW started to whine uphill. "Nicosia's temperature always is a good many degrees hotter than anywhere else in Cyprus. But, as you should know from Virginia, it isn't the heat that gets you, it's the humidity. What little rain manages to waft as far as Cyprus from Europe usually drops its moisture here on the northern slopes of the Kyrenia Range. These mountains serve as an effective barrier to moisture reaching the central plain. We're just here on a day when the wind is blowing from Europe. Whatever comes from Turkey or north Africa is usually dry. On the dry days, the air is so clear that you often can see the hills of Turkey from up at Bellapais. I'm afraid that isn't likely to happen today."

The heat and humidity did dissipate a bit as the convertible climbed the foothills toward Bellapais, which, dominated by its huge, slope-clutching, stone-clad abbey, had come into view off to their left. From this distance the village looked quite charming. Well-kept stuccoed and stone bungalows, with individualized brightly colored shutters and doors, dotted the hillside. One house, painted stark white and standing apart from and higher than the rest, looked particularly interesting to Caitlyn. Its three stories climbed a steep, rocky incline from which stately cedars rose and framed the building. Each story sported a balcony and each balcony was covered and faced with two high arches. As they drew closer, the house took on an increasingly insistent aura, and it commanded Caitlyn's total attention. She was about to point it out to Paul, when he spoke and redirected her attention to a point further down the slope and more in the center of the village.

"When a portion of the abbey at Bellapais burned and the remainder became virtually disused during the Ottoman period," he was droning, "the village began a long economic decline. During the 1950s and 1960s, writers and artists from Europe—primarily from Britain and Germany, with Lawrence Durrell having been the most famous writer in residence—discovered the village and its arresting views of the sea and northern coast. Over time they took over much of this and another village, that of Karmi, which is located at a similar altitude on the same mountain range but to the west of Kyrenia and directly in the shadow of St. Hilarion.

"By the time of the 1974 conflict, both villages had become very prosperous and represented a significant steady infusion of foreign capital. As the Turkish troops were storming the beach to the west of Kyrenia, the foreign artists made a deal with the Turkish Cypriot leader by which Bellapais and Karmi would be declared special districts that were to be off limits to the Turkish troops in return for money up front and the promise of a continued influx of foreign capital."

"Thus far this arrangement seems to have been working to the benefit of both the European part-time residents and the Turks," Paul said, as he drove into the only street in the village that was negotiable by car. They pulled up to a patio restaurant that took up the bulk of what had been the village square. Across the street, occupying the entire down slope by the square, were the brownstone ruins of the Bellapais Abbey.

As they were getting out of the car, Paul continued: "Of course, it hasn't worked that well for the Greeks who had to abandon their houses and their businesses and evacuate to the south. This had once primarily been a Greek-dominated village.

"On a brighter note, first lunch and then the abbey," declared Paul, as he guided Caitlyn toward the restaurant.

"This is what has poetically—literally poetically in several works produced by the resident writers—been named the 'Tree of Idleness' restaurant." Paul announced this with a flourish, as he started climbing to the restaurant's trellis-covered roof via a stairway that rose through the actual branches of the tree that had provided the restaurant its name.

"Of course, it isn't the tree itself that is idle," Paul quipped. "As this also functions as the town square, this is where the local men of the village gather for their morning, afternoon, and evening coffees, while their womenfolk remain busy keeping life moving."

"You'll also find another restaurant by this name in a suburb of Nicosia," Paul noted. "This restaurant had been owned by a Greek family as far back in history as anyone could remember. When they were forced to move from here, they recreated their restaurant as best they could on the Greek side. No tree incorporated as a staircase there, though."

"Not that this is a one-sided tragedy," he added. "There were plenty of Turkish Cypriots living in the south who had to give up everything without recompense and move to the north, as well. While the Greek owner of this restaurant has tried to replicate his family's restaurant in Nicosia, the current Turkish proprietor here was forced to abandon *his* ancestral restaurant in old Paphos harbor and evacuate to the north. While living in paradise, each only has yearnings for the specific locale of their own separate roots."

They had reached a straw matting-covered terrace on the restaurant's rooftop.

"The view is exquisite," Caitlyn cried, as she looked across the abbey ruins, down into Kyrenia harbor, and along the Mediterranean coast. Look as she might, however, she couldn't make out the coast of Turkey some forty miles offshore. Caitlyn felt she could idly sit here herself for the rest of the day, not the least because the day's activities were beginning to take their toll on her energy level.

Having ordered a hearty lunch of mixed grill with village salad and a bottle of Chankaya Turkish white wine, Caitlyn gazed out over the view and sighed contentedly.

"Penny for your thoughts, Caity," Paul interjected, breaking Caitlyn's spell and causing her to round on him with a bit more ire than she had actually intended.

"Please, I'd really very much rather that you didn't call me 'Caity.' Only my family—and one other—have ever called me that, and hearing it used outside the family setting puts me on edge."

"Okeydoke, I'm sorry. I didn't know it had that effect on you," Paul said with a false bravado. The hurt in his eyes was obvious. "I feel that 'Caitlyn' is a bit too stuffy, though. Would it be all right to call you 'Cait'?"

"Oh, I don't see why not," Caitlyn responded quickly. She had not intended to be quite so rough or direct in her objection and was anxious to make amends so that the rest of the day would not be reduced to disaster.

"Would I be out of line to ask why 'Caity' creates such bad vibes?" Paul pressed his luck. "Does it have anything to do with the 'someone other than family' you indicated had used that name?"

"I guess there's no big secret involved," she sighed. Resigned to the situation and deciding just to get it past her one more time, Caitlyn drew a breath and continued: "I was engaged to a man several years ago. His name was Kurt Schwin; he was at the university with me, and he called me 'Caity,' just as my family did." She paused, gathering strength to continue, and this time Paul did not press her to hurry her story.

"His father was a German industrialist. One summer when Kurt had gone back home on vacation, he was kidnapped by a German terrorist group—or so they claimed in their demands—and held for ransom." Caitlyn swallowed hard, fighting the tears, but then quickly finished off the story. "The ransom was paid, but we never got Kurt back. I've never been sure that they tried that hard to find him. Kurt had been a little wild before he left Germany, and the police there kept hinting that he might have staged the kidnapping himself. But that's not the Kurt I knew. To put your parents through that . . ."

"I'm sorry," Paul murmured. "I would not have pressed if I had suspected . . ."

After a brief period of silence, during which both Paul and Caitlyn looked off into the sea, he said: "I wondered why you seemed so on edge and somewhat remote." And then, in a slightly jauntier tone in an effort to take the pall off the air: "I also wondered why such an American beauty rose was still untaken."

45

"Thanks for the compliment at least," whispered Caitlyn with a wan smile and through an almost imperceptible film of tears. "I've been told it helps to talk about it, and I suppose that's true. I hadn't mentioned it to anyone in Cyprus as yet, and I suppose it was getting too bottled up inside me. Most of my friends in Virginia know the situation, and it helps in our relations that we all know, even if— probably especially because—we do not actually talk about it anymore."

"Well, here's our meal, so let's tuck in and talk about more pleasant topics," Caitlyn said, attempting to sound bright.

During the meal the conversation turned toward the houses around them and the identities of some of the artists in residence.

"What I'd really like to know," said Caitlyn after having discussed several of the closer houses, "is who owns that lovely home high on the hill; the one with the arched balconies."

"I don't know who occupies it now," responded Paul, "but it's funny you should have asked about that one. Up until the 1974 conflict, that was the mountain home of a French industrialist family named Piccard. You know of Eleni Piccard, I'm sure. She owns the Ledra Consolidated companies. They are big in the shipping industry in the Mediterranean. In fact, I think the family started off as pirates and smugglers. Rumor has it that their flagship still has a hidden stateroom in it where gold bullion was shunted around between the Arab states a decade or two ago. Mrs. Piccard also is the director of the Ledra Foundation they support. That's the foundation that is financing your archaeological project."

"Yes, of course," said Caitlyn. "Mrs. Piccard met me at the airport." Caitlyn didn't go on to tell Paul that this had marked the beginning of her strange feelings of familiarity with Cyprus. The initial sight of Mrs. Piccard had set off a spark of recognition that had perplexed Caitlyn ever since.

"Yes, it's certainly a coincidence that I've been attracted to her house. Why is it that you say that *used* to be her mountain home, and is there a Mr. Piccard?"

"Ah, now *there's* a mystery—and a tragedy," answered Paul. "Guy Piccard was French, as I said, but Eleni Piccard is a Greek Cypriot. She cannot come to this side and thus has not seen the house since 1974. I understand, though, that some European friends who live in the village permanently took over the house and have ensured that it is maintained in good shape and is rented to other European long-term visitors. At least it hasn't been taken over by strangers or left to molder unattended."

"But what about *Mr.* Piccard?" Caitlyn broke in. "You said there was some sort of mystery." It wasn't just idle curiosity that motivated Caitlyn's query. The mere mention of a mystery attached to the Piccards had inexplicably set Caitlyn's nerves on end.

"In fact," responded Paul, smoothly changing gears and taking note of how attractive Caitlyn was when she became intensively interested in a topic, "she last saw her husband, and, incidentally, her young son, Pierre, as well, on the same day she last saw that house. It was just one of the many tragedies of that chaotic 1974 period. When the Turkish troops came ashore, the Piccard family was vacationing at their Bellapais house and was trapped here by the events. As I have said, the European residents of Bellapais had concluded an agreement whereby the Turkish troops would bypass and not enter the village. When the fighting had died down, the Turks agreed to permit a limited number of convoys of both Greeks and Europeans who wanted safe passage from the occupied area to the Greek side to travel unmolested. The Piccards had originally planned to take the same convoy from Bellapais to Nicosia. But on the appointed day of departure, Guy Piccard told his wife he had an important business meeting to attend down on the coast before he left. He told her that she and the Greek servants should travel on ahead in one car. He and the son, Pierre, would follow in the next convoy in their other car."

Paul paused, gazing up at the Piccard villa. Caitlyn's attention already was riveted on the tiers of arches clinging to the hillside above them.

"Eleni Piccard never heard from either her husband or son again. They have been formally listed as missing persons and presumed to have been killed somehow in the confusion of those weeks of fighting. Eleni continued running and building the Cyprus arm of the family shipping and export businesses from Nicosia and the southern port city of Limassol—and has continued waiting in the hope of realizing a personal miracle in the return of her family."

"Oh, how awful for her," Caitlyn murmured, her eyes still captive of the mountain mansion that was shimmering in the afternoon sunlight.

"Yes, certainly," responded Paul, "but not untypical of tragic stories that many families on both sides of Cyprus's Greek-Turkish conflict could relate or of the memories they have to endure of family members, property, and possessions lost."

* * * *

The first thing that struck Caitlyn about the Bellapais Abbey after they had left the restaurant and crossed the street was the peacefulness of the informal garden that was laid out in the ruins of what had been the kitchen court and that overflowed with both cultivated and wild flowers in a riot of color. Her attention then moved to the four majestic funeral cypress trees that rose well above the abbey walls in a square pattern in the central cloister.

"What beautiful trees," Caitlyn exclaimed. "Are these cypresses the source of the island's name?"

"No," Paul chuckled, well-accustomed to the newcomers' victimization by the sound of the two words, "the words aren't related at all. Cyprus, the name of the island, is Greek for copper and reflects the importance of the Cypriot copper mines to the Mediterranean basin economy in the early days of the region's trading system."

"Copper mines?" Caitlyn looked sharply at Paul in an attempt to discern whether he was pulling her leg. "I've never heard about copper mines in Cyprus."

"Just bad timing," was Paul's amused response. "The mines played out a long time ago, but Cleopatra and her cronies took them seriously enough when Alexander's heirs were carving up shares of the region."

"Well, at least the color of copper is shining on in the flowers." Caitlyn waltzed around the pleasant abbey grounds. As her eyes lifted again to the four sentinel cypress trees, she once more was struck by a sense of déjà vu. "This is so familiar that it seems as if I've been here before," she gasped, seriously in danger of entering another of her reveries of ancient times.

"More than likely you've just subconsciously recognized the picture of the cloister garden on the Cyprus one-pound note," Paul burst her bubble. "Or perhaps you've just caught glances of this motif being put to use—and sometimes overuse—throughout the south, where this is one of the primary symbols used by the Greeks to depict what they have lost."

It seemed to Caitlyn that she was not to be so easily put off by cold reality, however, because, as she stood there drinking in the beautiful spring flowers that were running rampant through the ruin, she was increasingly convinced she heard the echo of monks chanting from somewhere within the abbey. The music was weaving its magic about her, and, closing her eyes and leaning against a stone pillar, she let her mind began to waft back in time. But, rather than drifting into to a scene of pure tones and quietude, the spectacle that was forming before her closed eyes, although the swirl of monk's habits most certainly was in evidence, was shockingly lurid and raucous. She was fighting to bring it all into focus, where she could start to sort out the incongruities.

"What the . . .? Where's that music coming from?" exclaimed Paul, as he tramped off toward the huge refectory perched out over the valley. Once more, Caitlyn's forming vision popped and fell like confetti before her. She caught up with Paul just as he encountered several men exiting the lofty chamber.

"Lovely acoustics," intoned one of the men with a somewhat chagrined look and a Flemish accent, as he brushed past. Caitlyn stood there like a startled deer. This was all becoming just a bit too surrealistic for her.

"Well, that explains that," Paul muttered, as he turned back from the entrance into the refectory.

"Explains what?" Caitlyn answered a bit too sharply.

"That Belgian church choir that's singing down at the archbishopric in old Nicosia. They must be filling in their days with sightseeing. Nice sound," he continued. "These walls certainly could use the cleansing of genuine Gregorian chants." The two had moved to the middle of a large stone-walled chamber that rose more than two stories to a cathedral ceiling. A pulpit cantilevered into the room about halfway up the outer wall, a wall that was pierced by tall, stone-laced arched windows that overlooked the hillside undulating down to the sea. The windows were open to the elements, the floor was beaten earth, and the current rulers of the realm were a large flock of doves, whose copious droppings provided the room's only current ornamentation.

"And what's *that* supposed to mean?" retorted Caitlyn. She continued to feel off balance and a bit woozy as well.

"This was once one of the most important centers of church power on the island," explained Paul. "It has had a Christian connection at least as far back as the seventh century. At one time it rivaled the cathedral in Nicosia in popularity and wealth to such an extent that it became the subject of all sorts of jealous attacks. The monks here were accused of being involved in all manner of debauchery. The order was near to being put down by the local church authorities when the Ottoman Turks entered the scene and saved the church in Nicosia the trouble by scattering the monks and closing the abbey themselves. It never did regain its abbey status."

"And that explains that," Caitlyn declared. The world was starting to regain perspective for Caitlyn. Although she had no idea how the vision of raucous monks had come to her, at least now the logic of the image made sense. It was Paul's turn to be nonplused. But before he could pursue the meaning of Caitlyn's answer, she had walked over to one of the large windows that overlooked the sea and had nearly lost her physical equilibrium after so recently having regained her mental balance. There was a sharp drop off of some four or five stories, the whole abbey structure being firmly built up from foundations of hewn rock. The view from the window was magnificent. The panorama, along with snatches of music still wafting from the Belgian tourists as they explored the rest of the abbey, held Caitlyn at the window.

The patch of slope running down from the base of the abbey complex and two-thirds toward the edge of the sea was largely covered in neatly patterned orchards. They had visited the abbey in precisely the right season. The almond trees were just about to lose their once-abundant white blossoms, while the fruit of the lemon, orange, grapefruit, and fig trees was just beginning to take on its color. Most of the rolling ground was devoted to olive trees, which could clearly be distinguished from the others by their dusty gray-green leaves.

The rockier areas of the landscape were planted to what Paul had informed her were carob trees—squat, bushy trees with gnarled trunks. Paul had said that these trees had once dominated the fields, just as the carob they produced had once dominated the economy of the Kyrenia region. Carob had been the single product that had for centuries supported the warehouses—now the harbor-side restaurants—of the small port. The product had been so important to this coast in earlier days that it was still referred to by locals as the "black gold of Cyprus."

Among the orchards that descended the slopes could be seen flocks of sheep and of goats. This sylvan setting merged into the more modern visage of pretty stuccoed holiday villas on either side of the road that paralleled the sea. Although a few small, sandy beaches could be discerned from Caitlyn's perch, most of the coastal margins ended abruptly in dark rocks of igneous origin that reached into the sea. The Mediterranean itself started in a turquoise color close to the land—the water here being so clear that Caitlyn could see the rocks covering the sea bottom even from her far-off perch—and merged into deeper shades of blue off toward the Turkish coast.

The bucolic setting was perfect, and both the scattered bungalows of this and other villages and the massive abbey complex—by right of its centuries-long presence—were in complete harmony with nature.

"Yes, I can see why the Cypriots would cling to this setting as a key part to their identity," Caitlyn thought.

As they returned to the car to depart, Caitlyn once more lifted her gaze toward the villa of the Piccards. "I already feel a strong affinity to Eleni Piccard," she thought. "We both have suffered great loss without the luxury of having had that loss defined as final and irrevocable. Yet, she seems to have been able to continue life for two decades and to have prospered without having let bitterness overtake her. How long I have feared that my own loss would cripple me emotionally. I'll have to learn where she has found her strength to go on."

But was it only this affinity in loss that linked her with Eleni Piccard? Caitlyn wondered. There seemed to be something more, something Caitlyn couldn't quite grasp.

Paul was completely oblivious to the contemplative mood Caitlyn had developed, as they folded themselves into the convertible for the gingerly negotiated trip through the narrow, twisting village street and back down the hillside. She was jarred out of her reverie by the uncomfortable feeling that they were being watched—and not just by the village grandfathers gathered with their pipes and their brandy glasses at the other end of the square. No. The old men were viewing them with a benign clash-of-worlds' amusement. What Caitlyn felt reaching out to her was more of a malevolence. She scanned the sides of the square. There was movement at the edge of the abbey complex, where there was a rock-strewn parking apron. But the movement there proved only to be the Belgians boarding their tourist bus.

Caitlyn turned to say something to Paul about her feeling, but, when she did, she encountered a hard stare from Paul himself. She was about to upbraid him for scaring her, but then she saw that he was looking past her, toward the embarking Belgians. He quickly backed the BMW out of the cramped parking space and was gathering up dangerous speed long before they careened into the opening at the top of the square that led into what barely passed as the village's main street.

Caitlyn was too concerned about what Paul had seen in the square and whether or not that was connected with the feeling of dread she herself had had back there to waste any worry on Paul's reckless driving. The quicker they got away the better she liked it, although she had no idea why she felt that way. All in all, this was not developing into the free-spirited day Paul had promised her.

Chapter Four

Paul gunned the responsive sports car out of the village and down the winding road toward the coast as if he were trying to qualify for the Grand Prix. Caitlyn held off on comment—in fact, she held on for dear life. When they were well away from the village, however, she made a point of totaling up "violent mood swings" in the debit column of her assessment of the American diplomat. She was even more determined than in earlier low points of their day's outing that she would quickly cultivate entirely different friendships to enrich the remainder of her time on the island. When she got back to Nicosia . . . no, *if* she got back to Nicosia alive, she corrected herself, as Paul swung around a corner and showed every intention of occupying the same space as an oncoming motorcycle, it would be "Good night, great time, see you in the States someday"—but not someday soon.

Three-quarters of the way down the slope, where the road dead-ended into the road they had taken from Kyrenia a couple of hours earlier, Paul made a wheels-squealing right turn and then, almost immediately, a sharp left. The car approached the outskirts of a village, where Paul cut the speed considerably. He didn't really have much choice. A small herd of goats was wandering aimlessly across the one-lane pebbled road.

Paul took a searching look over his shoulder, let his breath out for possibly the first time in the few minutes since he had jumped in the driver's seat up in Bellapais, and maneuvered the BMW sedately and expertly through the assorted goats. The latter seemed to have no appreciation for the possible death-producing capabilities of an automobile.

"That was nicely done," intoned Caitlyn, meaning to be taken sarcastically but not succeeding, whether through Paul's blissful ignorance or his intent not to further alienate.

"You *do* acquire a knack in Cyprus," Paul cheerily responded. "Everything prefers to play in the road—people, goats, cats, dogs, snakes, donkeys, sheep . . . chickens," he added, as an afterthought, as he approached two unconcerned roosters strutting towards his bumper.

Caitlyn's ire began to melt again. "What was I saying about gigantic mood swings," she sighed to herself.

Shortly after the car entered the village proper, Caitlyn had completely lost her sense of direction.

"I'm glad Paul knows where he's going," she thought. However, the third time they passed between the Happy Garden Restaurant and an abandoned Greek Orthodox chapel, she abandoned trust.

"Oh, well. Let *him* figure it out," she mused. "He hasn't admitted he's lost and shows no sign of dropping his self-perceived macho image long enough to ask directions."

Immediately thereafter, however, Paul returned to a direct course. This abrupt transition invited Caitlyn's suspicion that he had been rambling on purpose for reasons he wasn't about to volunteer—or just to try to get a rise from her, which seemed the most likely explanation. Very soon the BMW turned back toward Kyrenia. Caitlyn, of course, wondered why Paul had taken the unnecessary diversion into a village that was not in a direct lane between Bellapais and Kyrenia. But she was just too tired and disgusted to pursue the point.

In short order, they had passed through the upper reaches of Kyrenia and were ascending the road through the Kyrenia pass. Caitlyn traced the silhouette of St. Hilarion Castle with her eyes. Paul told her about the other two castles that crowned the Kyrenia Range, as he reestablished a steady driving pace. But he was still driving faster than she would have attempted with these road conditions. As both Caitlyn and Paul were otherwise distracted, they were startled when the BMW was overtaken by another vehicle. Accompanied by a single blast on a car horn and with only inches to spare, a small white van swept around the convertible as if the BMW were standing still.

At the same time he was struggling to maintain control of his car, Paul let out a yelp.

"Viktor! I wonder what *he's* doing here! And I wonder where he's headed at such a pace and in a van. I would have thought. . . . But, no that does make sense."

"Viktor? Who's Viktor?" Caitlyn croaked as soon as she was able to breath—she had been on the down-slope side of the BMW's attempt to fly out toward the coastline. "And what do you mean that it makes sense?"

"Victor's the madman in that UN van up there." It became fairly obvious Paul wasn't going to answer Caitlyn's second question.

"How do you know that's a UN van?" she asked aloud, while thinking to herself with exasperation that Paul seemed incapable of answering one question without raising others.

"By the registration plate color—blue for UN. And Viktor Gorodov is quite definitely UN, although what he is doing driving a van on this road is beyond me. But it's also very interesting," Paul added after a thoughtful pause.

"Why?" was Caitlyn's simple response, as she had become completely lost somewhere in this conversation.

"Gorodov, who you will meet sooner or later—probably sooner than later, considering his reputation for homing in on every lovely lady on the island—is the deputy United Nations coordinator for Cyprus. This makes him very high ranked, and it certainly makes him much too high ranked to be driving a UN van around alone in the Kyrenia Mountains like a maniac. As the name implies, he is Russian. He has somewhat of a reputation of being a real wheeler and dealer in the growth of entrepreneurial types in the former Soviet Union states following the breakup of socialism. The American embassy was not pleased he got this assignment, as we have to work very closely with the UN coordinator's office. We've worked quite hard over the years to keep the Russians out of the Cyprus problem altogether. But Viktor doesn't seem to appreciate us either, so we appear to be even."

Caitlyn could see that this Viktor fellow was a sore spot for Paul, but, thinking that this might help keep his speed down if he had a discussion to concentrate on, she decided to backtrack to repeat an earlier question. "So why," she asked, "if you are surprised to find such a high-ranking UN official here, did you also say that it made sense for you to see him here?"

Paul clamped his jaw shut.

"Oh, come on, Paul," Caitlyn jabbed. "I think I'm looking forward to meeting this Viktor. He sounds intriguing, and you seem to be exaggerating his bad character."

"Look, Caitlyn," Paul said after a pause. "I really shouldn't be going into this with you, but I will say this much, if only because it indicates what a dangerous man he is. While we were at the top of the castle tower back there in Kyrenia harbor and you were looking down into the harbor, I was looking in the opposite direction, at the piers of the new harbor. I saw Viktor there, standing beside a white van. There was a small ship at the pier that shouldn't have been there. Northern Cyprus waters are denied to all but Turkish vessels, as all other nations recognize these as waters of the Greek Cypriots. But the ship I saw there obviously wasn't Turkish."

"And so?"

"And so—there were wooden crates being loaded from that ship into the van. I could see that Viktor was up to something, but it is very interesting to have found out that he was driving the van himself. There was another man there with Viktor, a blond guy."

Caitlyn felt the hairs at the base of her neck inexplicably stand up at the mention of the "blond guy," but she ignored the reaction. "And so?" she repeated. She was beginning to enjoy this.

"So, this means Viktor quite evidently wants as few as possible to see him breaking a whole handful of international laws. These start with being a partner to an illegal port entry and move on

59

to receiving what are quite probably contraband goods in an illegal location and most likely taking those illegal goods back across the border into Greek Cyprus in a van protected by diplomatic plates. That's why I wasn't, in the final tally, surprised to see the van on this road. But, boy is he taking a chance. Any one of these acts would be enough to get a diplomat thrown out of the country. And Viktor's not just any diplomat. He's the number two UN official here.

"Oh, I see," Caitlyn mumbled. Now she was sorry she asked. But she had to admit to herself that this didn't make the Russian any less interesting to her. Her relationship with Kurt had proven that she was a sucker for naughty boys.

During this tirade, Paul had been adjusting the rear-view mirror that somehow had been pushed out of kilter while the BMW was contemplating whether it wanted to take a closer look at the ravine bed. With a grunt, he broke off his attack on the Russian official, hunkered down in his seat, and stepped on the gas.

"Oh, no, Mr. Hyde's back," Caitlyn moaned, as she checked her seat belt and closed her eyes tightly.

The BMW almost left the roadway, as it turned a corner and shot into a blind curve on the road. Within yards, just about at the point the road was to start its descent into Cyprus's central Messaoria Plain, Paul swerved hard to the right into a gravel road. He pulled up behind a few trees and out of sight from the main road.

"Just be a minute," Paul said cheerily, as he jerked off his seat belt. The only explanation he gave, as he leaped from the car and moved back toward the main road was, "Just remembered that the side road I wanted to take back to Nicosia had been washed out near where it leaves the highway. If I look over the side, maybe I can see whether it's still closed."

With this, Caitlyn was unceremoniously deserted, dust still settling on—and in—the car. The heat quickly began to clutch at her now that the air conditioning created by the convertible in motion had been switched off.

Paul returned within a few minutes. "Nope, the road's fine. We can use the old road back to Nicosia."

Halfway back down to the capital on what had been the old road linking Nicosia with the Kyrenia Pass before the Saudis had paid for a new highway, Caitlyn softly asked after considerable contemplation: "The truth, Paul. The road hasn't really been washed out, has it?"

"Nope," Paul answered with resignation. "I had to check the road behind us. I just thought you would find that a more comfortable explanation than that we have been followed all the way from Kyrenia. And, if my eyes haven't deceived me, by the same man we saw in the Kyrenia Castle moat who wanted to take a test drive in my car."

"And that's who you saw up in Bellapais just before we tore off down the mountain." This was more a statement than a question.

"Yep. He was watching us from the upper terrace of the Tree of Idleness."

"And you weren't really lost in that village down by the sea. You were backtracking to try to shake him off. Right?"

"Right. Thought I'd managed to do that too. I'm sorry, Caitlyn, it hasn't been a good day. It's probably the green diplomatic tags on my car. Sometimes we can come over here and just enjoy ourselves, and sometimes the local authorities want to put on a show for us. I didn't think the time was ripe for you to see the inside of the Turkish military headquarters yet."

"I grew up thinking diplomacy was all about striped pants, cocktail parties, and telling outrageous lies with a gracious smile," Caitlyn muttered wearily. "Just take me home, Paul. I just don't have the energy to keep up with all this intrigue."

But, in the end, she wasn't really to have that choice, either.

* * * *

Paul retraced their path to the Kyrenia Pass, in the shadow of St. Hilarion. But, once back on the central plain, he turned off on the old Kyrenia Road rather than proceeding to the capital on the new road the Saudis had built. The old road was much more bumpy and had more curves than the new one. But it only took Paul and Caitlyn about twenty minutes until the walled city of Nicosia could be seen in the near distance. After negotiating a short stretch of rolling sand dunes topped with scrub, the convertible was traveling through the newer part of Turkish Nicosia and was approaching the old city walls at the Kyrenia gate.

"Great," Paul muttered. "Just as I feared. Our friendly shadow is back. He undoubtedly just waited here to ensure we were accounted for. Well, a Turkish tailgunner will have to break surveillance at the checkpoint, which is nearby, and the streets here are too congested for him to try anything funny. So we should be all right."

Caitlyn wasn't all that amused by Paul's use of the word "gunner" and, try as she might, she couldn't see any car tailing them. In fact, now that she thought about it, other than the incident in the

Kyrenia Castle moat, which could have been chalked up to curiosity, she hadn't herself seen evidence of anyone purposefully following them all day. Could this be Paul's sense of a good joke on the new girl in town? From today's experience, she wouldn't put such behavior past him.

Paul cut in front of a bus as he followed the curvature of the wall toward the west and turned at one of many traffic circles, dominated by one of many war memorials. He picked his way through two blocks of shops and homes set back from the street behind concrete walls and negotiated an intersection with ancient traffic lights that appeared to be working only toward one direction. He then pulled up to the left of the two-story Turkish Cypriot border and customs checkpoint. This checkpoint was located on the bank of the old city's dry moat. Taking note of the BMW's green diplomatic registration plate and having received Caitlyn's day-pass exit form, the policeman on duty smiled congenially and lifted the barricade.

Within less than a hundred feet, the car passed between rolls of concertina wire and past a UN blue- and white-colored shed that stuck out in the road to prevent a direct line of sight between the Turkish and Greek checkpoints. They had entered the no-man's-land buffer zone, which was populated only by UN troops and which provided a token barrier between the two ethnic factions. Nearly all of the buildings here were abandoned and most had become bombed-out ruins. Perhaps most forlorn of all was the once majestic Ledra Palace Hotel, which now served as the dormitory for the UN troop contingent assigned to the Nicosia sector.

They were now approaching the end of the UN zone, which was marked by a zigzag concrete wall placed across the road. Without notice, Paul sat upright in his seat and hissed an "Oh, damn!"

Caitlyn's answering "What now?" clearly revealed her irritation.

"He's followed us into the buffer zone, so he can't be Turkish security," Paul muttered.

Caitlyn barely had time to brace herself against the dashboard as the BMW shot through the zigzag barrier and past the Greek checkpoint. The Greek border guard, in turn, only had time to drop his jaw and his clipboard before the car had entered still another traffic circle, this one mercifully devoid of a war monument, and careened toward the left, heading toward yet another traffic circle. The BMW was now running alongside the city wall once again at a point where there was actually no buffer zone at all. The street they were traversing was in the Greek zone, but the old city walls immediately above them and the dry moat immediately below them were Turkish territory. Two flags, the white on red flag of mainland Turkey and the mirroring red on white flag of the Turkish Cypriots, floated over their heads. Occupied machine gun nests, identifying the Greek Cypriot outposts here, were located in the upper stories of blocks of apartments on their right.

The first exit off of the next traffic circle they entered was the Paphos Gate, which also marked the first Greek-controlled point of entry into the old city on the western side. The road that spiraled off the circle from the opposite side of the Paphos Gate, the one Paul now took, entered directly into the new city's central block. The city park; the municipal theater; an open-air café; the nation's unimposing parliament building; and the Cyprus Museum, headquarters of the Antiquities Department and where Caitlyn was to do much of her work, were all located in this block. As they crossed the next intersection, they entered straight-on into Byron Avenue and now were only about four blocks from Gladstone Street, where Caitlyn was living. This section of the city having also been the British administrative center before independence, several of the streets still bore names appropriate to that period or still rendered in anglicized spellings—Byron, Gladstone, Egypt, Homer.

The BMW sped down the pleasantly tree-lined Byron Avenue, past, first, the Greek embassy on the right and, then, St. Paul's historic Anglican "Cathedral" (cathedral in name; not in size) on the left and subsequently between a procession of decaying colonial mansions.

"Under the circumstances, I'm afraid I'm just going to have to drop you off quickly and try to ensure that I've lost this character," Paul apologized. "I have no idea who from this side would be following me around the Turkish zone—very few people have such access to both sides."

"Yes, I suppose that would be best," answered Caitlyn in a level voice, trying her best to hide her relief. She had wondered how she could gracefully separate herself from the disturbing—and quite possibly disturbed—diplomat without scheduling a follow-up torture session.

But, as he turned into Gladstone, yet another crumbling mansion- and tree-lined street, and as if he had read her thoughts, Paul suggested: "Next week, if you like, we can do Salamis. Same day, same time?"

"Salamis!" Caitlyn exclaimed, her resolve dissolving at the mere suggestion of an opportunity to see the archaeological jewel on the east coast, which also was located in the Turkish zone.

Salamis, located just to the north of what now was the port of Famagusta, had been the center of many major civilizations marching back into the Neolithic period. The city specifically known by that name had, by tradition, been founded in the eleventh century BC by a hero of the Trojan Wars. It had remained a major Mediterranean city state for the next two thousand years, finally being destroyed by a series of earthquakes that dropped a good portion of the original city into the sea. The ancient city even had significance to the Christian era. St. Paul had been reputed to have arrived in Cyprus at Salamis, with Cyprus's native apostle, Barnabas, on one of his celebrated journeys in the western Mediterranean. Salamis. Salamis.

"Yes, probably, let's see if we can set it up definitely later in the week," Caitlyn involuntarily heard herself replying, as Paul screeched to a stop in front of her house and she hopped out.

And, with a roar and a loud "Good-bye, Cait," Paul was gone.

Caitlyn briefly looked back down the street, but she still could see no evidence they had been followed.

As she turned at the gate of the Petrou mansion to begin preparations for that evening's reception, she ran smack into . . .

. . . a Greek god.

* * * *

Caitlyn stuttered out an "Oh, excuse me," and pulled back out of the aura of Zeus. Yes, that was it—Zeus. He wasn't an Apollo, because he didn't have the perfect, slim build of a youth. In fact, he

66

was rather thickset, although he certainly left the impression of being solidly and beautifully put together on the whole. It occurred to Caitlyn that all Greek men tended to make her a bit weak about the knees—although, on reflection, she couldn't recall having known that many Greek men. At the moment, she was feeling like jelly down to her ankles.

Zeus was, of course, inhumanly handsome. His curly black hair, graying a bit at the temples, his laughing eyes, and his heavenly smile, with its playful hint of a tease at the corner, held her speechless and clinging to the tall stuccoed gatepost. He stood there in a classic senatorial pose that seemed to come to him by natural right, an observation that Caitlyn was to remember later and mark as prophetic.

"No, it is I who am sorry, Miss," the god spoke with a melting smile. Then, leaving her there, still speechless, he glided to a nearby aging Alfa Romeo coupe and drove down the street in the wake of Paul's BMW.

When she had regained her composure and recovered from the embarrassment of her obviously fawning behavior during this brief encounter, Caitlyn turned and gazed appreciatively up at the grand old mansion. She still could not believe her utterly good fortune to be staying here. This had been, from the time it was built, the primary home of the Petrou family—local Greek Cypriot notables for centuries on end and judicial system administrators for the British during the recent colonial period. It currently was the residence of Nora Petrou, a French Canadian national, who had met the brilliant Greek Cypriot lawyer, Nicos Petrou, in Paris directly after World War II. During the war Nicos had lost his first wife in the London blitz.

From the very beginning, the union between Nora and Nicos had been a strong marriage of two very ambitious and capable people. They had returned to Cyprus, where Nicos had eventually risen to be founder and chief of a major political party and, briefly, the nation's second elected president following the 1974 Turkish invasion of Cyprus. While stalwartly supporting Nicos's political climb, Nora Petrou had become a power in her own right in the business world through her managing directorship of the wealthy Engomi National bank. She had also subsequently added a large and successful international travel agency to her portfolio. The ultraconservative views promoted by Nicos through his New Democratic Party—the NDK (Nea Demokraitiko Kommo)—had eventually lost him the political support necessary to pass legislation, so he had stepped down as president. He had, however, with the full, active help of his wife, maintained control of the NDK and continued to fight his positions as a member of the Cypriot parliament. In more recent years, however, he had encountered a growing power struggle within the party, led by his son and only child from his first marriage.

The son, Vassos, had spent considerable time at universities in Russia in the 1960s, when a socialist education was fashionable among the Cypriots. He eventually returned to Cyprus, founded a firebrand liberal newspaper, *Rizospastis*—the Radical—and gained a seat of his own in parliament through the family's NDK. His campaign had not enjoyed the enthusiastic support of either his father or his stepmother.

And then, two years ago, Nicos Petrou had been assassinated, in broad daylight in the parliament building parking lot, not more than four blocks from this quiet house and this peaceful street. His killer or

68

killers had never been found, and both he and his grieving widow—who continued to function as an influential force in national affairs—had now been accorded legend status. Nora, in fact, remained so omnipresent in the upper echelons of both society and politics that a popular columnist had once referred to her as Queen Nora, and the name had stuck with her in press comment.

More pertinent for Caitlyn, however, Nora Petrou was also an honorary, but very active, member of the Fulbright Commission Board, which had brought Caitlyn to Cyprus. Upon hearing that Caitlyn needed a place to stay that would be convenient to the Cyprus Museum, Mrs. Petrou had immediately and graciously volunteered room and board in her ideally located mansion. She said that the house had become too lonely and quiet for her to bear by herself.

Even more fortunate, the house was also within a short walk to the Fulbright Commission offices, which were located on Egypt Street, just behind the museum. The house itself was a two-story, square colonial mansion with a newer, but complementarily designed two-floor wing off to one side and a detached garage block in the rear. As with much British colonial residential architecture, it combined British stalwartness with local embellishments. Thus it was built of large stone bricks, stuccoed in a light ocher color. Balconies and raised terraces were located with a greater concern for use than for artistic balance, which, in the end, provided far more charm and architectural interest than if they had been placed with greater care for symmetry and prevailing style. The house had a red tile roof, and its shutters, doors, and trim were painted in a dignified, yet glossy forest green. The approach to the house was via an impressive European-style marble staircase, but the door itself was presented in the best of

Cypriot town house tradition. There were heavy double doors, with intricately designed iron window grills. The same grill pattern was continued in full-length side windows and in a window above the door. One of the most distinctive features of the overhead window grill was a stylized rendering of the crusader-period Lusignan coat of arms. This had been placed there, it was said, when the building was first built by a Petrou, who claimed direct family linkage all the way back to the Lusignans.

In addition to the tall pine, funeral cypress, palm, and eucalyptus trees lining the street, an adornment that was not present on many Nicosia city streets any more, the mansion's facade was covered with bougainvillea vines in the most vibrant shade of magenta Caitlyn had ever seen. The long-established side and rear gardens were among the most verdant in the city. This was primarily because the mansion was located directly beside the city's river. Although the river's bed was dry ten months out of the year, it did have enough year-round subterranean water flow to nourish the trees on its banks as well as any gardens that stood immediately adjacent.

Caitlyn sighed with pleasure and, as she quickly admitted to herself, with pure physical fatigue, as she opened the door and entered the front hall. At this point her mood was burst by a screech in Greek that could not have translated into a nice phrase. Immediately thereafter, Caitlyn heard a crash of broken glass. She rushed to the large lounge that ran the full depth of the house on the river side.

Nora Petrou, a now-stout, but still very presentable woman with jet-black hair, jet-black eyes, a jet-black blouse and tailored suede skirt, and a flash of diamonds and gold was standing stiffly in the middle of the room and facing the fireplace. A now-unidentifiable pottery figurine lay shattered on the hearth.

Upon hearing Caitlyn pull open the pocket door to the hallway, Mrs. Petrou jerked around, eyes flashing, fists bunched, spangle bracelets spinning. She immediately relaxed, however, and automatically shifted into that gracious facial expression and body stance of welcome and interest that must be taught worldwide in Advanced Political Wifery courses.

"I'm so sorry, dear. I didn't hear you come in," she oozed. And then, after a brief pause, "Do look what naughty kitty has done."

Upon closer inspection, Caitlyn did, indeed, see "naughty kitty" cowering under a nearby Chippendale wing chair. But it was her strong suspicion that "kitty," in this case an aging Siamese that would have been hard pressed to reach the figurine let alone knock it off the mantel, was reacting more nearly like the attacked than the attacker.

Caitlyn's attention focused on the portrait over the mantelpiece, which seemed to be what Mrs. Petrou had been trying to bore her eyes into when Caitlyn had arrived at the scene. The portrait was of a magnificently handsome man, totally mesmerizing in spite of his physical absence from the room. Caitlyn couldn't remember having focused on it before, but this undoubtedly was the lost Nicos Petrou.

The presence of the man in the portrait was so dominant in the room that Caitlyn couldn't imagine why she had overlooked the painting earlier. Perhaps it was the sudden familiarity of the face. Snatches of her reveries of earlier in the day were racing back at her, and, although she couldn't make out detail in these flashbacks, she knew, without knowing why, that the face had been there in more

71

than one instance. Perhaps, she reasoned with herself, this was all a case of the power of suggestion. Perhaps she had actually seen the portrait without it having registered in her consciousness. And perhaps the strong features had intruded themselves into her imaginings earlier in the day. She was almost convincing herself that this had been the case.

But that wasn't all. She suddenly realized that the face was also that of the Zeus of her front gate encounter just now. That had been no illusion.

"We'll be leaving for Jacques's party at about half seven, my dear," Nora Petrou prattled as she led a confused, but subdued Caitlyn back out into the hall and to the foot of the massive semicircular marble staircase. "You have just enough time for a bath and a short nap."

"A bath and a short nap," Caitlyn repeated in a distant voice. She didn't think she had heard two such glorious suggestions all day. She didn't have to be prodded a second time to drag her weary bones up toward heaven—a heaven containing a bathtub and a bed.

Chapter Five

It was twilight when Nora Petrou's old, but still grand seven-seat Mercedes rolled up to the front of the Eleon swim and tennis club. At this time of the evening the retreating light showed off the predominantly white buildings, red tile roofs, tropical greenery, and multicolored shutters to an effect that was only rivaled by the brilliance of the noonday sun in a cloudless sky. But, of the two, Caitlyn picked twilight, which was guaranteed to soften both the heart strings and the resolve to ever depart the Greek isle setting.

It was also getting decidedly cooler and breezier, but not so cool that Caitlyn did not pity the French ambassador, who had taken the host's position under the suburban club's front portico. The ambassador perfectly lived up to his role by way of distinguished looks, a suave manner, erect stance, steady hand and gaze, and comfortably mid-life handsome visage. He was swathed in an elegant brown silk pinstripe suite, with a bold, colorful tie and pocket handkerchief such as only the French seem to be able to bring off successfully.

Although suitably impressed, Caitlyn's first thought was whether diplomats assigned to the tropics wore specially designed suits with secret waterproof lining in which they could keep ice cubes. She lamented that she herself had chosen, locale in mind, a low-necked long Greek chiton cut to be flattering to the figure and in a soft green and white pattern designed to evoke a sense of clouds. All well and good, but the gown had turned out to be a cotton blend that didn't breathe as well as she had thought it would. At Nora's insistence, she had also brought a shawl in a reverse pattern to that of the dress and cut in the shape of the traditional Greek pella that ancient women had often draped diagonally over their shoulders and around the hips over their chitons. However, Caitlyn didn't see now how she would be getting cool enough to require the shawl. For her part, Nora, as always, was wearing her signature black silk; solemn in color but as well-styled as her ample figure allowed and fairly dripping in diamonds.

Nora had regaled Caitlyn with the full life's story of Ambassador Jacques Piccard on the way over in the limousine. Nora was quite obviously smitten with the man and appeared to believe that those feelings were fully reciprocated, even though she must have been a good deal older than the diplomat. The first thing about Piccard that struck Caitlyn was the name. Nora had confirmed that it was no coincidence that he had the same surname as Eleni Piccard.

"Jacques is a nephew of Eleni's deceased husband, Guy. He had, in fact, been trying to work his career toward the Mediterranean area for some years so that he could eventually retire here and help Eleni with the Cyprus branch of the family corporations. If truth be known, he has already begun the transition and is overseeing a good part of the shipping end of the business. This leaves Eleni more time to develop the philanthropic foundation."

"My goodness, you certainly know a lot about the ambassador's background," responded Caitlyn.

"I always fully research my investment possibilities." Nora fairly glowed with happiness. "Jacques has had an interesting, if not flashy career," Nora continued. "He got a late start in the corps, as he began his professional life in France, working with the Marseilles branch of the family's shipping empire. But he tired quickly of business and became a commercial attaché, serving in French embassies in Russia, Canada, Belgium, Turkey, Bulgaria, and Lebanon over a fifteen-year period spanning from the sixties into the seventies. He then was attached to the French defense ministries for some time before having been rewarded this final ambassadorship tour."

"He sounds like an interesting person," Caitlyn had commented to be polite. Mrs. Petrou's ability to reel off the ambassador's pedigree so precisely seemed to reveal a cold, calculating side to the woman that Caitlyn didn't fully admire.

"Yes, he's fascinating," Nora bubbled with enthusiasm. "I'm sure you'll find him as irresistible as I do."

And now, as Caitlyn was being introduced to the ambassador in the flesh, Nora's infatuation was becoming clear. Caitlyn could tell instantly that Piccard was quite the ladies' man and was smooth enough to have to watch every moment. She hoped that Nora was not just being taken into a one-sided relationship solely on her ability to open political and social doors in the capital. These fears were only increased, however, when her gaze made contact with Piccard's for the first time. His roving and glittering eyes actively tried to take full possession.

"And this must be our visiting archaeology professor, Dr. Spencer. I am delighted you were able to come this evening. We feel so privileged to have you with us in Cyprus. I, too, am a bit of a history buff. But during my initial months here, alas, I have not been able to do much exploring. We will have to discover the island together. Eleni, Love, you will have to assign your new archaeologist as my ward for her field trips."

He had turned to Eleni Piccard, who stood on his right and who evidently was functioning as hostess for the bachelor diplomat (actually, twice divorced, Caitlyn had already been informed in scandalized undertones by Nora). Caitlyn was once more struck with the simultaneous and inexplicable emotions of affection and protectiveness as she came into contact with Eleni Piccard for a second time since arriving in Cyprus. The reputation of Eleni Piccard that had been provided to Caitlyn before she left the States was that of an iron woman. But, from their first meeting, Caitlyn had seen through to the vulnerability.

Tonight, the petite, exquisitely turned-out Eleni wore a deceptively simple cream-colored shirtdress, with suit-like bodice, billowy sleeves to the pearled wrists, and a softly pleated three-quarters-length skirt. The ensemble was not complicated, but it most certainly came straight from one of the better Paris houses. Even though—or was it because?—she seemed not interested in doing battle with the aging process, she had aged very well. She had allowed the gray to streak into her black hair, and she had not invested her millions in cosmetic.

"Unless, of course, both of the Piccards devote their cosmetic allowances to maintaining tubs of talcum to ensure dry receptions," Caitlyn chortled playfully to herself.

But, Caitlyn had to admit, with admiration, that Eleni had the carriage and quiet grace of a queen, and her face was still as smooth and unlined as a young girl's. Amazing, thought Caitlyn—and especially so now that she knew the tragic waiting loss Mrs. Piccard had faced these past two decades.

Caitlyn had managed to clear the reception line without falling into Jacques Piccard's arms, or, she hoped, without Nora having noticed how completely he had tried to undress her with his eyes. However, Piccard was holding Nora back, teasingly begging her to stand the reception line as well to greet the remainder of the guests. Nora was feasting on every ingratiating phrase, the pleasure at being asked to stand by Piccard shining across her face.

"Here, Dr. Spencer. May I call you Caitlyn? What an absolutely charming name. I'm afraid we need Madame Petrou to embellish our welcoming line. If you don't mind, we'll dragoon one of the passing gentlemen to take you on in and share you with our other distinguished guests. Ah, yes, there's Mr. Conte. Excuse me, Mr. Conte . . ."

Caitlyn could have died on the spot as Paul sauntered over, intoned an amused "Not at all; I'd be delighted" to the ambassador's request for an escort, pinched two of Caitlyn's fingers between his own, lifted her arm in a stylized and affected court pose, and drew her into the club's garden.

* * * *

Paul guided Caitlyn directly toward the covered bar area snuggled in the L provided between the diving area and shallow end of the club's pool, apparently purposefully oblivious to the attention-demanding voices emanating from a group they were sweeping by on their left.

"I say, Paul, aren't you going to introduce us to this Greek goddess?" twinkled the ruddy-complexioned man Caitlyn and Paul had seen on the Harbor Club balcony earlier in the day. And at his side, the platinum hair now swept up into a magnificent crown, stood his companion.

"Oh, hello, Alec," Paul responded with an exaggerated jolliness that was tinged with reluctance. "We were just going to the bar. This young lady has declared her refusal to meet one more British high commission political lackey until she has quenched her thirst."

Caitlyn flushed and was about to put an immediate lie to this assertion, when Alec intervened.

"Well, this is her lucky day. She can do both simultaneously and effortlessly. The man with the drinks tray is just here. What will you have? Ah, I see you hesitate. I strongly suggest the island's specialty, this pinkish one here. It's a brandy sour. Made, by rule, with the cheapest Cyprus brandy, the best British lemon squash, and any brand of grenadine and soda—that's real soda, mind you, not what the Yanks call soda, which is something completely different—Coke or Pepsi. You *are* a Yank, are you not? Yes, I thought so."

Caitlyn warmed to Alec immediately and Paul relented in the face of this patter. As Caitlyn helped herself to a brandy sour, Paul turned back to introduce her to the two men and one woman who stood in a tight group before them.

"Cait, excuse me, Dr. Caitlyn Spencer, let me introduce you to Mr. and Mrs. Murray and to . . ."

Before Paul could complete the introduction, Caitlyn had extended her hand to the man from the balcony and had said "Glad to meet you, Mr. Murray."

"No, I'm sorry," Paul said in a decidedly uncomfortable voice, "*This* is Mr. Murray." He indicated the second man, who had been standing on the other side of the woman.

Caitlyn reddened noticeably and quickly shook the man's hand, as she struggled to regain her bearings.

Paul went on: "Jill Murray is the American embassy's economic officer. Her husband, Bob, works for an offshore British pharmaceutical distributor. And *this* impertinent bloke is Alec Stuart, a political officer for the British high commission."

As far as Caitlyn could tell, neither Jill Murray nor Alec Stuart showed any sign that they realized they had been seen together earlier in the day, and both seemed somewhat nonplused that Paul was reacting to the introductions with considerable embarrassment.

Alec was the first diplomat Caitlyn had seen at the reception who seemed to be aware they were in the tropics, and who was suffering in that knowledge. He was wearing the apparently obligatory suit, but it looked like it had spent its recent life wadded up in a corner. And, although he had his shirt open at the collar with his tie knotted at half mast, with his flame-red hair and his sunburned complexion, he looked like a fire in search of a water hose.

Jill Murray, in contrast, was as cool and as formal as a penguin. She also was gorgeous. Caitlyn immediately felt that she herself, as striking as she knew her own looks to be, had picked a very bad field on which to take her stand for the evening. At closer inspection than the harbor scene had permitted, Caitlyn could see that Jill's long platinum-blonde hair was not her most striking feature. That proved to be a voluptuous figure that had been unnecessarily emphasized by the figure-hugging, plunging neckline cut of the black silk sheath shot through with silver threads. Caitlyn's first instinct was to wrap the woman in her own shawl, with the hopeful possibility that the woman would suffocate during the procedure, and the second was to wrap her own inferior bustline in the shawl.

However, when Jill spoke, which she did in a low melodic voice, she proved to be both friendly and intelligent. Caitlyn then felt somewhat ashamed for having jumped to her first conclusion that this was a man-hunting dumb blonde—although she was on guard enough to feel that everything was not as it should be here.

For one thing, the two diplomats had, indeed, looked very cozy together in Kyrenia this morning. And Bob Murray was the other reason. Like Paul, he had looked very unhappy and frustrated when they had first walked up, and he continued to do so now. Part of this, of course, was that he looked withdrawn and as if he felt altogether out of place in this venue. He wasn't bad looking, but he didn't have the assured air the rest had acquired, probably as a requirement for their careers. He was the sort of person who would be easily lost in a crowd. He appeared to be a good fifteen years older than Jill, who could not have been older than Caitlyn's own twenty-eight years. If his marriage was in trouble, Caitlyn highly suspected that he couldn't muster the ammunition to fight the enemy off. One look at Jill's cleavage was enough to convince Caitlyn that there probably had already been innumerable attacks on this union.

After a couple of minutes of exchanging meaningless pleasantries and with a somewhat worried look, Paul asked if he could withdraw and talk a bit of urgent business with Alec for a moment, during which Caitlyn could continue her discussions with the Murrays. Not wanting to be left alone with the pair and genuinely being hungry, Caitlyn suggested that she needed to go off and search the bar area for something to eat. She said, with no discernible enthusiasm, that Paul could join her there later.

As Caitlyn quickly drifted away from the Murrays like the proverbial deserting rat, Paul and Alec withdrew several paces and launched into an intense exchange of whispers.

* * * *

Caitlyn was in luck. There was a well-provisioned table of food near the pool bar, and she leaped into it like a Viking. Try as she might, she had not been able to adjust to the Cypriot mealtimes as yet. Her family in the States had eaten dinner at the formally accepted time of 8:30 in the evening, which was more than two hours after most Americans customarily ate their evening meal. She had discovered, however, that the Cypriots did not even start appearing in the restaurants and taverns until almost 10 PM. This may, indeed, fit in nicely with their mid-afternoon siesta times and with the cooler evening temperatures, but Caitlyn had yet to have been able to put off her dinner hour that long.

Having feasted her fill—mostly of exotic foods that she could not recognize and only knew were delicious—Caitlyn once more was thirsty. The brandy sour had been light and flavorful, and she was ready for another one. Turning once more toward the bar, she froze, as her heart leaped into her throat and the name "Kurt" sliced into her brain.

The man at the bar who had evidently been engaged in an intense but quite private conversation was swept up in the crowd swirling around the bar immediately after their eyes had met, leaving Caitlyn in a cloud of confusion. It couldn't have been. She had gotten no more than a glance, and, although she had suffered several false sightings of Kurt in the first year after he had been kidnapped, these stabs at her heart had long since abated. Her imagination was certainly putting in a lot of overtime today. But why had there been such a strong sense of recognition?

A voice saying "And up from what bath did this Aphrodite arise?" drifted into her consciousness in cultured, if not wholly grammatical, tones.

Her first thought when she focused on the source of this comment was "that's who Kurt was talking to." Her second thought, as she fought to force this silliness out of her mind, was "Is there no end to handsome men on the island?" This specimen was good looking in a rough, Slavic way. Strong, fair features, military bearing, a sturdiness that looked very good when the subject was fit—and this man was very fit—but that could easily go to fat and take with it the fine edge of the chiseled facial features. Another well-tailored, if severe suit. (The quality of the material suspect, however.) Yet another pocketful of ice cubes.

"Good evening, I am Viktor Gorodov of UN. And you are?"

"Hello, I'm Caitlyn Spencer, an archeologist here for a short time on a foundation grant. And somehow I would have guessed who you were."

"I do not understand; surely my reputation not so bad it has before me come."

Caitlyn didn't respond to this fractured challenge. She had a more compelling question. "Excuse me, but who was that you were speaking to just now?"

"Speaking to just now? No one that I remember," he answered, trading evasion for evasion. "But, was just about to tell you I think you would look beautiful in the setting of Ayia Napa and to suggest we leave this terrible party immediately and I take you there."

"Sorry, I'm sure it would be lovely, but I'm here with friends. I said I would have guessed who you were because I saw you near Kyrenia today."

Viktor looked perplexed.

"No, rather, Paul—that's the American diplomat Paul Conte—said *he'd* seen you. All I actually saw at that precise moment was my past life racing before my eyes."

Viktor looked even more perplexed, although a steely glint had also entered into his expression.

"Oh, I'm sorry, I'm not explaining this right. That's just an American idiom—"

At this point, Paul broke in and saved Caitlyn, probably in more ways than one.

"Hullo, Viktor," Paul said cheerily, "I see you found my date unprotected. How's tricks? Done any dirty work in the north lately?"

Viktor snapped up his head in shock, a gesture that he quickly covered with a belligerent look. "I was not in north today."

He then turned a more studiously charming gaze on Caitlyn, saying as he folded back into the crowd, "You are enchanted. The invitation always open."

"And what invitation was that?" asked Paul, appraising Viktor's departing broad back until it was no longer in view.

"He said he saw me in the setting of someplace called Ayia Napa and wanted to take me there. What, do you suppose, he meant?"

"Ayia Napa is a topless beach on the southeast coast," Paul laughed.

"Oh," Caitlyn squeaked.

"Of course, there's a fine old monastery in the center of the town there also. Maybe he just envisioned you as the woman at the well."

Caitlyn slapped at Paul's shoulder with a soggy potato chip.

"Come with me," Paul continued. "There's someone else you should meet, as long as we're talking suggestively. Someone you're sharing a bed with," he sniggered.

* * * *

Paul had caught the eye of the newspaper editor and MP, Vassos Petrou. Following his line of sight, Caitlyn confirmed that the Zeus she had encountered this afternoon was, indeed, Vassos Petrou. His likeness to the portrait of Nicos Petrou at the mansion had nagged at Caitlyn during her bath to the point of realization that it must have been the prodigal son she had tripped over on the front steps. She had also become fast enough on the uptake on Paul's little jokes that she readily connected the probability that Vassos must at some time have lived in the Petrou mansion and might conceivably have occupied the same room she now was occupying.

When she was introduced to Vassos Petrou, he very graciously made no reference to their encounter earlier in the day, and, upon the second meeting, Caitlyn found that she was beginning to be able to control the melting sensation prompted by her strong natural attraction to the parliamentarian. Vassos's personality and conversation lived up to his looks. He and Caitlyn had a lively and intellectual discussion on the archaeology project she had been assigned to, and, before she knew it, they had agreed on his acting as her guide to the Paphos area on the west coast sometime early in her stay in Cyprus.

"But I'll have to put it off long enough to be able to trust myself alone in a room with him," Caitlyn thought.

Vassos wasn't the only person present in this little group. His stepmother, Nora Petrou, was also there, her arm possessively linked with that of Jacques Piccard. To all appearances, she had been having a very pleasant and congenial conversation with her stepson, which brought this afternoon's pottery attack into Caitlyn's memory and made her wonder once again what that had been all about. Caitlyn had entered the mansion right after Vassos had left. It had become quite clear that the foul mood Caitlyn had found Nora in had been a direct result of her stepson's visit. "Nora Petrou would not be someone I'd want as an adversary," Caitlyn thought, with a shudder.

Eventually, Paul introduced her to the last person present, who turned out to be a Cypriot police official by the name of Takis Koniotis. He looked young, serious, and a bit on edge—as if he were here on business rather than to enjoy free food and drink.

"What do you do with the police, Mr. Koniotis?" Caitlyn ventured in a polite attempt to balance the long conversation she had just had with Vassos.

"I'm with the International Investigations Division," Koniotis replied. "We handle everything arising specifically in the foreign or tourist community—things like smuggling, foul play against foreigners, illegal importation of cabaret girls, bank fraud, drugs . . ."

"My, that is quite a broad area of responsibility," responded Caitlyn. "You must find your work very rewarding."

"Well, I don't really think of it as 'rewarding,'" Koniotis answered a bit grimly. "It is necessary work, and I do get some satisfaction from having helped maintain Cyprus's reputation as one of the few remaining safe places to live. It is an uphill battle, however, which can also be quite frustrating."

"Yes, I was very pleased to learn that it was safe to walk around freely in Cyprus," said Caitlyn, although she quickly added "safe from the standpoint of crime, I mean. I've already seen that safety from erratic traffic behavior is an entirely different matter. If there's no domestic crime, then what is the source of your 'uphill battle'?"

"I didn't mean to imply that there is *no* domestic crime in Cyprus," laughed Koniotis. This was the first journey Caitlyn had seen the police official take away from deadpan seriousness, and the trip had done wonders for his expression. He really was quite handsome, she could see. "We do have our occasional 'husband bashes wife' family crime problems. And I don't mean to imply that these are not serious crimes as well. However, Cypriots are a very religious, family-oriented, if impulsive, people, with a strong sense of right and wrong and of honor and integrity. Also, Cyprus is such a small island and the people here are so closely interrelated that nearly all crime that is not a spur-of-the moment crime of passion would victimize someone connected to the family. Thus the perpetrator certainly could not go far or enjoy any ill-gotten gain without the rest of the community learning about it. A bad behavior mark against the individual here inevitably is totaled up equally against the family. That would be devastating, because a family cannot escape generations of disgrace and ostracism here simply by moving to another locale, as they would be able to do in America."

"And you know all about American society?" Caitlyn teased.

"Enough to avoid it," Koniotis countered. "I went to university in America."

The police official continued his dissertation, seemingly oblivious to the flush of embarrassment that had crossed Caitlyn's face. "The frustration I have to deal with is that, after centuries of a trusting, honest, honorable atmosphere, Cyprus has not maintained defensive barriers against the evil intentions and activities of the world around it. At the same time, it continues to suffer from the mixed blessing of being located on the crossroads of the world. International crime is being imported into the island—not necessarily to be played out on the island, but as a conduit to other locations. We are a ripe host for such parasites. My division was set up only a few years ago to focus on this type of international crime. And I've already become swamped with the work."

"But he's already very, very good at it," interjected Paul, the focus of his attention actually drawn to the corner of the sports complex.

His attention and that of nearly everyone else as well, Caitlyn noted, after having made a sweeping inspection around the club grounds. Most of those who were close by were watching surreptitiously and with various combinations of concern and calculation—Nora, Vassos, Jacques, Viktor, Eleni. All were watching Jill Murray and Alec Stuart slip into the darkened squash court. Bob Murray was also watching, but with an entirely different expression. His look was one of forlorn frustration.

But then Caitlyn noticed that Takis Koniotis was not watching the retreating pair. Instead, he was watching the watchers, one by one.

"Very interesting," thought Caitlyn, "and, at the same time, a bit frightening." She had come to Cyprus to delve into the past, and here she was being overwhelmed with intrigues—international and personal—of the present. But then, she'd always thought that intrigues of the present were grounded in the past. She wondered how true that was of what was causing the palpable tension in the air this evening.

Chapter Six

Caitlyn turned down several proffered dinner invitations before she left the Eleon, saying that she was just too tired and that, having gorged at the reception, she was just not hungry anymore. She had not been able to get away, however, without promising the French ambassador that he could take to her first traditional meze dinner the following Monday. She had also accepted Eleni Piccard's offer of breakfast and a ride up to the Kaliana dig the same morning for an introduction to Caitlyn's colleagues on that project. It would be no problem, Eleni had said, because she had to travel up to the village hotel she owned in Kakopetria, which was just up the slope toward Mount Olympus from Caitlyn's dig. Normally, one of the Ledra Foundation drivers would be at Caitlyn's disposal to take her to wherever she needed to be, and there were periodic shuttles from Nicosia's Cyprus Museum to the excavation.

Nora Petrou dropped an exhausted Caitlyn off at the Gladstone Street mansion and went on to a private dinner with Jacques. Nora was in seventh heaven in her view of her developing relationship with the ambassador. As she got out of the car, Caitlyn thanked Nora both for the lift and for cajoling her into taking her shawl. As it had turned out, the temperature had dropped enough that she had needed the wrap.

"I wonder if Jill Murray and her plunging neckline have managed to keep warm," Caitlyn meowed to herself, as she climbed the front steps. Jill and Alec had not reappeared after having slipped into the Eleon's squash court, and the reception had begun to wind down not long after the couple's disappearance.

Once in her large bedroom and with the air conditioner running, Caitlyn again counted her good fortune at having been given these accommodations. The bedroom was on the upper floor of the new wing. It was at the end of the addition and spanned the entire wing. French doors led out to small balconies off both the front and the back. The front balcony was covered with bougainvillea, and the back with a luxurious vine of sweet-smelling white jasmine. A large canopy double bed dominated the room, and a fireplace was centered on the end wall.

"How nice of Nora to give me an air conditioned room in the new wing," Caitlyn murmured to the mantelpiece. She found herself gazing at a photograph in an ivory-inlaid frame of a much younger Nora astride a camel, with a broken marble column surrounded by rolling sand dunes in the background. This mansion had been built in the British colonial period, and she had visited relatives in England enough to know that the British seemed to want to suffer in their homes. The houses were built in such a way that they couldn't get quite cool enough in the rare instance of summer heat but were downright impossible to heat to comfort levels in the winter. Except for the new wing, Caitlyn had noted that the Petrou mansion had been faithfully constructed to these same British specifications.

Caitlyn turned out the lights in her bedroom, although she left a light on in the connecting bathroom, as she still wasn't familiar enough with the room to be wandering around in the dark at night. She quickly relaxed toward sleep, still feeling the effects of the multiple brandy sours she had consumed during the evening and being lulled by the steady humming of the air conditioner. As she drifted off, she mulled over some of the events of the day, but she had to admit that she couldn't figure them out.

She also admitted she couldn't figure Paul Conte out or sort out, as yet, her feelings for the young diplomat. He was frustrating, amusing, exacerbating, and mysterious all rolled into one. She also reviewed all of the other interesting men—nearly all very much available and most obviously interested in her—she had met today. Then she thought of Kurt and rationalized away the possibility that she had seen him at the reception. Over the past several months, she had fantasized enough about him that he had often seemed to be near her in the flesh. And she still could not think about him without dying a bit inside each time she did so.

Since it was this point at which Caitlyn entered sleep, her initial dreams *were* of Kurt. She was at some sort of masquerade party. She was in a crowd of people who were dressed in Elizabethan-period costumes and who were swirling around a bar standing precariously close to the rocky edge of a cliff. Two men, one tall, thin, and elegantly clad and the other muscular and somehow coarse, were crowding in on her. Their masked faces and the brandy sours they were both forcing at her fought to fill up her full range of vision. But she kept looking past them, trying to focus on what she somehow knew was Kurt. Kurt was trying to get to her and she was trying to get to him, but the two masked men and a swirl of dancers, the men all with flaming-red hair and the women all with flowing platinum manes that whipped around in the air, were keeping Caitlyn and Kurt apart. The two men were crowding Caitlyn closer and closer to the edge of the cliff, and she could hear Kurt screaming. But she couldn't quite conjure up his features and, in her sleep, she became very upset at not being able to do so and began to think of herself as a traitor. She felt no fear at being forced ever closer to the cliff edge herself. She was completely focused on the feeling of being a traitor for not being able to see Kurt's face.

This dream folded into a sensation of falling interminably, with an aching pain in her side, which changed in sequence to a feeling of isolation and dread, as if being locked in a dark tomb. Eleni Piccard was searching for her, frantically running up and down stone passageways overhead and calling her name. Caitlyn was pulling herself up to a small barred window that looked out onto a passageway at the base of a wall. But she had climbed to this position just in time to see Eleni being herded down the corridor by someone wearing a jeweled crown and riding a camel. The masts of a ship were set against the nighttime sky at the end of the passageway.

Suddenly, Caitlyn's view was obliterated by the elegantly dressed masked man from the party, who leaned down in the passageway and put his covered face to the barred window. The masque was grotesque and the man was laughing at her. She fell back into the tomb with the sensation of cold steel on her ear. She tried to brush the sensation away, but her hand became ensnared in long platinum blonde strands of hair. There was a painful burst of expansion within her brain, getting hotter and wetter, hotter and wetter.

Caitlyn woke with a start. The room was pitch black and the air conditioner was not working. The air in the room was stifling, and her nightgown was soaked. The power must be off, she realized.

She struggled out of the bed and moved to the rear balcony door, stubbing her toe painfully on a chair en route. She pushed back the drapes and opened the door to the evening breeze, which also brought enough light into the room for her to move across the room to the front balcony in safety. She pulled back the drapes on this side of the room and opened this door as well. She stood in the doorway for a considerable time, enjoying the cool night breeze and willing her nightmares to be gone when she returned to the bed.

After a couple of moments, she began to realize that she could hear muffled voices somewhere below her in or near the garden. Both male and female voices, but how many of each she could not say. She also slowly became aware that they were speaking neither English nor Greek. It also wasn't French or any other European language that she might readily have identified, even if she couldn't converse in them.

"Arabic," she whispered. "It sounds like what I'd think Arabic might sound like. Although it could just as easily be Turkish or Persian, I suppose."

Since she couldn't understand the language and could only barely hear the voices, in any event, she entertained no thought that she might be considered to be eavesdropping.

She was about to return to the bed, when the bathroom light lit up and the air conditioner hissed and once more began to hum.

Almost at precisely that moment, Caitlyn heard a surprised exclamation, followed by the closing of a door or window. The conversation in the foreign tongue no longer could be heard. It was only then that Caitlyn realized that she still stood at the front balcony, now fully silhouetted by the bathroom light behind her.

Sighing slightly, no more room in her thoughts for mysteries, Caitlyn closed both front and back doors and drapes and sank down on the bed, this time to sleep the remainder of the night and most of the following morning without dreams and without cares.

Chapter Seven

Caitlyn's arrangement with Eleni Piccard on her first, Monday morning, visit to the archaeological dig at Kaliana in the northern foothills of the Troodos was that Caitlyn would breakfast with Mrs. Piccard in her Nicosia home before they drove up into the mountains. Caitlyn had been surprised to discover that the Piccard house was not in one of the older residential areas of Nicosia but, rather, was near the buffer zone and the UN encampment in the western suburb of Makedonitissa.

"Oh, we did once have one of those piles of stones on Byron Avenue," Eleni explained while driving the four miles from the Gladstone Street mansion to the western edge of the city, "but I abandoned it to be used by the Greek embassy shortly after I evacuated from Bellapais."

Caitlyn listened quietly and sympathetically as Eleni gave her a somewhat abbreviated version of the story of the disappearance from Bellapais of her husband and son, which more or less matched Paul's version. Caitlyn did not, however, reveal that she had heard the story already and had seen the family home in Bellapais, reasoning that this would probably only upset Mrs. Piccard as she couldn't go there herself. Nor did Caitlyn relate her own loss of her fiancé to certain death at the hands of terrorist kidnappers in Germany. This was still just too private to her, and she certainly didn't want to leave the impression that she wanted to upstage Eleni's tragedy with one of her own.

Eleni revealed that her current home was, in fact, the fourth house she had occupied in Nicosia since 1974. She said she liked to move to areas where new architectural styles were being tested. She did think, however, that she might settle in the current house, because it had a drawing card that no previous house in Nicosia had possessed. As they drove up onto Eleni's street in her Jaguar saloon car, Caitlyn could plainly see that the villa's drawing card was the view.

In this part of the city there were three distinct north-south ridges running parallel to Morphou Bay, in the distant west, toward the city proper in the east. The main UN encampment, located in the buffer zone, was spread along the top of the western-most ridge. At its southern end, this ridge broadened out into a plateau, which was occupied by the ill-fated Nicosia International Airport. Nicosia's airport had opened briefly in the early 1970s, only to be closed down during the 1974 Turkish invasion, when it became trapped in the buffer zone. The city reservoir, along with the glitzier of the city's newer mansions, crowned the eastern-most ridge.

Eleni's house was located prominently on one of the highest spots of the middle ridge. The front of the house had a full-range view of the UN encampment ridge. The vista was also bordered on the north by the western end of the Kyrenia mountain range and on the south by Mount Olympus and the rest of the distant Troodos range. Mount Olympus, naturally, was the highest peak in Cyprus.

96

The highest spot in all Greek regions—by legend the realm of visiting gods and goddesses—was usually named Mount Olympus. The sun would set over the plain running to Morphou Bay and directly between these two mountain ranges, a view, Eleni said, that was, in itself, worth the exorbitant cost of the lot.

If this was true, the view from the house's rear terrace area provided a huge additional fringe benefit. A full-range view of the Kyrenia Mountains dominated this side of the house, hovering over the spectacle of the built-up Makedonitissa Valley. The view into the valley offered up the standard vibrant sun-splashed colors of white and ochre stucco, red tile roofs, lush green trees, and iridescent flowers. The vista would be equally enchanting at twilight or at night.

Immediately below the base of the hill was nestled the ancient Makedonitissa Monastery. For centuries, this complex had served as an isolated way station on the road from Nicosia to Paphos. It now was in the middle of a busy new community—so new, in fact, that the dominant sound now was not the Orthodox priests' chants but the constant sound of bulldozers and hammers.

"What a delightful house," Caitlyn truthfully exclaimed, as Eleni pulled into the short drive of one of only three structures on the hilltop. Caitlyn could see that Eleni's place was of a particularly modernistic design, but one that was faithful in style both to the neighboring dwellings and to traditional Cypriot house design concepts. Most unusual for local customs, the building was outfitted with large windows that captured the beautiful mountain and valley vistas from all angles.

Once inside, Caitlyn also exclaimed with delight at the decor she found, which was heavily accented with carved pine furniture and what Eleni explained were native Cypriot textiles, rugs, pottery, and basketware. Obviously pleased at the interest Caitlyn was showing in the decor, Eleni became unusually animated.

"This is where the worlds of my activities merge. Most of these handicrafts were made in my workshops. The motifs come from the historical research and archaeological projects being supported by my Ledra Foundation. Anything beautiful and unique that you find in your own archaeological dig will be translated in my workshops into Cypriot crafts."

"How interesting," Caitlyn responded. "Something of a bridge from the past to the present."

"Yes, exactly. My handicraft company is a subsidiary of the Ledra Consolidated Company. This, of course, isn't our only export line, and our vessels carry many different types of goods. But the Cypriot handicraft industry represents my own life's interest."

"It must be quite rewarding," Caitlyn said with warmth.

"Yes, very. You must come to the workshop and see how we translate the historical bits and pieces we find into handicrafts."

"I'd very much like to do that," answered Caitlyn.

"Then it's a date. Perhaps Friday afternoon, if you are available." The two quickly scheduled the visit; Caitlyn would spend the morning at the Kaliana dig and the afternoon at the Nicosia handicraft workshops.

Caitlyn was beginning to understand how Eleni Piccard had managed to cope with her tragic loss. She had buried herself in her work in an endeavor that enabled the rich heritage of her native land to be rediscovered and shared in beautiful form with the rest of the world.

"She's always taken such pride in the Cypriot heritage," Caitlyn mused. But then she wondered why that thought had entered her mind. She had only recently met Eleni Piccard. Why had such a thought occurred to her? And why did she feel such an affinity for the older woman? Not for the first time, Caitlyn found the independent workings of her own mind a bit frightening.

* * * *

The road departing Nicosia toward the southwest in the direction of the Troodos was a study in sharp contrasts. Starting out as a modern highway, it quickly turned into a secondary road before once more gaining some semblance of a major artery for the run up into the mountains.

"The road was once much better than this," explained Eleni, as she careened around an ancient truck on a blind curve. "The primary road from Nicosia to the west coast was cut in the invasion. Now much of it lies either in the buffer zone or the Turkish zone."

"But that was some time ago," Caitlyn commented. "I would think that, if this is the main route into the Troodos from Nicosia, a new road would have been built by now."

"You must try to understand the Greek Cypriot mentality," Eleni countered. "And the road isn't the only example. Didn't you notice a new sign back there indicating the turnoff to the Nicosia International Airport. That illustrates what I'm trying to say."

"The international airport," Caitlyn said, her voice full of confusion. "You're right. Now that you mention it, I did see that sign. But the international airport is fifty miles away in Larnaca. I thought you said the Nicosia airport had been closed for more than twenty-five years."

99

"It has," Eleni answered sadly. "We Greeks are ever the optimists, and we also refuse to accept any sense of fait accompli in this Turkish occupation of a third of our island. Thus we won't build a new road to the Troodos because we already have a perfectly good road that we expect to get back at any moment. And when we *do* build a new stretch of highway, such as this section coming out of the new area of Nicosia, we go ahead and put up new signs noting the turnoff to an airport that isn't functioning and that we can't reach from here at the moment.

"We can be a little unrealistic, I suppose. But we live in the hope and expectation that the world will focus on our plight and we'll get our territory back soon."

Shifting down hard, as if to channel her frustration with the political situation on the island, Eleni turned off the winding, narrow road onto firmer asphalt for the nearly straight run up into the mountains. Caitlyn could barely make out the broad curve of the now unattainable Morphou Bay off to the West. The elusiveness of the hazy blue waters of the Mediterranean was punctuated by the occasional blockhouses in the near distance that were variously flying Greek, UN, or Turkish flags. Until the Jaguar reached the quickly approaching foothills of the mountains, the buffer zone ran very close to the road.

More to take Eleni's thoughts off the smothering presence of the cease-fire lines—which seemed to be affecting her driving—than for any other reason, Caitlyn sought further clarification on the day's schedule.

"You said you could take me up to the Kaliana dig and would pick me up later—that you were going further up the mountain for the day to a village called Kakopetria. What calls you up into the mountains? Does it have anything to do with your shipping business or with the handicraft center? I understand Kakopetria is a popular destination for tourists."

"Yes, it's a favorite summer retreat for Cypriots and foreign tourists alike. It's at the head of the Solea Valley, which sweeps down the mountains and into Morphou Bay. The fold in the mountains that the village occupies provides the quickest access to our tallest peak, Mt. Olympus, from the floor of the central plain. I guess its greatest attraction, though," Eleni continued with real warmth in her voice, "is the water. The river—I'm sure you'd call it only a trickle—is one of the few sources of year-round running water on the island. The valley has been settled for unknown centuries. Perhaps your project will provide us a good idea how long the area has been inhabited."

"You seem to glow with a genuine affection when you speak of this mountain valley," Caitlyn noted with a broad smile. "It must be a special place for you." Indeed, Caitlyn herself had felt her spirit rising with each lift in elevation in the road.

"Does it show?" Eleni responded. "I'm glad. As a matter of fact, my husband and I established a popular restaurant and small exclusive inn in the large, old stone mill located near Kakopetria's town square. The mill is the reason for Kakopetria's existence. The village is located where two streams converge to form the river. That's where I'm going today, to visit the inn. I have an apartment at the top of the mill.

"This valley is also where the Ledra Foundation has marked its greatest involvement in archaeology. The Kaliana dig is the culmination of our efforts here. That's where a young village boy unearthed a cruciform-shaped soapstone doll-like object that was almost identical to those being excavated elsewhere on the island. The digs where the other figures have been found have been dated to the Chalcolithic era, the period spanning from 3900 to 2600 BC. This find was very exciting for the Cypriots, because this was the first indication of settlements from that era in this area of the island. It was exciting for everyone, but in particular, for our foundation, because this was the first major discovery in Cyprus by a team of home-grown archaeologists."

"The team under Andriko, you mean?" interjected Caitlyn.

"Yes, our very own Professor Andriko Visiliou," Eleni answered with pride, as she stretched her petite frame to try to catch a glimpse of the road ahead beyond a slow-moving truck. She couldn't see far because of the frequent curves, however. At first she relaxed back into the driver's seat with a resigned sigh, but then her eyes flickered into life and she gripped the wheel tightly and swung around the truck. As if in vindication, no oncoming vehicle was in sight. "I keep forgetting," she continued the conversation, without giving any indication that she had just blindly trusted not only her own life but that of her passenger completely to fate, "that you know Professor Visiliou. That's a major reason why you're here, isn't it?"

"Oh, yes," Caitlyn responded enthusiastically. "I met him at the University of Michigan. He trained there and in London, and I trained at Michigan. I found his skills quite impressive, and I have full confidence in his abilities."

"That's good," Eleni said, with a smoothness that put Caitlyn on guard. "The team Professor Visiliou has put together here comes entirely—or did so before Andriko declared he needed someone from

102

the outside of your caliber who specialized in artifact dating techniques—from the first set of archaeologists turned out by the new University of Cyprus."

Then, while Caitlyn was mulling the implications of this statement, Mrs. Piccard threw in a second zinger: "Andriko's married now, you know. To a nice Cypriot girl, who was one of his more promising students. She is expecting rather soon."

"Yes, I know," Caitlyn responded as evenly as she could. "I received the announcement of the wedding. Andriko certainly sounded smitten in the nice letter he included." And then, to put the other point to rest as well: "I'm really looking forward to working with the team. I'll only be here for a short time until I can help get one of Andriko's own team members trained in carbon-dating techniques."

The two looked at each other with increased regard. "Now I'm beginning to understand how such a delicate-appearing woman was able to prosper in the business world," Caitlyn thought. She would approach Eleni with no less respect and admiration but with considerably more care and deliberation in the future.

After they arrived at the Kaliana excavation site and when she had been introduced all around by Eleni and the professor, Caitlyn drew away and began to walk the hillside above Kaliana. She could almost feel the ancient civilizations trying to burst through the ground. She was in her element, and she was fully absorbed in participation in the early planning for the dig, which had to be mapped out and executed as precisely as any major battle. She passed the entire day without giving a single thought to any of the disturbing events of the previous weekend.

* * * *

Late that evening, as Caitlyn sat in Nora Petrou's fully glassed penthouse in the striking, yet completely incongruous Engomi National Bank building, her thoughts were of the two strong-willed women she was encountering. This had come as a surprise to her. She had always understood that Greek cultural was heavily paternalistic. Her experience thus far with Eleni Piccard and Nora Petrou belied that view. At the same time, however, she could see where her understanding of the dynamics of Greek social structure had originated. Everywhere she turned, she caught glimpses of the continuing workings of a male-dominated society.

She did not have to look any further than the reasons she was now sitting here at the bank building to see the dynamic at work. The driver who had brought her back from the Kaliana dig had only spoken Greek. He had quite obviously been given the wrong directions on where to deposit Caitlyn and was so much of the old Greek school that he had no intention of listening to Caitlyn's pleas that she was to have been delivered to the Petrou's house, not Nora Petrou's bank. Caitlyn had been too tired from the day's activities to put up much of a fight, however.

The bank building was located almost directly across the dry riverbed from Nora's Gladstone Street mansion. The austere glass tower thankfully was shielded from the mansion's view by tree cover, however. Therefore, Caitlyn had thought she would just walk home. The driver had had other ideas, though. In his world, woman were heavily protected and supervised, so Caitlyn ultimately found herself hustled into Nora's office. Mrs. Petrou was not in residence, however, and Caitlyn sank into the overstuffed cushions of a clear acrylic chair

104

to wait. She felt like she was floating without support above the edge of the old city. Everything around her was transparent, including the walls and the desktop. The carpet was stark white, and there was no clutter to provide grounding.

Caitlyn's eyes slitted, as her focus shifted and she started to drift off in thoughts of the afternoon. Although it had been her first visit to the Kaliana dig, she had felt a familiarity with and affinity for the locale that she could not comprehend, an affinity that evoked senses of both happiness and chilling fear. A visual sense of an ancient community at Kaliana was beginning to form in Caitlyn's mind, when all was shattered by a piercing and obviously angry voice that flipped Caitlyn both forward to her return to Nicosia from the Kyrenia adventure and into the present.

In the reception area beyond the glass-walled office, Nora Petrou had just propelled herself from an elevator like an aircraft carrier under full steam. She was surrounded by a bevy of concerned tenders, who were obviously lashed within her support fleet but who equally obviously wished they were sailing over the horizon to less stormy waters. Nora was hefting a nasty-sized crystal paperweight in one clinched fist. Her facial expression was very similar to the one that had greeted Caitlyn the day she had returned to the mansion as Vassos Petrou was leaving. Caitlyn consequently found herself shrinking as far as possible into the cushion of her chair in case there would be a repeat of the figurine shot-put performance Nora had given on that occasion. Nora, thrifty businesswoman that she was, had the presence of mind not to exhibit her hurling ability in her expensive glass tower, however.

In her almost blind anger with her staff, Nora quite evidently hadn't seen Caitlyn yet.

"What in the hell was Vassos doing here?" she bellowed, as her minions flitted around her, trying to calm her. "Right under my nose, he walks in, asks to see the books of both the bank accounting department and the travel agency, and you donkeys let him look at whatever he wants."

"But he's your . . ." one tall, thin—and soon to be gone—elderly bank official bravely—and stupidly—started to offer.

"He's my nothing!" Nora spat out. "He's not *my* son. He's just a newspaperman and a politician. He is nothing to this bank or travel agency. These are mine. His father didn't have any stake here. Can't you people get that through your thick skulls? It doesn't matter in this male-plagued society that Vassos was Nicos's son. I've always had full control here. You work for me, not Vassos, and I'll only have people here who understand that."

Caitlyn observed this scene less in dismay than in bemusement. She had already seen her hostess in her "Queen Nora" performance. The thought of the royal appellation sent inexplicable buzzers off in Caitlyn's head. Nora seemed so familiar to her, but what was coming to mind was entirely a different woman and a different time. Nothing seemed to come into focus, however, because Nora's demeanor had altered drastically.

As if she were alone, Nora was continuing in a strained voice: "I thought I'd taken care of his meddling last Saturday. Why is he worming his way into my affairs now. All the questions about Nicos's death were silenced years ago. Is this all for his newspaper? Does it have something to do with the NDK?"

Then Nora swept the reception area with a vehement stare that cleared the room and wearily entered her office, all fight at least temporarily drained from her. Still not noticing Caitlyn's unexpected presence, she crossed to the window overlooking her family home and the walls of the old city and rested her head against the now-cool glass.

"Vassos, Vassos," she murmured softly but distinctly. "What is your game? And just where were *you* when your father was killed?"

Caitlyn's acrylic chair complained, as she involuntarily shifted her weight in response to a cramped hip. Nora's head snapped up and around. The initial look on her face was both startled and malevolent, but this was quickly replaced by her silken hostess visage, as she rushed to cover the moment by inundating Caitlyn with questions of her unexpected visit, her lunch with Eleni Piccard, and her first day on the job.

* * * *

Caitlyn was determined not to let her hostess's volatility intrude into her own enjoyment of the Cyprus experience. She had been supercharged by the invigorating afternoon at the dig, and she fairly bounced out of the house and into Jacques Piccard's Citroen sedan that evening when he picked her up for their prearranged dinner. She immediately went on guard, however, as Jacques registered her effervescent spirit and misinterpreted her mood as a sign of openness to his advances.

The French ambassador moved very close to her in the commodious back seat of the embassy limousine and only backed off a bit when he sensed that she was stiffening. Caitlyn already felt guilty enough about going out with Jacques for an innocent dinner without

Nora's knowledge, let alone her blessing. She didn't want to have those feelings of guilt deepened by having to beat off passes from the man, especially while they were still sitting in front of the Petrou mansion. Of course, Nora had already told Caitlyn that she had a dinner engagement that night in the southern port city of Larnaca before Jacques had extended the invitation, so it wasn't as if Caitlyn was sneaking behind Nora's back.

Jacques had managed to reel Caitlyn in for dinner by announcing tongue-in-cheek as she was leaving the Eleon reception that it was against Cypriot law for anyone to be in Cyprus for a week without having taken in a traditional meze dinner. Caitlyn hadn't wanted to be rude to a member of the family heading the foundation that was largely underwriting her research project, let alone an ambassador. She also had read about that special form of Greek feast and had been disappointed that she hadn't had occasion to attend one earlier. Therefore, she hadn't hesitated long when Jacques said he wanted to introduce her to the meze. She hadn't realized, though, that Jacques had invited no one but her.

Caitlyn had read that "meze" translated as "tidbits" and that the institution of meze dinners had started when diners were permitted to order a sampling of all of the foods the restaurant had prepared that day. This menu had become so popular that it evolved into specialty restaurants that only served meze style. For her first experience, Jacques had chosen the Ambelokipi Restaurant, which was located near the presidential palace and across from the posh English School and which was classed as a connoisseur's meze restaurant.

Jacques seemed somewhat crestfallen, but Caitlyn was relieved, when, on entering the restaurant, they discovered that Jill and Bob Murray had also just arrived and had suggested that they make it a foursome. Caitlyn was soon finding that the food fully lived up to its reputation, as did the light white wine. The Murrays also seemed to be getting along well this evening. Caitlyn was in such a good mood that she only had a tinge of regret when Jill queried where Nora Piccard might be, saying she would have expected to see Nora with either or both Caitlyn and Jacques.

"Nora had a business dinner to attend in Larnaca this evening," explained Jacques.

"Oh, perhaps that's why I couldn't get her when I tried to call earlier today," said Jill. "I'd like to try to set up an evening meeting between Nora and an American travel agency sometime this week."

"Well, I don't know too much about her availability this week, but I do know she has another business dinner in Larnaca on Thursday," Jacques answered.

"Well, I suppose I might try something next week," Jill concluded.

Later, as the wine started to take its effect, Jacques began to goad Jill on business matters.

"You know, Caitlyn," he said, pretending to direct his comment at Caitlyn but really addressing the table at large, "the word is out that Jill is playing in a heavy-duty sand pile with some sort of money laundering issues, presumably involving the East Europeans. The Americans are leaning very heavily on the Cypriots on offshore banking issues and on foreign currencies circulating on the island, especially that of the Yugoslavs. They've even been, how do you say, nosing into the possible involvement of some Cypriot members of parliament."

Then he addressed himself directly to Jill: "Is that so, Jill? Where is all of this taking us?"

Jill didn't look at all pleased at this turn of the conversation, and Bob Murray looked like he might choke.

"Yes, Ambassador," she responded somewhat stiffly, "we *are* worried about the origin—and the destination—of some of the money floating through Cyprus. And we are concerned about the Cypriot's policies and attitudes in this regard. We could use all of the Permanent Five, including French, help we can get to keep this from getting out of hand."

Piccard continued. "I understand you've been showing a lot of interest in Vassos Petrou. He's pretty big game in Cyprus—not only because he's an MP and from a prominent family, but because he controls his own newspaper. Of course, with his Russian education and leftist leanings, he could be counted on to look favorably on the East Europeans. I'd be careful about Vassos, if I were you, though."

Jill had opened her mouth to reply, but Jacques had turned immediately back toward Caitlyn, saying, "Yes, Vassos Petrou would be a very good person to avoid. I wouldn't think *you* would want to get involved with leftist politics while you are here, Caitlyn. There are so many more pleasant things to do and places to go."

Caitlyn reddened, but she did not reply. Had Jacques seen her attraction to Vassos at the reception the other night? Was this whole conversation, she wondered, directed at keeping her from becoming involved with Vassos? For her own good, or to narrow the field for Jacques?

110

The traditional last dish was served. It was Kleftiko, a succulent roasted lamb dish that translates as "thieves' meat," because it traditionally represented meat that had been obtained by stealing someone else's sheep. The purloined sheep was slaughtered and then hidden and slow-baked underground to escape detection. This dish was finished off by fresh fruit, brandy, and coffee, and then the foursome found themselves in front of the restaurant. Jacques suggested a nightcap at the Navarino Lodge, the haunt of the press corps, but the Murrays gracefully declined and headed for their car. Caitlyn herself was apparently not going to be given a choice in the matter and couldn't say much, as she didn't have her own transportation.

As Caitlyn and Jacques reached the street, the lights on a car parked a considerable distance down the road flashed three times. She couldn't be sure that Jacques had seen this strange behavior as well, but he seemed to tense as the driver walked around to open the rear door of the Citroen.

Having reached their black Mercedes, the Murrays drove alongside the Citroen and, in passing, tooted their horn and waved good-bye.

While she was being handed into the back seat, Caitlyn clearly saw the car that had flashed its lights maneuver a U-turn in the middle of the narrow street and bear down on the Citroen, accelerating its speed as it came closer.

Caitlyn gave a little cry as she sank into the deep upholstery. But then the car had swept by—following the Murrays into the traffic circle in front of the presidential palace.

"What's wrong?" Jacques asked with concern, as he entered the car.

"Nothing, sorry, just an overactive imagination," Caitlyn whispered.

"Well, I think perhaps we should call it a night as well," said Jacques. "We can try the Navarino some other evening."

The limousine moved toward the old city.

"Hm, that was quite a switch in gears," Caitlyn mused. Turning her attention to the passing night lights of the city streets, she couldn't rid herself of a nagging concern that belied the delicious meal she had just consumed.

"An overly consumed meal," she corrected herself. "That must be my problem."

Chapter Eight

Drugs. Money Laundering. Illegal Arms. Unassigned. It was late Thursday afternoon, and Takis Koniotis was sitting at his police department International Investigations Division desk, staring intently at the four growing piles of note cards in front of him. Each note card represented a nugget of information, a question, or a theory connected with one or more of the cases he was pursuing. Nothing was making sense yet, and, indeed, most of the bits of separate data were included in more than one of the piles.

He flipped over the top note card on the Unassigned pile, which represented the last piece of information to have been gathered. All that was written on the card was "Bulgarian steamer?" After pondering the card for several moments, he shuffled hurriedly through the Unassigned deck once more, extracted a card, and placed it beside the first. On the card were written the words "Unidentified fishing boat/'as prearranged'."

"Right. Now we're getting nowhere." Koniotis dropped the cards and spun around toward the window—the one with a full view of the window in the homicide division in the building across the alley. It didn't really matter what the view was, however, as the police official was fully engaged in thought, trying to bring the data on the note cards into some semblance of order.

"A. Today is Thursday. On Friday night last, our coastal patrol, while searching for a Bulgarian vessel it has suspected of having illegally docked in the Turkish zone, intercepted a distress signal from what was identified as 'the fishing boat' off the coast of the Greek island of Rhodes.

"B. The signal was in Turkish and was addressed to Antalya, the closest city in Turkey.

"C. According to the translation of the signals, the ship claimed its engine had broken down and that it required help 'as prearranged.'

"D. On Saturday afternoon, a small Bulgarian steamer was hailed off the Paphos coast by the coastal patrol. It claimed it was bound for Haifa, Israel, from Crete, and denied that it had entered the denied Turkish area of Cyprus.

"E. Upon later check, the authorities in Crete denied the steamer had stopped there.

"F. After much discussion, the Israelis acknowledged that the Bulgarian ship docked in Haifa, as scheduled. City of origin: Varna, Bulgaria. Cargo: machine tools.

"G. Likely story; I wasn't born yesterday."

Koniotis started ticking off questions on his fingers. "Is there any reason not to believe we're only talking about one ship here? If so, why was the ship in northern Cypriot waters? Why did it radio for help to the Turkish mainland? What does 'as prearranged' mean? Why did its captain lie about sailing out of Crete?"

He sat immobile for several minutes, trying to think of all the possibilities. After a while, he gave a frustrated grunt and flipped the two cards into the Illegal Arms pile. "Seems as likely as anything else," he mumbled. He then took a card from the Illegal Arms pile. It said "Embassy help?"

"Now what was that about?" the policeman wondered. "Ah, yes, the anonymous tip that had been traced to a telephone exchange in the British sovereign base area of Dhekelia in the southeast sector of the island. Could this have been pointing to the British high commission?"

"Both the high commission and the American embassy have seemed to be cooperative," Koniotis mused, "but those three—Stuart, Murray, and Conte. Always appearing to be helpful, but always seeming to be holding something back. 'Embassy help.' Both the Brits and the Americans are major arms dealers, although they both act like they want to stamp out arms proliferation. Stamp out every other nation's arms deals but their own is more like it. No, I won't rule out the British or the Americans."

Then he took the top card off the Money Laundering pile.

There were two entries on this card. At the top, written in ink, was the phrase "Large transaction to Geneva." Below that, in pencil, having very recently been added to the card, were the words "Engomi Bank (Petrou)."

"Petrou, Petrou. Where have I seen this before in this pile of cards?"

He sifted into the pile. Near the bottom he found the card he sought. This one had three entries written on it. The top one said "Legislation enabling Yugoslav bank setup. Diplomatic demarche by

Americans." Below that was the entry "Vassos Petrou," with an arrow drawn to the first sentence. And at the bottom of the card was the entry "Economic officer Murray," with an arrow drawn to the second sentence.

Koniotis started mulling again. "Bulgarians. Yugoslavs. Petrou. Banks, Yugoslavs. Embassies. Arms. Americans. Murray. Petrou. Yugoslavs. Bulgarians. Arms. Drugs. Petrou. Petrou."

On a hunch, Koniotis reached for the telephone and tried to call Vassos Petrou at his parliamentary office.

"I'm sorry," Petrou's secretary intoned. "Mr. Petrou has gone to Larnaca. He likes to take his sailboat out on Thursdays when it's nice."

Koniotis sighed and returned the phone to its cradle. He wasn't even sure what he would have asked Petrou if he had been able to get through to the parliamentarian. He had had faith that something appropriate would have come to him, though. It was just this process that had helped him crack most of his cases. The evidence was continually being sifted in his subconscious and would suddenly surface in a hunch that almost always put him on the right path. Petrou. He knew that must be a key to something.

Absently, he withdrew a note card from the middle of the Drugs pile. All the card said was "Larnaca marina."

Koniotis rose from the desk, reached for his car keys, and headed for the door.

* * * *

Bob Murray had been pacing the floor for hours. "I can't take this anymore. She has to stop!" he cried bitterly to himself. "This is more than I can stand. I know she is compelled and that this is so

116

very important to her. But everyone has seen them. It's out in the open, and it's so much more dangerous now. It must stop now. Surely she can see that we can't live any longer with this hanging over our heads."

The man had built himself up to a violent state and he began throwing objects around the apartment—first pillows, harmlessly; eventually, a heavy silver lighter, which, unfortunately, landed precisely in the middle of the center pane of the glass china cabinet. The burst of glass proved that the cabinet did indeed contain china and stemware.

The crash seemed to mobilize Murray. He headed for the door, almost sobbing. "I know where they are! It's time for this to stop!"

A single, repeated strangled word screamed up from the stairwell—"Jill, Jill, Jill." The street door slammed, and the apartment, now looking much like a war zone, returned to silence.

* * * *

Vassos Petrou was enjoying the onset of evening shadows, as he tacked his sailboat back and forth across the Larnaca seafront. Larnaca, Cyprus's longest permanently inhabited town, couldn't be considered to have a real harbor. An old seaport on the southern coast, Larnaca did, at one time, have a harbor. That was when it was the ancient city state of Kition, so old that it was said to have been founded by a great grandson of Noah. But the original harbor had silted over, and now Larnaca only had a European-style seafront promenade, albeit it was a very nice promenade.

To Vassos Petrou, Larnaca was a second home. This was because it provided the closest access to the sea from Nicosia now that the northern coast was inaccessible, and because it still boasted the largest marina on the island for private boats. Petrou always felt most alive and free when he was sailing with the sea breezes off the southern coast. However, now he saw that he would have to come back around and head into the marina if he was to make his evening's rendezvous. Tonight might be dangerous. Tonight he'd best be at his most alert.

* * * *

Alec Stuart and Jill Murray were beginning to relax a bit as twilight set in over the Larnaca seafront. They had been sitting outside the old Four Lanterns Hotel in one of the many open-air cafés that literally covered the three hundred-foot-deep promenade that stretched from the hotel fronts to the seafront road and then to the mixed pebble and sand beach for a distance of a mile.

While they sat and watched, they were trying to seem as inconspicuous as possible. Alec was dressed in the darkest clothes he had been able to find. Jill had also opted for dark and baggy clothes and had tried as best she could to hide her distinctive hair under a billed cap.

Both were miserable and looked it. They both knew they shouldn't go on like this, but it was too late to back down now. It meant too much to both of them. Still, Jill could almost cry at the effect all of this was having on Bob. If only they hadn't been seen together. But they needed to meet; they could not do otherwise until this had all spun out to the end.

Night had now fallen across the waterfront and the old globe street lights had come on. Alec tensed and sank down into his cushioned seat, muttering the name "Vassos Petrou" and inclining his head toward the street. Jill picked up her menu and buried herself behind it as best she could. Petrou passed by them at some distance, not seeing them among the evening crowd that was gathering at the café. Stuart stood, dropped some money on the table and moved toward the street.

"See you later," he said *sotto voce*, as he left Jill. "You know where."

Jill only had to wait a few more minutes until she too found it was time for her to slide out of her chair and carefully move toward the street.

Jill was too intent on her own movements to notice the man who had been sitting in the adjacent café and who had been watching the couple for some time. "Jill," he muttered under his breath, mouthing the name lovingly with a cruel grin, his eyes fixed with a half-crazed glare. When Jill rose and moved toward the street, so did he—in the same direction and measuring his pace to hers.

* * * *

Paul Conte had had no idea this road was so bad when he had started out from Larnaca. It was already dark and the dirt and stone road—"dirt and *boulder* road" he grimaced to himself, as he took a jolt that just may have destroyed his transmission—would have been almost impossible to negotiate even in the daylight. The road, as marked on the map, had certainly looked like it should be passable. The track followed and closely hugged the coastline running between Larnaca and Limassol. One would think, therefore, that it should have been paved with asphalt to attract tourists looking for the most scenic route between the two towns. Not that Paul was playing the tourist just now.

There was the old, inland road between the towns. And even more recently, a dual-lane highway had been constructed even further inland. But Paul definitely did not want to be seen by anyone who would take significance from his presence on this coast tonight. He didn't want to become as dangerously conspicuous as Alec and Jill had become in their supposedly clandestine meetings. And he was pretty sure he had caught Viktor Gorodov engaging in unclean activities on the Kyrenia pass road on Saturday. The Russian had almost dropped his teeth when Paul had asked him at the Eleon reception, with full calculation, what dirty work the UN official had been up to.

Saturday. There were a lot of perplexing activities in evidence on the Turkish side on Saturday. "Luckily," thought Paul, "Caity . . . umm, Cait Spencer had not seemed to notice anything as being out of the ordinary. Nice girl. But a little spaced out. Well, guess I can't blame her. But I wonder how long she'll permit herself to carry the torch for this dead German guy? Maybe, if I'm lucky, I'll be around when she comes around. She certainly seemed to enjoy the day—and my company."

Another grinding encounter with a boulder brought Paul back to the business at hand. "Zygi. Got to rendezvous at Zygi in time. And got to make sure this is all very private.

"Damn those rocks! Why do they even bother calling this a road?"

* * * *

Ambassador Jacques Piccard and his aunt, Eleni Piccard, bustled out of the front door of the plush Limassol Le Meridien Hotel. As she bundled into the Citroen limousine, Eleni gazed out

120

over the glittering lights of Cyprus's glitziest hotel strip, glowing in the knowledge that several of the smaller hotels dotting the hillside above the coast were her property. Eleni had started investing in this area just to the east of the country's major seaport and second largest city when the only claim to fame of this stretch of seacoast was in having once been one of the island's oldest and wealthiest city states. From this earlier civilization had come the coastal strip's name—Amathus.

For its part, Limassol was just a sprawling urban area, spreading along the coasts and up into the slowly rising hills. It sat between two areas of ancient civilization—Amathus to the east and Curium to the west. Curium now existed as one of the earliest and most extensive archaeological excavations in Cyprus, representing the Greek and Roman periods. Other than Curium and a couple of crusader's castles—the seafront castle in which Richard the Lionhearted married Berengaria and Kolossi Castle, where the island's grape and wine industry started—Limassol was a bit shy on culture. It was the unabashed business and shipping center for the island, however, and, thus, was the real center of the Piccards' Cypriot holdings.

The city, which boasted the only deep-water port on the Greek side of the island, was strategically located only a hundred and fifty miles from the Syria-Lebanon coast, two hundred and fifty miles from Tel Aviv and Haifa in Israel, and just three hundred and thirty miles from Port Said, Egypt. It, thus, was one of the major ports of the eastern Mediterranean.

Jacques and Eleni had been attending a Ledra Consolidated board of directors' dinner meeting at the Le Meridien when the call had come through.

Eleni walked quickly to Jacques's chair and whispered in his ear: "They've told me she's left. She's headed back to Nicosia. We *must* intercept her before she gets to her superiors."

Jacques instantly understood, and the two quickly gave their apologies and good-byes. The big, black Citroen was waiting at the front entrance and immediately pulled away and onto the Limassol-Nicosia highway and into the night.

* * * *

The three people, one woman and two men, stood on the stony beach, below the sea wall and next to the fishing pier. The pier jutted out from the middle of the village of Zygi, clearly establishing the claim that the livelihood of the village, located halfway between Larnaca and Limassol, centered on fishing. If you had asked a local inhabitant, however, you would have been told forthrightly that Zygi was a smuggler's village rather than a fishing village and had been so for centuries—and very proudly so. It was better known now, especially to the tourist trade, as the best place to go for good salt-water fish.

Those three were not here for the fish, though. They were staring anxiously out to sea. Their vehicles were located as close to the dock as the pier-side restaurants would permit. The evident leader was dressed in dark clothes and was chain-smoking, stopping every once in a while to audibly encourage the small fishing boat to appear. The other man, a tall, hunky middle European type, had returned to one of the vehicles, a station wagon, and was nervously fiddling around with something in the back seat. The woman was just as nervous, continually twisting her rope bracelet around and around her wrist. Her long blonde hair whipped around in the wind, and she continually brushed it away from her face. They all wore gloves, although she kept taking one of hers off to scratch her forearm, apparently having been bitten by mosquitoes.

The trio seemed to know that they had no reason to be afraid of the local authorities. This indeed, by custom and through regular payoffs, was the accepted smugglers' port for small entrepreneurs engaged in surreptitiously hustling goods back and forth from the Lebanese coast.

The leader's attention was arrested by a low whistle emanating from the darkness, out to sea, and just to the right of the long fishing pier. He squeezed the woman's elbow, and she gave three quick flashes of the flashlight she held in her hand. Something bumped woodenly against the side of the pier just beyond the light being cast by the open-air restaurants and the couple moved to the vehicle as quickly as they could without attracting undue notice from the large groups of tourists all around them. The tourists appeared absorbed in gorging on the battered and fried squid dish called calamari and on grilled swordfish, all washed down with endlessly provided bottles of Keo beer. The fish in Zygi must have lived up to its reputation, as no one in the restaurants was paying the slightest attention to the movements around the station wagon.

Well, almost no one. There was one diner, sitting back in a landward side corner, who was very much aware of the trio's activities, although you would not have known it unless you were watching him very closely. The three, intent on moving their three crates from the station wagon to the small boat as quickly as possible, were not, in fact, watching him—or anyone else—closely.

There was a brief boat-side discussion in Arabic, which was followed by the exchange of the last crate for a briefcase. The boat cast off, as the leader and the woman walked back down the pier, this time in an embrace that would be taken as two lovers out for an evening stroll by anyone who had not seen them heft the crates in the other direction a few minutes earlier. A moment later, the other man materialized from the darkness of the pier and entered the driver's side of the station wagon. The woman hurried over to a small sports coupe that was parked nearby and drove off into the night.

After the leader had transferred the contents of the briefcase to the specially constructed compartment under his passenger seat floor mat, he made a quick sweeping inspection of the area, quickly climbed into the vehicle, and the two men drove away. The observant diner was not far behind.

* * * *

Caitlyn had eaten alone that evening. She had taken a taxi to the Mignon, a French restaurant between the Gladstone Street mansion and the American embassy. There were very few diners on the restaurant's grapevine-covered patio that evening, but she was happy for the solitude. The service was impeccable; the atmosphere superb. The meal had made her so mellow—and full—that she chose to walk the short distance back to the mansion. The evening was balmy, and she enjoyed the walk.

The mansion was deserted when she returned, and she took the opportunity to inspect the ground floor rooms. Nora Petrou had a lot of nice things, and Caitlyn had not yet had time to focus on them. Now that she did, she was surprised. Almost all of the accents in the room appeared to be from the Middle East. Caitlyn had not realized

124

that Nora had an interest in that region. She had assumed that the French Canadian would be more oriented toward Paris and other European locales.

Caitlyn also realized that she was very tired and decided she would not wait up for Nora's return. She withdrew to her room and went straight to bed after a warm bath, very quickly slipping into the sleep of the dead.

* * * *

Jill Murray was traveling in her Miata coupe toward Nicosia at a rather fast clip.

"Well, that's that," she thought smugly to herself. It had worked perfectly, she decided, and now she felt prepared to face Bob. She was feeling so pleased with the night's work and was so engrossed in devising just how she would phrase her report that she didn't even see the big, black car swoop down on her from behind. The saloon car pulled up beside her, and its driver hit the horn hard. Jill was jerked out of her musing and involuntarily turned her head toward the unexpected, loud sound. As she did so, the other car made a pronounced and deliberate swerve in her direction. Caught completely off balance, Jill pulled her wheel hard to avoid a collision. In doing so, she left the roadway at high speed, and the small coupe soared over and behind a roadside hillock and into a clump of pink- and white-blossomed oleander bushes.

The car landed at a sharp angle, its hood pushed into the soft, sandy earth. Jill was unconscious for a brief moment. Luckily—at least for the moment—she had been wearing her seat belt and there was little damage to the passenger compartment. When she came to, she was still extremely disoriented and, most probably, in shock. The first thought she had as she pushed the crumpled car door open into the bushes was: "Oh, pretty pink and white. Pretty oleander. But poison. Mustn't taste. Could kill."

That was her last thought as well.

Just as she managed to force the door open, a gloved hand reached in, grabbed a handful of her long, platinum blonde hair, and forced her head sideways.

She had a brief sensation of cold steel in her ear, followed rapidly by an explosion of pain, her head expanding and disintegrating, followed by . . . nothingness.

Chapter Nine

She was at complete peace. "I feel like I must have died and gone to heaven," Caitlyn sighed contentedly. She sat up, stretched her back, and readjusted her head scarf. The morning sun beat mercilessly down on the Kaliana hillside. Although she had remembered to bring her sunscreen when she left Nicosia this morning for the dig, she already was burnt. And she was loving every minute of it.

The atmosphere at the dig had been electric when she arrived at the site just as the sun was peeking up over the eastern fold of the valley. On the preceding afternoon, one of Professor Visiliou's brightest assistants had uncovered shards of red polished ware from the hillside. This pottery was associated with Anatolian settlers who were known to have been displaced from the Asia Minor area around 2000 BC and to have scattered further into the Levant. And what this find really meant was that the archaeologists had probably pushed the dating of the settlement of this valley from the Middle Bronze Age into the Early Bronze Age, a period that dated from about 2300 to 1850 BC. This timing would date the site as the earliest confirmed settlement of this area of the island, although habitation here during this era had long been academically assumed.

As soon as she had arrived at Kaliana this morning, Caitlyn had started to work. And now she was delighted to be able to celebrate this achievement with her new colleagues. But, at the same time, she had been very disappointed she had not been part of the find. It was very important for her to be able to make a significant contribution to this project, given the great sums that were being expended on her grant. The entire morning she had worked feverishly, but with the extreme care and expertise of the fully trained archaeologist that she was.

A large part of the gentle rising hillside had been excavated to a depth of about four feet, an impressive feat considering that, after the initial breaking of the surface growth, all digging had been done on hands and knees with precision tools closer to the size of spoons than shovels. A squared network of string had been staked out in a grid over the entire area so that each find could be precisely cataloged and sited in situ. After the staking of the area, several photographs—using more than one camera—would be taken of the location of any halfway important find. Any areas in which building foundations were discovered or that revealed significant groups of objects were also quickly covered with tent-like tarps. There were as many archaeologists making sketches or carefully cataloging finds as there were excavators. And there were legions of other helpers painstakingly bagging all of the artifacts that were to go back to the Cyprus Museum for processing. Just as many support personnel were running around doing odd jobs.

Caitlyn's role in the project would normally keep her out of all of this hustle and bustle. Her principal responsibilities were to help determine the age, through the techniques of carbon dating, of the more significant finds being transferred to the Cyprus Museum down in Nicosia. The majority of this work would be performed at the laboratory that had been assigned to her in the basement of the museum. But today Caitlyn wanted to become fully attuned to the project, and she believed she could only do that by being out on the hillside and by digging alongside her new colleagues.

On a hunch, albeit an educated hunch, Caitlyn had been working all morning at some distance from the rest of the archaeologists, who were concentrating in the area of the red polished ware find in hopes of finding further evidence of Early Bronze Age habitation.

Caitlyn had stood for some time, looking at the site and letting her imagination run free in an effort to capture the ancient time and its flow of life. On the basis of this daydreaming, she had chosen to work near a large rock outcropping in the upper, southern quadrant of the excavated site. Her choice was not all that mystical, even though there was an unexplainable familiarity and feeling of comfort—although a comfort tinged with surprise and fear—about the location. The choice was scientifically reasoned even though, when she closed her eyes and let herself drift, the site brought to her senses voices, sounds, and snatches of visions that had no relation to either the excavating work that was proceeding nearby or to the present time. Even if she had not somehow "known" to come to this spot, her expertise would have led her here. Her choice had been based on a combination of considering how the environment would have looked over 4,000 years ago and how inhabitants of that era would meld their lives to that environment. Added to this was Caitlyn's detailed academic knowledge, thus far untested by the limiting experience of her Virginia projects, of what to look for in evidence of Bronze Age civilizations that would survive the scourges of time and nature.

She hadn't found anything in the five hours she had been digging, but she was delighted to be actually working and was becoming increasingly mentally attuned to this exciting new project. "If this is all I accomplish today," she told herself, "than that will have been enough for now."

But that wasn't going to prove to be all she would accomplish on this day. The growing heat of the day had caused Caitlyn to concentrate her work in the shadow of the large rock outcropping. After more than an hour's time of working directly at the base of the rock, what had been up to that time a tight mixture of packed soil and rocks began to come away in clumps. Some of this composite then surprisingly fell away into what appeared to be a pocket of open space where the ground met the base of the rock. Excitedly, Caitlyn began to dig with more concentration and as quickly as her training would permit. Yes, there was an open space. The space became larger the more she dug and began to take on definition as the top of a human-carved doorway into the rock.

There was carving on the top of the doorway—mere scratchings, but Caitlyn knew immediately the message they were trying to convey. She stood up straight and rigid, floating off in a trance, her body cold as ice despite the oppressive heat of the day.

It was the name of her best friend, an older woman than she, but one who had taken her under her wing, guided her, and taught her the healing skills that gave them both purpose and the right to live in the village after both of their men had failed to come home from separate hunts. That's what was written over the door. A name. This had been the door to her home, her home for eternity as well as for life. The weight of the grief of the loss was almost too much to bear, and she reached out to the carving in the stone both for renewed connection with her lost friend and for physical support.

Caitlyn bruised her fingers against the uneven rock, as the weight of her body fell against the stone. This was enough to evaporate the vision.

Shaking her head vigorously, and having looked accusingly up at the beating sun, Caitlyn regained her equilibrium and let her expertise take charge. She called down to Professor Visiliou, who was working with and guiding the other excavators further down the hill. She had not been able to keep the exuberance out of her voice, so everyone quickly began moving in her direction.

"You'd best bring some light," Caitlyn called, and a few of the helpers turned away to find flashlights.

Following much painstaking clearing away, a narrow passage was revealed that evidently had been a natural cave formed by space having been left at the base of two large rocks that leaned into each other above the surface of the earth. But the natural space had quite obviously been enlarged and squared off by human hands into what appeared to be a passageway. Being careful of the possibilities of snakes or other undesirable contemporary inhabitants, one of the smaller archaeologists and Caitlyn began to work their way down the passageway.

"Just as I dreamed and hoped," thought Caitlyn with exultation when they reached a small chamber several yards beyond. It

131

had been turned into a tomb. Clearly discernible to Caitlyn's trained eye were several funerary artifacts directly associated with the Early Bronze Age. These were special goods to help the dead cope with the afterlife.

The first goods Caitlyn noticed were the glass beads heavily strung around the shriveled, mummified mound that once must have been someone's loved one. The mere sight made Caitlyn's heart lurch, and images gripped at her in the dark and close tomb, accompanied by a feeling of loss and woe that threatened to pull Caitlyn into the darkness. But she violently shook her head and willed her attention away from the mound of beads. She forced her thoughts into scientific paths, grasping hard onto the observation that they must have achieved the archaeologists' highest and most rare gift—to have discovered a site that had not previously been found and ransacked by robbers.

Caitlyn's determination to keep her attention focused in the present rewarded her with the vision of small gold and copper articles, the former glittering in the beams from the flashlights. What remained of the copper ware had turned a moss-green color. Her attention then moved to shards of clay pottery with faint designs of what appeared to be oxen yoked to plows as well as bulls and snakes. The most interesting find of all, if the object was what Caitlyn thought it was— she could only look at this point; the whole area would need to be carefully excavated, cataloged, and processed—was a cylinder signature seal. The other items Caitlyn had seen were associated with the early portion of the Bronze Age. Cylinder signature seals, imported and implying trading links with Syria and Egypt, did not start to appear in Cyprus until the later years of the period. "We may be able to date this find very precisely," thought Caitlyn.

After one more lingering look, she backed out of the tomb to leave it to the army of follow-up workers. An incongruous feeling of grief and loss was still clawing at her, but she would not let the exultation of her find be sullied by these silly feelings of hers. Enveloping a surprised, but equally exuberant Dr. Visiliou in a bear hug the strength of which belied her willowy frame, Caitlyn let out a loud whoop of triumph. Following this, she had the presence of mind to graciously make her way around the excited circle of workers to explain repeatedly what she had found and why she had chosen to dig at this spot—and to receive their congratulations. She kept reminding herself that this was a group effort and that she needed to acknowledge it as such. Her whole purpose in participating in the day's dig was to meld with her coworkers.

Eventually, Caitlyn made her way down the hillside for the ride into Nicosia, a well-earned bath, and her appointment with Eleni. She would not be needed—indeed, she would not be wanted—at the site for several more days. All effort would be concentrated on the detailed and painstaking excavation of the tomb, and all of this work now belonged to others. Knowing Andriko Visiliou, she knew that the tomb and its contents would be treated with the utmost respect by the Cypriot team—and for some unknown reason it was very important to her that this tomb be treated with respect.

Chapter Ten

Takis Koniotis got out of his car and dragged his weary body toward his office door. His mind was racing with the developments of the night, both of which, he could feel in his bones, helped move one or more of his cases closer to resolution. One of the tragedies, he sadly thought, he might have helped prevent if he had worked faster and more effectively.

He entered his office with a cup of coffee in hand, collapsed in his chair, and raised his feet, with some difficulty, onto the desk. Within seconds, his investigative assistant, Maria Solonos, hurried into the office. She looked disheveled, as if she had been up all night as well, which, in fact, was not the truth; she had not been called into the office until 4:00 AM.

"Where have you been? And have you heard the news?" queried Maria, looking hard at Koniotis until he got the hint and removed his feet from the desk and onto a chair.

"I went to Larnaca on a hunch last evening; one that didn't work out. Don't look so amused and smug! My hunches often work out; this is just one of those that didn't. However, while I was in Larnaca, I got a call patched through on my car phone and all hell broke loose. But, yes, I've heard the other news. Tragic. And very disturbing. What have you gathered so far? I do assume this one has dropped on our desk."

"It certainly has, I'm afraid," Maria sighed. "But you first. What hell broke out?" With that, she swept Koniotis's feet off the only unoccupied chair in the room and sat down, notebook at the ready.

"Well, we're now making headway on one of our cases, although I have no idea at this point what—and who—is involved."

Maria said nothing, her head bent over her notebook and her eyes squinting in the faint light in the office. Koniotis continued. "On a hunch I spent a good part of the evening at the Larnaca marina, checking out the boat of our favorite NDK parliamentarian, Vassos Petrou. I had just missed him when I arrived. He had just been out in his sailboat, and I thought I might be able to find something on the boat that would tell me why I think the name Petrou is tied up with our cases. It took me some time to convince the marina guards to let me search without notifying Petrou, and it took me even longer to find that the boat seems to be clean as a whistle."

"When I returned to the car, the phone was ringing. The Larnaca police station was telephoning to report that Paul Conte of the American embassy had called and provided the tip-off that he had just seen a suspicious boat-loading activity at the Zygi fishing pier. Both the Larnaca and Limassol coastal patrols were quickly put in the water in search of a possible smuggler.

"By the time I had gotten to the Larnaca coastal patrol station, it had intercepted a small boat that was trying to reach a larger one and that, very interestingly indeed, contained three crates of AK-47s."

Maria whistled appreciatively.

"I've been at the Larnaca station, working on the boatman, all night. But he obviously doesn't want to talk. My guess is that he's Lebanese or Syrian; he only speaks Arabic—when he speaks at all, that is. For much of the time I wasn't questioning the smuggler; I was trying to track Conte down. Finally found him at the American embassy—significantly at 4:00 AM. He didn't react to my suggestion that he worked odd hours. I thanked him for the information he had provided on the smugglers and tried to find out both why he had conveniently been in Zygi to provide an eyewitness account of the arms transfer and whether he could identify any of the perpetrators. He said he loves fish and would—and did—travel across the island for a good fish meal. He also said he was sorry but he didn't recognize any of the smugglers. I think he's lying. He didn't seem half surprised enough when I told him the cargo was assault rifles. I can't get too rough with him, because he *did* tip us off—and because he does have diplomatic status. But I think we need to start watching Paul Conte very closely."

"Done," said Maria, as she lifted her pen and her head from the notebook with a flourish. "My turn. What do you know about Jill Murray?"

"I was notified of the murder about 10:00 AM. I hadn't notified the office I was at the Larnaca police station. I trust most of that lost time was in deciding that this is a case for us and not just an unfortunate road accident. You say it's our case?"

"Yes, but the kicker for later," Maria responded. "Here are the prelims. We figure she was killed at about 11:00 PM. It took a while for someone to notice and investigate the rubber marks veering off the road. There were two separate sets of skid marks, incidentally. She didn't crash all by herself. The car had completely cleared a small hill, so it could have been out there for days before someone found her—if it hadn't been for the skid marks. Then, for a few more hours the highway police were adding it up as just another of the many high speed- and alcohol-related deaths on the Nicosia-Limassol highway. The skid marks carried quite a distance and the severity of the accident impact was judged as sufficient to have caused the extent of the head injury. She didn't have a seat belt on, and her head went into the windshield.

"Of course, it started off as a sensitive case, because her green registration plates clearly identified the vehicle as diplomatic. They started working double time when she was identified as a senior American embassy official. And they went into a tailspin and called us in as soon as a doctor saw the head wound and someone dug the bullet out of the passenger door."

Koniotis grunted in surprise, but quickly recovered and asked: "Husband notified?"

"Yes, he was found huddled in a corner of his apartment, car keys in hand, and mumbling to himself. Someone had had a terrific row in the apartment. Pillows and shattered glass everywhere. The neighbors said they thought the couple might have had a fight in the early evening. They said she must have run out of the building. He was heard stomping down the stairs, yelling her name, and roaring off in his big Mercedes. He didn't seem all that surprised she was dead.

137

Also, interestingly enough, there are fresh bashes on his car fender. Consistent enough, say the detectives on first inspection, to a helpful push off a road."

"Looks bad for him," said Koniotis. "So, why us? Why did you say this had a kicker? Although we do get involved in foreigner versus foreigner domestic killing, why isn't this an open and shut case, all ready for the prosecutors and the Foreign Ministry?"

"The gun," answered Maria. Koniotis gave her a questioning look. She went on. "I thought the method looked oddly familiar. So, I took a chance and put a priority on the check and comparison of the bullet. It matched perfectly.

"Jill Murray was murdered in the same way and with the same weapon, a Markarov pistol, that was used on Nicos Petrou in front of the parliament building two years ago. I checked on the Murrays. They weren't even living here two years ago."

Koniotis took a deep breath, covered his face with his hands, and began to concentrate deeply. It was as if Maria Solonos weren't even there. But she didn't resent his withdrawal; she had worked with Takis a long time. At length, Koniotis opened his hands and his eyes and straightened up in the chair.

"A hunch, Maria. Please check the ballistics tests with Interpol again. And as quickly as possible, please."

"Done yesterday," Maria answered and headed for the door.

"And, Maria," Koniotis called at her back. "You are brilliant."

"I've trained with the best," was all she said, as she swept out of the door. But her gait was sprier and her head was held higher than when she had entered the room.

Koniotis sat, playing with the stacks of note cards on his desk for some time, staring at them, heavy in contemplation. After several minutes, he took out a blank card and, with a flourish, wrote a word on top and lined it up with the other four piles on the desktop. He took two other cards, wrote "Nicos Petrou" on one and "Jill Murray" on the other, and placed them in the fifth pile.

The piles now read Drugs, Money Laundering, Illegal Arms, Unassigned, and—Assassination.

* * * *

He was absolutely stunned.

His secretary stood there in front of his desk, blubbering away and alternating between spinning that silly rope bracelet around her wrist and pulling at the strands of her long, blonde hair. She was having difficulty getting the full story out, and yet he couldn't snap at her and command her to shut up and pull herself together, as he very much wanted to do. He couldn't do this, because he had to get as many details from her as possible and she knew dangerously more than he could afford for her to know now that she had been involved in the previous night's fiasco.

He finally got her calmed down, and she reported the call she had received that the arms shipment had been intercepted. He then sweet-talked her out of the room, with declarations that her small part in the botched operation could not have been detected and with sugary details of all the things he would do to reward her for her continued loyalty.

Once she was out of the office, he returned to his desk, his mind racing.

"Where do we stand? How did the authorities know about the shipment? Could they have known all about the operation? Probably not. It was probably a lucky fluke by a routine coastal patrol boat that had just been in the area by coincidence. But we'll have to keep a closer eye on the German. I've never been sure about him. I had told them that Zygi was too obvious. We could have easily moved it out of either Limassol or the Larnaca marina, as we have done before. There even are possibilities of using Ayia Napa now."

He took a deep breath, the rationalization having relieved his initial fears greatly. "All right, calm down. No harm was done on this side. We have the heroin. And little harm was done on the other side. They all know there are risks involved. There are so many Lebanese factions to serve. If the Hizballah aren't prepared to write this off as their bad luck and to continue with the slate clean, there are several other groups that would love to have the service—and who can obtain the drugs from the Al-Biqa' Valley suppliers just as easily. What could the authorities know? We've had no inkling that they are getting close. I talked to that Inspector Koniotis the other night. If anyone is in the position to be tracing us down, it would be him. But, I didn't get any feeling from him at all that indicated he might suspect our activities."

He leaned back in his richly upholstered chair, once more full of confidence. "But, the secretary," he thought. "She definitely will have to go."

Chapter Eleven

Caitlyn was still walking on air when she arrived that afternoon at the Ledra Handicrafts Center. Although Eleni Piccard received Caitlyn graciously enough, she appeared quite weary—at least until Caitlyn started to describe her Bronze Age tomb find that morning at the Kaliana dig. Eleni then quickly got caught up in Caitlyn's animated enthusiasm and began to question her closely.

"You mentioned markings on the pottery. What sort of markings? Can you describe the designs or motifs?"

"Oh, no, It was too dark and close in the tomb. And I was too emotionally charged over the magnitude of the find to remember any of the details. You don't know how exhilarating it is for an archaeologist to find an intact site. I do seem to recall some sort of bull and snake pattern on bits of broken pottery, but I couldn't describe the motif."

This was not completely true. Caitlyn clearly remembered the bull and snake pattern, but she could not say in the confusion of the previous day's excitement whether she had seen the pattern in the tomb yesterday or if she only knew that the pattern was once there to be seen. She could hardly explain the workings of the knowing to Mrs. Piccard, when she had difficulty understanding it herself.

"What a pity," Eleni responded, her disappointment quite evident. "The ancient Cypriot motifs are vital for our work."

"Nothing is lost," Caitlyn smiled. "It will just take some time. The pieces will be coming down to me at the Cyprus Museum soon, and I promise to report to you quickly on the artistic aspects of what we find—with photos of the motifs."

"And the body itself. The body in the tomb. You say it hadn't been disturbed?" And then when Caitlyn indicated it had not, and that it probably would not be disinterred, Mrs. Piccard's pleasure was quite evident.

Some of the obvious tension surrounding Mrs. Piccard this morning was noticeably dispelled by Caitlyn's assurances about both the tomb and its contents. "I'm sorry, My Dear. Of course I can wait for your reports. The work at Kaliana is close to my heart. I also have an aversion to disturbing our ancestors. Not the possessions buried with them so much as their own remains. Also, I'm afraid I'm a bit out of sorts this morning. I was up most of the night and have not gotten much sleep."

Even though Caitlyn showed no curiosity for further explanation, Eleni went on to say: "I was in Limassol on business yesterday and had been working hard to convince a very talented young lacemaker to leave her present employers and join my handicraft company. Jacques and I had to leave a meeting in Limassol last night to meet with her. It took most of the rest of the night, but I do believe I have won her over.

"But enough of my administrative problems," Eleni declared. "After your visit to the handicrafts center today, I think you will understand my intense interest in any new designs you have found on the ancient grave goods you have uncovered."

Escorting Caitlyn around the showroom off the center's lobby, Eleni started into what was probably a standard pitch she gave all important visitors to her enterprise. "The archaeological activities of the Ledra Foundation and the work of this handicraft center are closely entwined. Like the government's own handicraft center, our company only works with designs and motifs that are authentic to Cyprus's ancient history. We acquire our designs by studying the artifacts being unearthed with the help of the foundation. Of course, we sometimes do new things with the motifs to make them marketable. We are, after all, a business and are also interested in promoting Cyprus and its goods and themes abroad. Thus the bull and snake images you think you found on some pottery shards in the tomb this morning quite likely may be faithfully reproduced on our pottery. But you are also very likely to see them on T-shirts. You have not yet, I assume, discovered any T- shirts from the Bronze Age periods?"

Both were laughing and all tension had been dispelled as Eleni conducted Caitlyn on a tour of the working area of the center. This area consisted of a series of thankfully air conditioned rooms that formed a square around a pleasant central atrium. One workshop housed looms on which artisans were weaving woolen rugs and cotton fabrics that incorporated traditional Cypriot motifs and colors.

"These motifs can come from any source of original rendering," Eleni explained. "It could have been on pottery or on cave walls. The only requirement that has to be met is that we must have documentation that it was found in Cyprus."

"This isn't all wool," Caitlyn exclaimed, as she watched the working of one of the looms. "This looks like silk. You don't use indigenous fabrics?"

"Silk *is* authentic to Cyprus," Eleni responded. "It was once one of the staple products of Kakopetria, the mountain village I was going to the other day when I took you to the Kaliana excavation."

"How interesting. I'd like to see Kakopetria someday."

"Yes, you must," Eleni responded warmly. "I'll arrange to take you there."

While moving from this room, Eleni further explained her business's relationship with the official Cyprus Handicraft Center: "The government's operation is run much the same as ours. We both started from a decision to preserve and foster the country's artistic traditions and from the need to help employ the displaced refugees from the 1974 Turkish invasion. The two operations manage to coexist and, in fact, work rather closely together. This is because the government center focuses on sales here in Cyprus, whereas the Ledra center—other than our showroom here in the building—focuses entirely on exports abroad. We both insist on authenticity of design and high quality of workmanship."

They had now reached and traveled through the jewelry-making room and were entering the largest room of all.

"This is where we make our pottery goods," announced Eleni. "This is the largest section of our operation, not only because pottery represents the largest percentage of the artifacts that have survived the ravages of time and of grave robbers, but also because we found that pottery sells the best abroad."

Caitlyn looked at the many pottery wheels that were in constant motion and then around at the tables where all forms of pottery goods were sitting in various stages of completion. She saw examples of the Early Bronze Age red polished ware that had electrified the Kaliana excavation team earlier in the week. Nearby was some pottery in the white painted style, which, for archaeologists, indicated the later Middle Bronze Age. Most of the pottery here, however, as with most she had seen in local gift shops and at street stalls, depicted the fanciful birds and fishes that were rendered in what was known as the "free field" style. This motif represented the much later Archaic period, which had dominated the island from about 750 to 450 BC.

Then her eye was caught by an artisan, evidently a senior artisan, working off to the side with white ceramic vases coated with a reddish brown color and decorated by running a comb along the surface before the brown color had dried. She turned and looked quizzically at Eleni.

"This represents our oldest documented age," smiled Eleni. "This is known as combed ware and has been traced to the Neolithic period, that is all the way back to the period spanning from 7000 to about 4000 BC. This particular motif was found at the Khirokitia excavations located just off the Nicosia-Limassol highway and near Limassol. You must visit that excavation soon."

"Yes, I must," Caitlyn agreed, "I studied reports of the excavation before I arrived here."

Beside this table was one that held some interesting terra-cotta figurines. These appeared to be a statuette or a child's doll rendered in a rigid cross shape, the shortened arms held exactly perpendicular to the elongated neck and head section above and legs and feet section below. Caitlyn picked one of the figurines up and curiously turned it over several times in her hands. It was textured on the front to indicate where the eyes, nose, toes, and fingers would be. There was an oblong opening at the back, which revealed that the figurine was hollow inside.

"That design is from the Chalcolithic period, the one stretching between the Neolithic and Early Bronze Age," intoned a refined male voice from over her shoulder.

Startled, Caitlyn turned to find Jacques Piccard standing in the doorway to the next room. Before Caitlyn could speak, Jacques continued: "The original finds of that form were small soapstone figurines, which our archaeologists believe were talismans, probably related to female fertility. The figurines had holes at the top, so they probably were worn on a string around the neck. Perhaps, under the circumstances, you don't want to handle that figurine too long." He ended this explanation with a teasing smile.

"It is a lovely piece of art. Thank you for the explanation, Ambassador," Caitlyn replied somewhat coolly and did not put the figurine down, if only to deny Jacques the pleasure of seeing her do so.

"What are you doing in the shop, Jacques?" asked Eleni somewhat sharply. "I thought you were going to restrict your activities to the shipping details. I also asked you to be in the office to receive those arriving for the British Council exhibition meeting."

146

"I wanted to check on the Chalcolithic figurines we are boxing up for the special order for Marseilles. Also, Alec Stuart, representing the British Council, and Vassos Petrou, who will coordinate the press publicity, have already arrived for the meeting on the exhibit. Alec asked to use the men's room. He looks like death warmed over. He may not be well. I asked them to meet us in the courtyard when they were finished there. They should be here any minute."

While Jacques and Eleni were conversing, Caitlyn had moved into the next room. This appeared to be the shipping room, where the handicrafts were boxed for export. On a nearby table was a small shipping crate, which contained more of the terra-cotta cruciform figurines. These had been very carefully cushioned both from each other and from the sides of the crate.

"They seem to be very careful about preventing breakage," thought Caitlyn, as she absentmindedly picked one of the figurines up and turned it over in her hands, tracing the smooth texture of the terra-cotta.

At this instant, she felt as if there were eyes boring into the back of her head. She looked first at the door through which she had entered. Both Eleni and Jacques were looking at her, the former with rather a distracted gaze and the latter with a look that was both intense and speculative. She smiled somewhat guiltily—although she had no idea why she should have such a feeling. She turned toward the door into the outer corridor as she slipped the figurine carefully back into the crate. Staring at her from that door were a grinning Vassos Petrou and an obviously distressed Alec Stuart.

As she moved toward the door to greet Vassos and Alec, something was nagging at the back of her mind. She had missed something over the last couple of minutes, but she could not, for the life of her, figure out what it was—or why her subconscious should indicate that it had any special significance.

Chapter Twelve

At the same moment Caitlyn was attempting to reason what important event she had unwittingly experienced at the handicraft center, Bob Murray seemed to be fighting hard for his life and sanity against events that were all too real to him. By all measures, he appeared to be losing the fight.

"Once again, Mr. Murray," Takis Koniotis said gently. "Can you tell us what you and your wife were fighting about yesterday afternoon?"

"I've told you repeatedly that we didn't fight about anything yesterday." responded Murray in a voice that reflected both exhaustion and the edge of hysteria. "I haven't even seen my wife since the early afternoon yesterday. She'd gone to Larnaca on business. I haven't seen her since. The neighbors could not have heard the two of us having a fight in the apartment early in the evening, because Jill wasn't even there. Jill was in Larnaca on business. Why can't you let me see Jill? Where are the embassy people? I need to have the embassy people here."

"Please keep calm," cooed Koniotis. "The embassy people are on their way." This was not precisely true. The American consul was, in fact, pacing impatiently in a downstairs waiting room and had been doing so for almost a half hour now. Koniotis had to make one last stab at getting information out of Murray. He didn't really rank the husband high on his list of suspects in the murder, but Murray seemed to know more than he was revealing about why his wife might have been murdered—and possibly assassinated, if this was a politically motivated crime. Koniotis had to try to get this information—and fast. He could not hold the American consul off for much longer.

"I'm sorry, Mr. Murray," Koniotis continued, "But I'm sure that, in your current state, you really don't want to see your wife's body. It was a very bad accident. She has already been identified by someone from the embassy. I'm afraid we're quite sure it is her. Now, about this possible altercation between you and your wife. We understand—and I'm sorry I have to bring this up now—that you might have been having problems in your relations . . . that there may have been another man in your wife's life?"

"There was no other man," Murray fairly wailed. "I loved my wife and she loved me. I know what it looked like. God, I know what it looked like. I saw the glares people gave my wife and that man from the British embassy. But it wasn't what people thought." Suddenly, Murray just clammed up and sat there.

After a moment, to try to get the monologue going again, Koniotis repeated: "About the fight . . ."

Murray screamed, eyes flashing: "*There was no fight!*"

"But there was all that broken china and glassware."

"I did that myself. There was no fight. Jill was not there."

"But you were mad about something, then. Something about Mrs. Murray, certainly, because you were yelling her name when you left your flat."

"Yes, I was mad." And at great length, getting it out only with a struggle. "Mad and . . . scared. Yes, scared. Mad and scared, but not *at* Jill. Not *at* Jill, but *about* and *for* Jill. This has nothing to do with Jill and another man." The conclusion of this outburst drifted off into a quiet exasperation, and Murray sank into his chair, seemingly trying to disappear from sight completely.

"About the car bash," Koniotis started into a new direction.

"Where are the embassy people? I don't think I should say any more until I've talked to the embassy people," Murray responded stubbornly.

"Yes, just a minute. I'm sure they will be here directly. I will be told as soon as they arrive. Now, about the car bash . . ."

"I've told you a million times. I *was* looking for Jill. I *did* get tired and worried about waiting for her in the apartment. I *did* drive to Larnaca. I *was* in a state of high agitation—but I'm not going to say anything more about *that* until I've seen the embassy people. I *did* . . . I'm sorry, I didn't stay there, but I *did* hit a parked car while driving through a narrow street in Larnaca."

"Well, I do suppose that will soon be verified, if true," said Koniotis, not wanting to dwell on the subject, as it had already been verified, through the checking of paint samples, as very likely to be true.

"Mr. Murray. Mr. Murray, can you look at me, please?" And, when he did: "Mr. Murray, do you own a gun?"

Bob Murray collapsed into sobbing, and Takis Koniotis could see that this interview functionally was at an end. He gave an imperceptible signal, and Maria Solonos bustled into the room.

"Mr. Koniotis," she said with a great deal of dignity, "You asked me to let you know just as soon as the American consul arrived. He is here. Unfortunately, I think he has been here for about a half hour, but there was a misunderstanding downstairs, and they just told me about his arrival."

"Fine, thank you, Ms. Solonos," said Koniotis, maintaining his end of the charade. "Could you please show Mr. Murray downstairs. Mr. Murray, you are free to go. I'm sorry if we have inconvenienced you. I'm also sorry to say that we may have to talk with you again sometime next week. I know these questions are trying under the circumstances, but we do need to try to sort everything out—for your wife's sake. Please accept our heartfelt sympathy in your loss."

Bob Murray must have at least gotten the part about being free to go, because he rose, his face buried in a soggy handkerchief, and, still sobbing with great heaves, shuffled out of the room under the gentle guidance of Maria.

Maria was back even before Koniotis had gathered his thoughts for a review of the just-concluded session.

"Yes, Maria, you have something?" asked Koniotis somewhat absently.

"Certainly do. And it's another bombshell."

She had Koniotis's complete attention.

"The ballistics check with Interpol on the murder weapon was a beauty of a hunch. They are continuing to check, but they came up with a quick match on a previous international crime. Two years ago, only a couple of months before the assassination of Nicos Petrou. When a check was run right after Petrou's death, the paperwork from this other crime must not have made it into the records yet. The same gun was used then—in nearly the same manner—to murder a senior money laundering investigator for the World Bank. She was shot in Belgrade while pursuing a case involving Yugoslav banks. She was working on cases involving East Europe, the Cayman Islands, and various terrorist organizations at the time."

"Fascinating," said Koniotis. "Does Interpol have any leads?"

"Nothing specific. But since she was then in Belgrade and since she was very good at her job, the presumption has been that she was getting too close to a revelation on the Yugoslav operations."

"Once more the Yugoslavs," mused Koniotis, followed by: "Maria, you are still brilliant."

When he was alone, Koniotis took out another note card, scrawled the words "Yugoslav money laundering/Nicos and/or Vassos Petrou?" on it, and flipped it on the Assassination pile.

* * * *

Following dinner that evening at the Gladstone Street mansion, Caitlyn and Nora Petrou retired to the lounge and talked about their recent activities. Most of the conversation, of course, revolved around the archaeological discovery Caitlyn had made at the Kaliana excavation. They had not been conversing long when a telephone call for Caitlyn came through. It was Paul Conte, and he was sounding very solemn and subdued.

"Hello Cait."

"Oh, hello Paul. You sound a bit down."

"Well, yes, that's what I was calling you about. I'm afraid we're going to have to postpone our trip to Salamis tomorrow. I'll have to work." There was a peculiar catch in his voice.

"Oh, that's all right; perhaps another time." Caitlyn had mixed feelings about not getting to spend another day with the American diplomat on the Turkish side, even though she was dying to see Salamis. "But, Paul, what's wrong. You sound rather sad."

"Yes, well, I guess you'll have to hear about it eventually. There's been a bad accident. It's Jill Murray. I'm afraid she's dead."

Caitlyn more or less collapsed into the chair beside the telephone. She was griping the instrument so tightly that her knuckles were turning white. Paul related the entire story in terms of an automobile accident, and then, when Caitlyn had managed to absorb that news, he doubled back and told her that they had found that Jill had actually died from a gunshot wound. At the end of this discourse, there was a long moment of silence.

"Cait? Caitlyn? Are you still there?"

"Yes, Paul. I'm sorry. I just am having trouble taking it all in. I just had dinner with the Murrays the other evening. It's all so awful!" Then a horrible thought hit her. "Her husband. He isn't . . . ? He didn't . . . ?"

"No," Paul answered. "I'm sure Bob wasn't involved in her death. He has been questioned extensively and there was a bit of a problem with seemingly incriminating evidence—and he is, of course, in very bad emotional shape. But, I am quite sure he wasn't involved in this, and I believe the police are becoming sure as well."

"That, at least, is good to hear," Caitlyn replied. "One has to wonder, of course, with those encounters between Jill and Alec Stuart and her husband's apparent reaction to them. Oh my gosh! Alec Stuart. He must have known this afternoon. That must be why he looked so ill at the handicraft center."

"Yes," agreed Paul. "I'm sure he would have known by the afternoon. But, whatever people might be saying, Caitlyn, please don't believe that Alec and Jill were having an affair or even that Bob Murray thought they were. I can't say any more than that, but it's unfair to both Bob and Alec—and especially to Jill herself—for people to be thinking that now."

"All right, I understand. Or, at least, I am happy to accept your judgment on this," answered Caitlyn. "And I perfectly understand why it's best for us to call off tomorrow's trip. I do thank you for taking me to Kyrenia last weekend."

"It was my pleasure. Oh, and before I hang up. About Kyrenia."

"Yes, what about it?"

"Remember how I told you the Turkish antiquities people were about to start poking around in some of the long-closed areas of Kyrenia Castle? Well, our Turkish translator passed me a news clipping yesterday that they have started doing so, and guess what they found below the gatekeeper's chambers?"

Caitlyn felt a sudden chill coming on and experienced a very brief flashback of both her vision in the castle and her nightmare of the same night.

"Cait? Are you there?"

"Yes, Paul," Caitlyn responded in as even a voice as she could muster. "What did they find?"

"Human bones. More than one body, but they can't be sure. They were scattered by animals. There's also no telling how long they've been there. Isn't that strange?"

"Yes, that is . . . strange."

After she had disconnected her conversation with Paul, Caitlyn had to repeat it all for Nora, who had been sitting nearly at her elbow and who had been listening intently enough to Caitlyn's side of the discussion that she didn't really require all that much filling in. No sooner had Caitlyn finished with her story than another call came through, once again for Caitlyn. This time it was Vassos Petrou.

"I am so pleased I found you at home," Vassos began. "I meant to talk to you at the handicraft center today, but there were so many people around and I had to get publicity details straight for the British Council handicrafts exhibit. The reason that I called is that I find I have a free day tomorrow and wondered if that would be a good time for me to show you Paphos."

"Well, as it turns out, I just had my plans for tomorrow canceled, and . . . I do feel like it would be good just to get completely away from Nicosia for a day. Yes, thank you, a trip to Paphos tomorrow would be lovely."

"Perhaps I can press my luck a bit further," said Vassos a bit haltingly.

"Oh, in what way?" Caitlyn queried.

"Well, as you may know, Paphos is a good distance away." Caitlyn voiced assent, and Vassos continued. "It really will take more than just a day trip even for an introduction to Paphos—and especially for an archaeologist to even get her initial bearings. And it would also be very nice for you to see the contrast offered by the mountains. S-o-o, I took the liberty of making reservations for two rooms at the Forest Park Hotel in the Troodos Mountains for tomorrow night. We could stop there on our way back and return by the mountain route. I hope I haven't been too forward."

Caitlyn could feel her knees turning to jelly again, and she knew she should refuse outright. But he sounded so charming, he did have a point about the long distance, and he had specifically said he had reserved two rooms. But, still, she voiced her regrets in her reply.

"I understand, of course," said Vassos, not betraying any particular disappointment in his voice. "But I had thought, if we made it into a two-day adventure, that we could stop at the Khirokitia Neolithic site near Limassol on our way. I'm sure you want to see that."

That had done it. That and perhaps the reminder through Jill Murray's untimely death that life was too short not to take advantage of every opportunity to enjoy it.

"All right," Caitlyn capitulated, with a little laugh. "We'll give it a try."

"Thank you, I am very pleased you said 'yes.' And you can always change your mind. I am a good customer at the Forest Park, and they will not mind if I cancel at the last moment."

They made arrangements for an early start in the morning, and Caitlyn rang off.

Nora had not gotten much out of that conversation, although she certainly had made no effort to hide her interest. She also proved to be in a state of considerable agitation. Caitlyn told her who had called and why he had called, and Nora proceeded to criticize her stepson and to try to dissuade Caitlyn from developing a relationship with him. Seeing that she had not dissuaded Caitlyn, she concluded with the emphatic plea: "Please be very careful of Vassos and of yourself whenever you are around Vassos. It would be best to avoid him altogether. He is not a nice person, and he leads a dangerous life. He is not for you. Please, please, be on your guard, and do be careful."

Caitlyn quieted Nora down with assurances that she would be very careful around Vassos and that she had no intention of developing a relationship with him. She could not understand the root of the vehemence Nora exhibited toward the son of her departed husband, but she did not want Nora to be upset nor did she want to establish problems between herself and her hostess over the man.

As they began to wind their conversation down for the evening, Caitlyn strove for a high note ending. So she asked Nora about the Middle Eastern accents she had used in the room's decoration.

"Yes, I actually have close connections in the Middle East region," Nora responded, "connections that are rooted in my days in Paris, where I associated with many Middle Easterners who were getting their education or taking their holidays there. I continued the contacts when I started my travel agency, and my associations have been very beneficial for business. I regularly travel to such places as Morocco, Tunisia, Algeria, Libya, Egypt, and Lebanon."

"Not to Israel?" Caitlyn asked in pure innocence.

"No, not to Israel," Nora answered unequivocally, as she stood and started switching off lamps as an unmistakable signal that it was time for the two to retire.

"A very strong-willed and complex woman," mused Caitlyn, as she started up the stairs. "Libya and Lebanon. Very interesting. Not only ultraconservative Greek in her politics, but evidently strongly pro-Arab as well. Quite a combination."

Before Caitlyn ascended to the top landing, her world was shattered by the ringing, once more, of the telephone. The knowing rushed in and had nearly knocked the breath completely out of her when Nora handed her the telephone, with the note: "It's for you again, Caitlyn. It's a man, but he wouldn't give his name. Do you want to take it?" Something in Nora's demeanor indicated that the call had taken her very much by surprise, although she seemed more perplexed than dismayed.

Somehow Caitlyn knew she really didn't need to take the telephone. She had known at the first ring who it was, no matter how impossible it was. And, in knowing it was Kurt, her entire equilibrium was shot. The emotions of relief and desire were strangely subsumed by anger and disgust. At the same time she should only have had thoughts of joy that Kurt was alive and was coming back into her life, she was consumed by the anger of what this meant he had done to his family and to her by allowing them to think he had been dead these many months. The only thought she could muster on such an occasion was: "So, this is how love dies."

She grabbed for the telephone, and the tone of her response to the call must have all to clearly conveyed her emotions down the line. Only one word was spoken: "Caity?" This was followed by a prolonged silence when Caitlyn did not respond, and then the telephone went dead. Nora could only look on in amazement, as Caitlyn turned and stomped back up the stairs.

Chapter Thirteen

Nora did not appear for breakfast Saturday morning, which was unusual. She was an early riser, who normally spent considerable time devouring several of the papers for local political news while partaking of a leisurely breakfast on a shaded terrace before leaving for the office. Caitlyn had been surprised to find that the Cypriot workweek included Saturday morning, in trade for Wednesday afternoon. On this Saturday, Caitlyn was relieved that Nora had not joined her for breakfast. Not the least of the reasons for her relief was that she did not want to discuss her last telephone call of the previous evening. She was determined to relegate all thoughts of Kurt to her past, and the easiest way to do that was to pretend that last evening had never occurred.

Vassos arrived at the Gladstone Street mansion bright and early, as he had promised, for the trip to Paphos. As he was putting Caitlyn's overnight bag into the trunk of his car, Caitlyn glanced up at the window to Nora's bedroom at the corner of the old, central structure's upper floor. The curtains were parted and Nora could be seen observing the proceedings with what could only be described as a malevolent scrutiny.

"So, that's why she didn't come down to breakfast," thought Caitlyn. "She is still upset that I am taking a trip with Vassos. What difficulty between those two could possibly evoke such hatred from Mrs. Petrou? She otherwise seems such a pleasant person, if a little silly and naïve in her doting on Ambassador Piccard. It was probably very unwise for me to accept this invitation. I have a feeling she will not forget it easily or soon."

"Oh, well," Caitlyn sighed, as she entered the car for the trip toward the south, "in for a penny, in for a pound, as they say here in Cyprus. I might as well enjoy myself and try to smooth everything over afterwards. Perhaps if I don't follow through on the overnight stay, she will be mollified."

* * * *

Vassos delivered on his promise on a side trip to Khirokitia, and, in just under an hour's drive via the Nicosia-Limassol highway, he turned off to the right and up a hillside that directly overlooked the road. In the space of a few hundred yards and a few minutes, the two had spun back nearly 8,000 years in time to the Khirokitia settlement of the Neolithic, or New Stone Age. Caitlyn was fascinated by the site and immediately began closely examining the excavations. They were composed of an attached network of room-sized circular chambers, separated by low walls of irregular, but smoothly rounded stones. The walls evidently represented the foundations of dwellings and support buildings, each between ten and twenty feet in diameter. The buildings had been opened to reveal shallow chambers under the floors, which, Caitlyn knew from study, represented the graves of the inhabitants' ancestors. Dwellings in the later, Chalcolithic period were circular as well, Caitlyn knew. But they were distinguished from those of this earlier age by providing separate tombs outside of the village area.

After having closely examined the village area, Caitlyn spent several minutes in the middle of the excavations just slowly turning full circles and taking in all of the surrounding details.

"And what are you doing, young lady?" Vassos asked in a pseudo-serious voice but with an amused gleam in his eye. "You know, I don't think witchcraft and incantations are legal in Cyprus."

"They were prevalent many more centuries than they've been illegal," was Caitlyn's thought. But what she said in response was "Sorry, I was just getting acclimated to the site. Some archaeologists are very detail oriented and have a detached scientific approach to their work. I approach archaeology emotionally, trying to merge with the ancient time and place. I find that helps me in my research. It certainly was the method I used to discover the Early Bronze Age tomb up at Kaliana on Monday."

"And have you merged with this site?" Vassos queried, still with an amused edge to his voice.

"No, I've never been . . . I mean, yes, to a certain extent I can imagine what life once was like here." It was strange. This site, in fact, was not as familiar to her as the Kaliana site had been. How could that be? Why could she relate almost viscerally to one ancient site but feel only minimal familiarity with another one of the same period. This wasn't anything like she had experienced with what she called the knowing before. Yet, when she looked around this site, she could make some connections. But that, of course, was because of the similarity of life throughout the region in any given period.

"Caitlyn?"

"What? Oh, sorry. I'm afraid my mind was drifting."

"What I asked is, what have you learned from your merging with this site? From the trance you were in, I'd have no trouble believing you were channeling back."

"Have you been to the Kaliana excavation?" Caitlyn asked.

"No, I haven't. What does that have to do with this site?"

"That's exactly what I was trying to consider," answered Caitlyn. "Since I am working on the Kaliana project, and since our greatest hope is that our project site goes back in time as far as this one does, I was trying to discern whether the sites would have seemed equally satisfactory for settlement to the people of that time."

"And . . ."

"And, upon brief inspection, I find they are, but with one very interesting wrinkle."

"All right, first the similarities," said Vassos, suddenly changing to his investigative reporter style.

"I'm sure I could find others if I spent more time at it," laughed Caitlyn, "But three right off hand. First, the rise of this hillside is virtually identical to that of the hillsides—on both sides of the valley—at Kaliana. Second, the relationship to the surrounding sheltering hills is also the same. And, third, see the road below us?"

Vassos nodded pleasantly.

"Do you know what was down there many thousands of years before the road was there?"

Vassos shook his head pleasantly.

"A river," Caitlyn marched on, oblivious to Vassos's teasing nods. "That was naturally considered to be a good place to build a road down to the southern coast, because it once had been the bed of a river gently falling to the coast. And, do you know what that means to this site?"

Vassos began to nod and then thought better of it and shook his head, now all ears for Caitlyn's explanation.

"Well, two things. The most obvious is a nearby source of fresh water. Second, not so obvious, is a nearby source of building materials. A trained eye can quickly discern that the rocks used to build these walls were tumbled in water. Thus they most certainly came from the river bed down there when there was a river down there. At Kaliana, there was—and still is—a river at nearly exactly the same distance from the excavation."

Vassos applauded. "And now the interesting wrinkle?"

"Ah, the most exciting possibility of all. Come here and stand by me." Vassos did as commanded. "What do you see?" queried Caitlyn.

"Hills," answered Vassos.

"And beyond the hills?" In the haze beyond the hills?"

"The sea," answered Vassos at some length.

"Absolutely correct," said Caitlyn. "You see the water and, if you open to all of your senses, you can feel the cooling breeze rising up the valley from the sea."

"And what about this relation to the sea provides an interesting wrinkle at the Kaliana site?"

"Principally the observation that the current Kaliana site is turned away from the sea."

Vassos looked confused.

"The 'interesting wrinkle' in my observations is that, although we've already tracked the Kaliana site far back in time and have every reason to believe it goes even further back, dating the settlement of the whole valley back into earliest times, it may not be the oldest site. But I may now know where to start looking for that site. I would not be surprised if the Kaliana site went back to Neolithic times. But, after seeing Khirokitia, I would also not be surprised to find that the current Kaliana site was first settled in a later age."

Vassos looked even more confused.

"Have you been up that valley toward Kakopetria?" Caitlyn asked.

"Of course," Vassos answered. "All Cypriots have. It provides the direct route to Mt. Olympus from the central plain, and it is a favorite retreat during the heat of July and August."

"Well," Caitlyn continued, "If you crossed the valley directly opposite Kaliana, walked up the hill to the identical elevation, and turned around, what would you see?"

Vassos puzzled for a minute and then his face lit up in a broad smile. "You would see Morphou Bay."

"Precisely," confirmed Caitlyn. "Off in the haze, at nearly the same distance that we now stand from the southern coast, you would, from the valley hillside opposite Kaliana, see the water of the west coast."

"Therefore . . ." Vassos started to venture.

"Therefore," Caitlyn broke in, "My musings here today have told me that, if we can't find evidence of the Neolithic period at the current Kaliana excavations, we very likely only need to cross the narrow valley. I'm betting we'll find that the settlement of that valley indeed started on the opposite hillside and at least as early as the Neolithic period."

"Bravo," Vassos sang out, once again applauding, and this time with even more respect than he had accorded her earlier. "You are a brilliant detective. I most certainly would not like to have to match wits with you."

Caitlyn glowed with thoughts of the possibilities at the Kaliana project, and Vassos turned to introspection, as the two returned to the car and continued their journey toward Limassol, and, ultimately, toward Paphos.

* * * *

Within fifteen minutes of having traveled south and west from the Khirokitia site, the old Alfa Romeo had reached the southern coastal hotel district of Amathus and then traversed, at mid-hill level, the entire stretch of the sprawling port city of Limassol. Caitlyn found the view from the highway of the country's teaming commercial, shipping, and wine center fascinating. After having nervously navigated six busy traffic circles across the top of the city, the highway telescoped into a two-lane road, and, within minutes, the little sports car brought them to the second stop of the day—Curium.

Rivaled in Cyprus as a major excavated archaeological site only by the largely inaccessible ancient city of Salamis on the eastern coast and in the Turkish zone, Curium is probably the most-visited Greco-Roman site on the island. It is located in an area that stretches for more than a mile on top of chalk cliffs that unexpectedly rise from the coastal plan about ten miles west of Limassol. The Greek city state had been established on the site in the twelfth century BC. The first settlement in the area has been traced back to the Mycenean expansion of the fourteenth century B.C. and had flourished under the reign of the Ptolemies and later the Romans, only to be destroyed

166

and scattered during coastal raids by the Saracens in the seventh century AD.

Throughout the examination of the complex, Caitlyn maintained the appreciation and fascination that could be expected of a professional archaeologist visiting major excavated sites. Vassos guided her from the Greco-Roman theater to the Roman House of Eustolios, with its mosaic floors and breathtaking view of the sea; to the early Christian basilica; to the stadium; and to the sanctuary of Apollo Hylates, the god of the woodlands and patron god of Curium. But Caitlyn discovered that the excitement and the spark of a visceral link with the past seemed to be missing for her.

"I don't know," Caitlyn sighed and thought to herself, as she stood at the top of the largely restored amphitheater that was now used for cultural programs. She gazed out over the orchestra area and toward the sea below the cliffs. "Perhaps it's just that these excavations have been too picked over and jumbled around by succeeding civilizations, with access too ordered, and that there have been too many visitors trekking through for the spirit of this city to have remained."

She kept thinking back to her visit to Kyrenia Castle and Paul's lecture in justification of the dismantling and reuse of building material from previous eras. As an archaeologist, she felt she could only abhor the desecration of heritage and the disorder and confusion of civilization that resulted from successive use of settlement sites.

Having heard the sigh and having misinterpreted its meaning, Vassos, who was standing at Caitlyn's side on the theater's top aisle, quietly said: "Beautiful, isn't it?"

Caitlyn agreed, not wanting to disappoint Vassos in the feeling of incompleteness and dissatisfaction the site had evoked from her.

"Ancient, in ruins, and, yet, still living for my people," continued Vassos.

"Oh, how so?" asked Caitlyn, her interest stimulated.

"Perhaps I can explain it better in Paphos—there is a basilica there now called St. Paul's of the Pillar that expresses the concept best to me. But such sites as Curium provide Cypriots with a context for their connection over a long continuum of past civilizations and events with their earliest ancestors. And they do so in a way that seems to be most deeply internalized in island cultures such as ours."

Caitlyn now was fully attentive.

"When the average visitor comes to a place like Curium, they tend to see only ruined buildings, conceptually frozen in linear time. I'm not saying they don't appreciate and learn from what they see. They just don't really see what is represented here. When trained archaeologists such as yourself come here, they do see the site in its complexity—with the realization of the greater spread of time revealed by ruins. But they, even more than the casual tourists, seem to want to tuck what they see away in separate little labeled boxes as soon as possible. When they see what a developed site such as Curium has become, they tend to get lost in a feeling of disappointment that the site has been somehow vandalized by succeeding generations and that, even now, it has been 'prepared' for the tourist trade."

Caitlyn looked sharply at Vassos, amazed by and a bit frightened of his penetrating perception of her very thoughts.

"However," Vassos continued. "We Cypriots look at and appreciate our visits to this site, seeing them as a never-ending continuum of our history. We see and feel what happened here before the ruins you now can see were built and what happened here after that—and then after that. We know and accept that these very stones have been reused and refashioned to meet the changing, but real needs of our earliest ancestors and of all the many and varied succeeding civilizations on the island.

"Take that corner room of the House of Eustolios over there, for instance—the one with the beautiful animal mosaics that was located at the very edge of the cliff to take in the sea breeze. The casual visitors see the beautiful mosaics, marvel at the view, and appreciate the breeze. You archaeologists, through studying the changes and additions made to the building and deciphering the inscriptions in the mosaics, discern that this was a principal lounge area of a private, palatial dwelling of one Eustolios. You also see that it was built from stones pried from this then-deteriorating and unused theater, a dwelling that was later turned into a private bathing club. All very accurate, but also all a bit too clinical.

"We Cypriots stand here and make connections with our ancestors who lived and prospered here for generations, using building materials salvaged from previous generations and from structures that no longer had current-day use. And later ancestors who, when financial times got tough, were forced to turn their home into a business. And even later ancestors, who, when attacked by Saracens, removed whatever they could carry to the hills to rebuild and continue life in safety. And then nearer ancestors who returned to the site to build their sheep folds from the scraps of material they found here. Down the generations to ancestors who retreated here and died here in the short-lived fight to keep yet another invader, Richard the Lionhearted, from choking off the independent rule of the island's indigenous people. And thus down to the grand uncle who sat at nights in that very room, acting as a lookout for British military activity in our struggle for our final grab for independence.

"Tourists see—and appreciate—a simple snapshot of ancient history. Archaeologists see the context of civilizations represented here—even if only the ancient civilizations need apply. But they also tend to be judgmental of the seeming lack of respect of succeeding civilizations that have salvaged building materials and have built over the remains of earlier civilizations. Cypriots see their earlier Cypriot ancestors trying to stay alive and prosper and to leave their children and their children's children a better world than the one they inherited.

"Tell me," Vassos asked Caitlyn, seemingly changing subject, "where do you believe people go when they die, and where to you think the life essences of the newborn come from?"

"I've never really given it much thought," Caitlyn laughed nervously.

"Well, here's something to think about," Vassos responded. "Maybe successive generations are even more closely connected and entwined than just the continuous passing of memories in the short term and DNA in the long term. Maybe there's something more spiritual and cognitive that flows through the centuries. Don't you sometimes feel a very close connection with your heritage or feel that someone unseen is watching over you and guiding you through bad times. There, I can see from your expression that you know what I

170

mean. And I've been reading some of your articles on your work methods. I think what you call incredible luck and informed intuition in your unusual ability to sift through to the essence of your archaeological projects are controlled by talents and abilities that go far beyond physical science. I'm sorry, I didn't mean to lecture," Vassos concluded with a wistful smile. "But I encourage you to give the proposition some thought."

"No, please, don't apologize," Caitlyn answered quickly. "I *was* being just a bit disappointed in this site and probably exactly for the reasons you have mentioned. I fully appreciate what you are saying. And I certainly will mull over your interesting observations. I'm also amazed—and flattered—that you have taken time to read some of my studies."

"Well," Vassos laughed. "Perhaps your archaeologist's sensitivities won't be too ruffled if I go on to tell you that we Cypriots are still using this site for our needs. The theater is regularly used for plays and concerts—yes, I'm almost afraid to admit, even for rock concerts. But do try to remember that even the Romans in their later uses of the amphitheater had changed it into an animal-baiting arena. The site is a beautiful setting for an evening concert. And the most spectacular use to which it now is put is in the annual charity performance of a Shakespearean play. Virtually everyone who enjoys culture attends this production, which has been staged for more than thirty years. This year's production will be next week. You must come see it. As I said, Curium takes on a whole new, awesome presence when seen in the twilight."

"Yes," Caitlyn responded, as they walked to the car. "Yes, I think I do need to give this site another chance."

Fifteen minutes later, they were passing through the British sovereign base of Episkopi, with its typically British buildings strung out on seaside cliffs and its lush Happy Valley playing fields. After clearing Episkopi, the road to the west once again came very close to the sea and was suspended on hillsides high above the surf below. At this point, Vassos drove up the hill to a tourist pavilion overlooking Petra tou Romiou, a rock formation at the edge of the sea that had been celebrated for thousands of years as the traditional spot at which Aphrodite, the goddess of love, beauty, and fertility, rose from the sea. Ancient pilgrims traveled to the area of Cyprus stretching from here to Paphos to pay homage to one of the twelve Olympian gods and goddesses of Greek mythology. At the pavilion, Vassos and Caitlyn had a cooling drink, enjoyed the sea breezes that lifted up the hillside, discussed the deep-seated cult of Aphrodite that had made the island a chief tourist attraction during the Greek period, and planned the rest of the day ahead.

Caitlyn had been enjoying a strong sense of well-being that had not been present during her trip to the north with Paul the previous weekend. Vassos had yet to show any indication of making unwanted advances or forcing decisions on Caitlyn, and the further she traveled from the heavily negative environment of Nora Petrou and the Gladstone Street mansion, the more inclined she felt toward carrying through with the planned overnight stay in the Troodos Mountains.

This feeling of well-being was shattered, however, as they left the pavilion and headed for the Alfa Romeo. Caitlyn suddenly had the feeling of being watched. She looked around her and noticed a man who was sitting in a nearby car, a big, black Mercedes. Her first impression focused on the cruel smile she had caught on his countenance before he lifted and became closely engrossed in a large, unfolded road map. She involuntarily shuddered but did not say anything to Vassos, as she climbed into the Alfa Romeo.

It was not until they had descended back onto the road for the twenty-minute drive to Paphos that it hit her. She had seen that face before. It was one of the faces that had scowled at Paul's back in Kyrenia harbor the previous Saturday. It belonged to the man that she had last seen following Jill Murray out of Kyrenia harbor the previous Saturday. The Jill Murray who was now dead. Murdered.

Caitlyn shuddered again, turned her head toward the passenger window, and snuggled into her seat. Ringing in her ears was Nora's intimation the previous evening of the possible physical danger of being near Vassos. Thoughts raced through her mind.

"I've already made a connection between the man back there and Jill Murray. But, what is the connection between Vassos and that man? And is there a connection between Jill and Vassos? Is Vassos also in danger, or did Vassos have something to do with Jill's murder? And what does Nora know about all of this? I must think. I must not panic. That man. How is it that that man can be on both sides of the buffer zone? He cannot be either Greek or Turkish Cypriot. What *is* his nationality? I told Paul he looked Middle Eastern to me, and Paul just laughed and said Turks fit the bill and we were in the Turkish zone. But we're not in the Turkish zone now. However, I have no evidence he was at the pavilion because of us at all. I'll have to mull this one and observe—I can't mention it to Vassos. For all I know, Vassos and that man might be cohorts."

None of these movements nor Caitlyn's reticence escaped Vassos's attention. He glanced her way with concern and speculation. Everything had seemed to be going so well. What had happened to darken the atmosphere, he wondered. He did not know, but he did already know from observation that Caitlyn had to be handled quite delicately.

"There is more to her than meets the eye," Vassos thought. "I must walk very carefully when around this one. She sees and understands far more than one would imagine. And I do not yet know if she is merely an archaeologist, as she has presented herself. She has several interesting friends for just the short time she has been on the island. And she has already been in the right—or wrong, depending on how one wants to perceive it—place suspiciously often. No, I won't intrude into her thoughts now, but I must set my traps very carefully if I am to get what I want."

At the pavilion, the driver of the black Mercedes folded his map, turned on the engine, descended the steep mountain road to the sea, and turned west toward Paphos. The cruel smile and wild look in his eye never wavered. A much-used Markarov pistol rested on the floor in front of the passenger seat.

Chapter Fourteen

As they neared Paphos, Vassos stopped briefly at the side of the road to show Caitlyn where the original town had been located. From the coastal road, the area looked like a low-slung medieval stone fortress just a short way up the hillside, although the signs identified it as the Sanctuary of Aphrodite.

Pointing up toward a stone structure, Vassos explained. "The structure you see is the fifteenth-century manor house of the Lusignans' holdings in this area. By dumb luck, or, who knows, by some more logical plan that escapes us, the Lusignans built their manor house and sugar refinery on top of the most important temple to the Goddess Aphrodite located anywhere in the Greek world. The ruins of the temple have been traced back to the Early Bronze Age, so the Greek legend and the cult of Aphrodite must have been a development from and probably a perversion of an even more ancient deity. At the height of the Aphrodite cult's popularity, a festival was held every spring. All of this ended in the twelfth century BC, when an earthquake destroyed the temple and the harbor area. The inhabitants mostly drifted away, and new Paphos was founded in about the fourth century BC on the coast to the west."

Caitlyn had been drawn into Vassos's discourse, and she was trying her best to keep up with him now. But her mind had been racing off in other directions, starting about the time Vassos had begun to talk about the earthquake. When she had looked back up the hill from the old harbor area, her attention had been drawn by a black Mercedes, which had come up behind them on the road from Limassol, had lost power slightly as it came upon their car idling at the side of the road, and then had picked up speed as it passed them and moved off toward Paphos.

Vassos's brief introduction to old Paphos having been concluded, he too rejoined the road, and the Alfa Romeo followed in the wake of the Mercedes, which, as they motored into upper Paphos, Caitlyn was happy to note had disappeared. She soon had returned her full attention to the sights and to Vassos's guided tour.

Their first approach into lower Paphos was straight down the hill, past old stone warehouses that Vassos identified as the former center of the region's carob export business, and into the quaint old harbor, with its jetty and small, cube-like castle.

"Not quite Kyrenia harbor," Caitlyn thought. "But a passable substitute, if you can't get to Kyrenia."

They parked and immediately went to lunch, which they took at the harbor near the opening to the jetty and in a restaurant that featured a live pelican strutting around the tables. Caitlyn was amused but took on a mock air of concern until Vassos informed her, with a laugh, that pelican was not on the menu.

During lunch, Vassos explained that the jetty, current harbor, and castle were from the Turkish and British periods. "The original breakwater, which is now broken up and almost entirely under water, was south of the current jetty, and the Turkish castle was built on top of the ruins of a larger Byzantine castle that had stretched around to the end of the present-day jetty.

"At the height of its Greek existence," said Vassos, "The harbor was, in fact, further out to sea. This area has been struck by many earthquakes during ancient times—although none of recent centuries," he assured Caitlyn, who had unconsciously taken a firm grip on the edge of the table. "As a result, the original harbor area was completely submerged."

"Interestingly enough, Paphos also has the distinction of having become the first known Christian state, when its governor, the Roman proconsul Sergius Paulus, was converted in 49 AD by the Paul and Barnabas. Consequently, there are many ancient Christian basilicas here as well."

Following lunch, Vassos proceeded to support his claim of ancient Paphian wealth by showing Caitlyn the excavated houses of Dionysos and Theseus, which were located immediately inland from the old harbor and which had once been composed of hundreds of rooms each. These ruins contained the most beautiful and elaborate floor mosaics that Caitlyn had ever seen. As time was getting short, Vassos took Caitlyn on a drive within the same general area, past the only odeon—once a covered semicircular theater—yet to be found in Cyprus, to the remnants of the original fourth-century BC city walls, and past the agora—or Greek-period marketplace—and the Byzantine fort known as the "Forty Columns."

"The fort was called this not so much because forty columns now—or even once—rose from its ramparts," explained Vassos, "but because many salvaged ancient Greek and Roman columns had been

177

incorporated into the foundations of its walls and were found strewn about in the fort's ruins. I'm afraid it didn't have a very proud history."

The story of the columns immediately brought to Caitlyn's mind the columns embedded in the walls of Kyrenia Castle that Paul Conte had shown her the previous Saturday.

"Just a week ago today?" Caitlyn mused. "It seems like that day existed in another lifetime."

After a quick drive through this western section of the old city, Vassos quickly moved into the eastern part of the town—up to what had been the town's original eastern gate—because he wanted to be sure to show her the basilica he had referred to when they were in Curium.

"Here, this is another example of the continuum of Cypriot history. It was the first site to have made me think in these terms and to have raised in my mind what must also be the archaeologist's dilemma of putting relative value on history," said Vassos, as they approached a fenced-off excavation in the middle of a residential area.

"All right, Caitlyn, what do you see from here?"

"I see extensive excavations, with a very pretty little church sitting in the middle of the ruins," responded Caitlyn. "And I see columns in various stages of being raised back in place. I also see beautiful mosaics—and I see it all open to the elements," she added somewhat disapprovingly.

"Well, yes, I won't quibble about it being unfortunate the whole area hasn't been covered," Vassos agreed. "But, let me tell you what I've come to see here."

"From the top, I see the existing sixteenth-century church of Ayia Kyriaki, or what is presently known as St. Paul's of the Pillar, which currently houses services for the English-speaking community by both the Catholic and Anglican churches. Incorporated into that structure, I see the fourteenth-century Latin church of St. Francis. Below that structure and running in this direction, I see the excavations of a fourth-century Christian basilica, the church of Chrysopolitissa, which may turn out to have been the largest such basilica in Cyprus. Over here, in front of us, is the footprint of an even older, smaller basilica, probably the first church associated with that pillar right in front of you. That pillar has traditionally been identified as the one St. Paul was supposedly tied to for scourging—presumably before he converted the proconsul—and which is fittingly called St. Paul's pillar. And, the evidence of the last structure that we can see, but probably not the last one down there, is an older, undated temple, running in a southerly direction from under the corner of the current structure. That most likely was a pagan temple.

"Now, first of all, as I said at Curium, we Cypriots look at an excavation such as this and have an innate sense of the continuum of history—the continuum of *our* history and of *our* bloodlines. But, I also look at such sites as this and am struck by the dilemma of judging what has priority for examination and preservation—particularly for preservation. How far do we dig down through the layers of history, and how do we make the decisions concerning what to keep and what to destroy in the process? To us it is all important—perhaps not equally important to us on a individual basis, but certainly nearly impossible to prioritize on a national level. Every era is an integral part of our heritage."

"Yes, I do, of course, understand and agree with you," Caitlyn humbly responded. "I admit I have not been much bothered by this dilemma, although it is an acknowledged basic conundrum of the profession. I have never before experienced an area of such rich and deep cultural history. This all gives me much food for thought. I don't pretend to have a pat answer for you. But I do appreciate seeing your history through your eyes. Thank you, Vassos."

The two were very close at that moment. Vassos purposely held the moment, his arm around Caitlyn's shoulder. Both gazed into the excavation area, trying to separate the eras being unraveled before them. Then the moment was over and Vassos smiled and said: "One more area to show you in this short introduction to Paphos before we have to head back to Limassol and up into the Troodos."

They walked hand in hand back to the car. Near the center of the town and about half a mile up from the harbor area they came upon a raised, flattened hill, devoid of buildings. Vassos said that this was the city's acropolis area and thus hid below its current dusting of soil a wealth of historical structures, including an amphitheater. This structure was assumed to be in fairly good condition, as it was judged to have been buried far enough beneath the rubble of the fourth-century earthquake not to have been stripped of its stone over the years by new residents of the area. The most amazing thing that Vassos had to show Caitlyn in this acropolis area, however, was the series of hollowed-out caves around its perimeter that had, he said, been enlarged and used over the centuries as early Christian churches. Many of these had been located here to keep them secret from the non-Christian residents of the area.

Vassos took Caitlyn into one of the cave areas. They moved from one cavern to another. In an apparent moment of playfulness, Vassos drifted into the back of one particularly dark cave and disappeared into the far recesses of the cavern. Caitlyn turned nervously a couple of times and called for him. There was no answer. She went into several adjacent chambers, trying to find him, but she soon lost her bearings. The darkness and closeness and thinness of the air were starting to scare her. She was beginning to have the same clutching feeling of isolation and suffocation she had felt in the gatekeeper's chambers at Kyrenia Castle and later in her nightmares. In the dark, images were also beginning to drift into her consciousness, just as they had done in the darkness previously. But this was becoming all too real. The roof above was beginning to shake, dust was falling on and about her, and some larger clods of earth were thudding to the floor. Many large rocks were embedded in the cave roof, easily positioned to fall and crush anything below them if the earth moved sufficiently.

Swirling into her consciousness was the presence of another being. A sensation of rustling skirts. Eleanor? Lani? Or more ancient rumblings instead? The sensation of a comforting presence. Long, dark hair flowing to the tanned skins of a rustling robe, moving toward her, protectively enfolding her, and carrying her away. And before her eyes, the amulet swaying from the presence's neck. A human form, but also a cruciform form. There, in the midst of the confusion, attention focused on the amulet. Something very important about the amulet. she reached out for it, but the darkness was overwhelming. Choked with dust, she fell to the ground and began to lose consciousness.

Suddenly, Vassos was there by Caitlyn's side. As he lifted her and carried her in the direction that he had taken when he had disappeared, Caitlyn looked widely about her. This wasn't the cave she had been in when the earth had started to move. The entrance to the interior cave had been over there, but no entrance was there now, just a tumble of boulders. Just around the corner of the back wall of the cave in which Vassos had found Caitlyn there was another cave, its floor titling up. A pathway led from here into another chamber, which was open to the sky above. Having carried Caitlyn up this path, Vassos proceeded up a set of earthen stairs that took the pair above the caves and out onto the top of the acropolis.

"I'm sorry, Caitlyn," Vassos crooned, as he wiped at her face with his handkerchief. "I thought you were right behind me. I wanted to show you the secret way to the top of the acropolis. What happened back there? Why had you fallen and why was there so much dust in the air?"

"Didn't you feel it?" Caitlyn asked, her voice choked with dust. "There must have been an earthquake. I thought I was going to be buried alive."

"An earthquake? There hasn't been an earthquake around here in decades. You must have been affected by all that talk of the earthquake through the ages. I didn't feel any quake—and I certainly don't see any evidence around us that anyone else has felt one."

Caitlyn looked warily at Vassos but decided not to pursue the issue. She got up, dusted herself off, and walked around to force air back into her lungs. Her walk took her over to an area that must have been directly above the chamber in which she had been pelted with the earth. She certainly wasn't looking for it and was quite shocked when she saw it, but the dirt in the area had been violently disturbed. Someone had recently been stomping heavily on the ground, and several of the big boulders in the area had been moved out of position by a loose board that was still wedged under one of the rocks. She turned and looked intently at Vassos's shoes.

"Yes, they are quite dirty and scuffed up," Caitlyn thought. "But mine are also dusty from the walk through the caves, and, for the life of me, I can't remember whether his shoes were scruffy or clean before we entered the caves."

During this whole time, Vassos seemed to have been oblivious to Caitlyn's discovery and inspection and appeared to still be looking out over the city for signs of a quake. He turned and said: "Well, I'm sorry that our visit to Paphos has ended on such a frightening note. I think we need to get your bag and go back to the restaurant where we ate lunch. The owner is a friend of mine. I know he will let you use his small apartment at the restaurant to clean up. Then we must be off to Platres. Unless, of course," Vassos said meekly, "You have decided we must go straight back to Nicosia."

"No," Caitlyn said with perhaps a bit too much determination, "I very much want to go to Platres."

And, as the two descended the side of the acropolis and headed toward the car, Caitlyn set her chin and continued with her thoughts: "Yes, Mr. Petrou, I am now even more determined than ever to get to the bottom of this little mystery and to find out what is what and who is who in this little story of Nora and Vassos. And possibly of Jill Murray and the man in the black Mercedes, as well." This thought, which had entered her mind by surprise, caused Caitlyn to shudder again as she moved toward the car.

The hospitable reception by Vassos's restaurateur friend and the bath and change of clothes went far to restore Caitlyn's resilient good spirits. Her humor was very much back to normal as they drove the nearly hour that it took them to backtrack from Paphos to Limassol and then the forty-five minutes it took them to travel northward from Limassol up into the Troodos Mountains to the health resort of Platres. Vassos fed on Caitlyn's good humor and managed to orchestrate a continuous stream of charming and interesting conversation.

The shadows were being cast deeply into the folds in the hills when the Alfa Romeo chugged into Platres, which, being located at an elevation of four thousand feet above sea level, was not the highest mountain resort in the Troodos. But it was the most established mountain resort, with the plushest accommodations.

The landscape of the Troodos had intrigued and surprised Caitlyn. The hillsides were covered with pines, which, from a distance, looked like velvet. In the growing twilight, they took on a purple, mixed with blue, glow and had a smoky aura about them. The mountains weren't anything like the more arid and sharper Kyrenia Range that she had traversed the previous weekend. But, just as she had formerly likened the Kyrenia Mountains to the look of America's Rocky Mountains from a distance, the foothills of the Troodos now reminded her of the foothills of the Rockies as well.

After a week in Cyprus and having already gotten used to its stucco and red tile roofed buildings, Platres also came as quite a surprise. Having started life as a health resort and as a traditional summer hill station during the British colonial period, much of the architecture of the upper village reflected British Victorian architecture and had used red brick and wood, building materials that were largely absent in construction on the island's central plain and coastal areas. The town square area and the lower village tended to favor the typical Cypriot hill architecture, which reflected but did not emphasize the island's predominant Mediterranean styles.

Just as was the case with mountain slopes elsewhere in the British colonial empire, Platres had started life as a temporary retreat from the summer's heat of the rest of the island—and Caitlyn immediately noticed and appreciated the coolness and cleanness of the mountain air. And as elsewhere in the empire, it had grown to become the official summer seat of the government for several decades in the mid twentieth century as well as the year-round retreat for those who were rich and connected with the British. Thus, the houses at the top of the village were large and impressive. The largest and most impressive structure in Platres, and the one that hovered at the very top of the town, was the Forest Park Hotel. Typical of the grand old hotels of the world, the Forest Park had extensive, well-manicured grounds, elaborate and commodious public rooms, and an elegant ambiance that had to be earned by decades of excellence.

As promised, Vassos had booked two rooms. Although the hotel's public areas had retained the charm and comfortable "stuffiness" of the British colonial period, Caitlyn was delighted to note that her room, with its vistas over the village roof tops and down the mountain, had been updated to include every conceivable amenity.

After freshening up, Vassos and Caitlyn walked down into the village. The lights of the town were starting to come on, but, like any Cypriot village, the town was just beginning to come alive. The two spent some time wandering around the shops and the town square, but, since they were growing hungry, they soon moved farther down the hill to the open-air restaurant Vassos had selected for dinner.

It was a special night at the International Casino Restaurant. The local queen of artists, a refugee from Famagusta, who reigned over the naïve school of Cypriot village landscapes and who lived part of the year in Platres, was hosting a week's retreat of artists, who were closing out a working visit in the village with a gathering at the restaurant. Recently rendered landscapes of the Platres area were hanging everywhere. Everyone—Vassos and Caitlyn quickly included—was part of the festivities, and there were meze dishes and fine Cypriot wine in abundance as well as dancers and village music. Caitlyn had not felt so enthusiastic, free, involved, and happy in years. She moved with the flow, ate and drank her fill, conversed freely and deeply with the artists, thought nothing of her fears and worries, feasted on the beautiful art and the magnificent dancers and music, and grew ever closer to Vassos.

The two were fairly entwined when, hours later, they wove their way back to the hotel in the early hours of the morning. Vassos walked Caitlyn to her room and looked at her with open, questioning eyes. God's eyes. Vassos had never before been as desirable and as Greek and as god-like to Caitlyn as he was at this moment. Caitlyn could feel herself weakening. But she was not out of control, and she had not forgotten the many questions and fears she had concerning Vassos. She smiled, kissed a fingertip, which she then touched to the tip of his nose, and said: "Thank you for the lovely day and a wonderful evening, Vassos. I know what you are feeling, and I am feeling it to. But it's just too soon. Please understand."

With that, she opened her door and glided into her room. Vassos did not try to follow her. He stood there with his puppy dog look of longing intact, but his eyes were dancing with amusement. He could wait, and somehow he thought the wait would be worthwhile.

* * * *

Caitlyn felt like a queen as they breakfasted on the hotel's terrace the next morning. The food was divine; the service was excellent and unobtrusive; and the terrace atmosphere, with its wrought iron furniture, starched linen tablecloths and napkins, fancy china and silverware, and vivid tropical plantings, was just perfect.

Vassos was quiet but attentive; Caitlyn was glowing and responsive. She wanted Vassos to know that he had acted his part of the gentleman just right, that she was not a tease, and that they both were moving closer to a deeper, more meaningful relationship. Vassos did, in fact, seem to understand her thoughts without her having to say anything. As they finished their meal and prepared to drive, first a bit further up the mountain to the uppermost village of Troodos and then back down the other side of the mountain, past Kakopetria and the Kaliana dig, to Nicosia, Caitlyn could not feel any more happy and at peace with the world.

That is until she let her eyes rise for one last appreciate sweep of the exterior of the fine old hotel. There, on a third-floor balcony almost directly overhead, stood the man of the black Mercedes. He was openly looking at them, the stare as malevolent as ever. But Caitlyn could not tell if it was Vassos or she herself who was receiving this scrutiny. If Vassos, the parliamentarian seemed to be oblivious to the stare; If Caitlyn, the man of the Mercedes obviously didn't care if she knew she was being watched.

* * * *

It was early afternoon when Vassos rolled up to the door of the Gladstone Street mansion. Caitlyn had convinced him to stop at the Kaliana project site and to walk the hillside with her on the opposite side of the valley. She was even more sure after this visit that she had located a Neolithic settlement site.

As they were parting in front of the house, they were trying to establish how they could maintain contact, as neither could say at the moment when their schedules would permit free time.

"Suppose I try to call you at your parliament office sometime this week," said Caitlyn. "I have to move back and forth between the museum and the Kaliana dig, and," she put it as delicately as she could, "I don't think it would be too convenient for you to call me at home."

"No, I suppose it wouldn't," Vassos agreed, "but I will just have to try to get you at the museum. My secretary has gone to her mountain village for the summer, and I don't have anyone to answer my office phones when I'm not there. Actually, that's how I keep my parliamentary work at a minimum during the summer months."

As they performed a polite but restrained good-bye, Caitlyn instinctively glanced up at Nora Petrou's bedroom window. As Caitlyn suspected, Nora was there, in the same place and with the same expression she had had when they had left early the previous day. Caitlyn was almost unable to suppress a giggle.

"Why, I think Nora and the Mercedes man have taken the same course on menacing stares," she thought to herself.

But then the chill set in. "Just why would I think that was funny?"

Chapter Fifteen

The first thing Caitlyn did when she reached the Cyprus Museum on Monday morning was to contact Dr. Visiliou at the Kalinia dig and discuss with him her theory about the possible earlier settlement at the other side of the valley. He proved to be just as convinced by the validity of her reasoning as she had been and promised to obtain the necessary permissions to excavate at the new site. He said he would also bring in the electronic detection equipment as soon as possible.

Caitlyn then set to work carbon dating the artifacts that had been brought to the museum from Kaliana. No sooner had she started this, however, than she received a telephone call from Jacques Piccard.

"I was wondering if you might join me for dinner on a restaurant boat in Larnaca marina this evening," the ambassador queried. "Our sunset cruise off the Larnaca seafront is superb."

"That sounds interesting, but I'm not sure whether Nora has already planned dinner at home," Caitlyn responded smoothly. "If not, I would think she might enjoy an evening dinner cruise, as well. Also, even if I am able to make it, I'll have to meet you in Larnaca.

Your aunt has invited me to Limassol for the afternoon to tour the shipping company and to have lunch. She's lending me a car so I can get there and back to Nicosia this evening." Caitlyn had no intention of coming between Nora's plans for Piccard, and these arrangements would keep the drive from the capital to Larnaca from being an uncomfortable threesome.

"You're touring the shipping company today?" This news seemed to have put Piccard a bit off balance.

"Yes, do you see a problem in that?"

"No, no, of course not. The *Arsinoe* sails this evening and the docks will be quite busy. But, I suppose there is not much interest in seeing the operation when it isn't busy." And then the ambassador returned to the dinner plans. "Of course, if Nora is available, it would be marvelous for her to join us. I should have thought of that myself. Why don't you call her and then let me know what the two of you are able to do?"

Caitlyn rang Nora at the office, pleased that she had avoided another dinner with Jacques behind Nora's back. Caitlyn was determined to do all she could to remain in Nora's good graces. Nora had been extremely pleasant all day Sunday and at breakfast this morning. She had not mentioned Vassos once and had expressed only polite, passing interest in Caitlyn's trip to Paphos and Platres.

Caitlyn managed to get in touch with Nora and told her of Jacques's dinner invitation, stretching the point thin by indicating that he had invited them both from the outset.

"I'm sorry, my dear," Nora answered with a slight edge to her voice, "but I have a regular monthly dinner meeting of the travel agents' council to attend this evening. I'm surprised Jacques didn't remember that; I mentioned it to him only a couple of days ago. But that means I won't be home to keep you company at dinner either, so I suggest you go ahead and accept Jacques's invitation. The dinner cruise off Larnaca should not be missed."

Caitlyn started to demur, but Nora wouldn't hear of it and was almost making it a point of honor that Caitlyn should go. Caitlyn finally gave in, with the thought that whatever damage had been done was now already done and certainly was not her fault.

"Perhaps it would actually be doing Nora a favor to force her to realize that Piccard has a roving eye," Caitlyn thought, as she rather belligerently punched in the French ambassador's telephone number on her phone. Surprisingly, Piccard answered the phone himself and, ever the diplomat, voiced delight that Caitlyn could go to dinner. He clucked in proper disappointment that Nora Petrou would be unable to have dinner with them to Larnaca.

Somewhat irritated to have been cornered once again in the shuttlecock position in the tenuous relationship between Jacques Piccard and Nora Petrou, Caitlyn threw herself into her work for the next couple of hours. After a while, she began to feel the strain of the close and intense work and decided to take a break by roaming around in the museum upstairs for a while.

The museum was designed very well and had been perfectly set up for the casual visitor. It covered all of the many periods of civilization represented in Cyprus that spanned from the Neolithic Age to the Roman period. No one period was covered so extensively, however, that the casual tourist would be overwhelmed. Caitlyn had worked her way back to the Neolithic period, when she saw the wall painting that had been found at the Kalavasos-Tenta excavations near the Khirokitia site she had just visited. It was a schematic picture of a human male, his arms raised up as in homage to an undepicted god. The picture was simple, yet mesmerizing. It also seemed quite familiar to Caitlyn and evoked sensations of torch light, twilight, and hillsides overlooking the sea. Caitlyn let her mind wander as she was being drawn deeper and deeper into the painting. A pressure on her elbow, however, brought her out of her reverie and made her flinch.

"Excuse me, I am sorry if I surprise you, Caitlyn. I had call your name, but is apparent you did not hear me."

It was Viktor Gorodov, the deputy UN coordinator, all outfitted in a suave suit, every inch the accomplished diplomat.

"My goodness, Mr. Gorodov, It's a real surprise to see you here at the museum. I'm surprised you recognize me at all, let alone remember my name."

"Please call me Viktor," said the Russian, "and I am here especially to see you. I am afraid I might have seem a little, what you say, crass the other night at reception, and I want to make right."

"Oh, no harm was done," Caitlyn almost stuttered out her response. "I didn't find you crass at all. All of this diplomatic whirl is so new to me. I thought you were . . . interesting."

"You did?" Gorodov responded, his eyes suddenly showing an edge of calculation. "Well, as peace offering, and as sign I really am cultured person, I come to ask if you would go with me to Shakespeare play at Curium theater this Friday evening. Nearly everyone will there be. I would arrange, how you call it, picnic supper and everything."

"Why, of course, I would be delighted to go." Caitlyn had answered almost immediately, with little thought about whether she really wanted to go out with the Russian. She had been touched and amused by his almost Victorian manner and his struggle with English. Also, following Vassos's endorsement of the event—and Vassos hadn't invited her to go himself—she definitely did want to see the annual production at the ancient Curium amphitheater.

Gorodov thanked her profusely—almost embarrassingly profusely—made arrangements to pick her up at around 6:00 PM on Friday, and backed out of the museum like a schoolboy who had just successfully arranged his first date.

Caitlyn chuckled and returned to her work.

* * * *

"Where did you hear about the hidden stateroom?"

The innocent question Caitlyn had posed to Eleni Piccard as they stood at the window of the Limassol dockside office overlooking the loading of the Piccards' flagship cargo-passenger vessel, the *Arsinoe*, had obviously surprised Eleni.

"I don't really remember," Caitlyn responded truthfully. "It's just something I remember having been told about your flagship vessel. I remember being told you had a secret cabin on your flagship, and you just said that the *Arsinoe* out there was your flagship vessel."

"Well, yes that is true. What is now the owner's cabin on the *Arsinoe* is behind a concealed door. My husband's father had enjoyed his privacy and was known for his quirky sense of humor. There's nothing really nefarious about the cabin. I suppose you'd like to go over and see it." Eleni exhibited no indication of reluctance to show the cabin to Caitlyn.

"Certainly, if that's possible. It's such an interesting idea."

As they reached the top of the gangway, they heard barking, and turned to see several uniformed men, each with a dog on a leash, at the bottom of the plank.

"Who . . .?"

"Oh, that must be the drug dogs," Eleni responded matter-of-factly. "For some time drugs have been flowing into France from the Middle East by way of the Marseilles port. So, all of the national drug agencies in the region are being extra cautious with their inspections. The *Arsinoe* is bound for Marseilles, so it is routine that the Cypriot authorities will conduct a close inspection for drugs. I'm not worried, however. Drugs have never been found on any of our vessels. Come, I'll take you to the owner's stateroom, and then I'll come back here and monitor the inspection."

The concealed door for the cabin was both simple and effective. The *Arsinoe* carried passengers as well as cargo, so much of the space at deck level and of the next level down was outfitted with cabins. One of the mid-ship cabins below the deck level was outfitted as an office for the captain and was located next to a storage room. Both of these cabins were shallow, however, and a bookcase in the captain's office opened into a commodious hidden cabin.

While Caitlyn was waiting for Eleni and the drug dogs to show up at the owner's cabin, she walked the perimeter of the room, admiring the custom wood walls and shelving. It occurred to her that a secret cabin might additionally contain secret compartments, and she absentmindedly rapped her knuckles on the paneling as she circled the room. Sure enough, there was a hollow sound at one of the panels and, when she stooped and inspected the panel, she saw a release switch. The panel swung on a hidden hinge, and Caitlyn rocked back on her heels, surprised and shocked by the stench that was released from the compartment.

"Onions," she exclaimed. "Why would anyone hide ripening onions in a secret compartment in a hidden room?"

But then Caitlyn noticed that the compartment was much deeper than it was wide and that something was located behind the onions. Pinching her nose and looking more closely, she saw that it was some sort of wooden crate.

"Now where have I seen a wooden crate like that before?" she wondered.

"Nosy. Why are you being so nosy?" Caitlyn admonished herself, as she closed the panel and moved to sit very primly on one of the chairs at the other end of the room. Eleni had readily shown her this room, so there couldn't be anything here that Eleni wanted to hide. She'd just sit here quietly and wait for Eleni and the drug dogs to arrive.

But, when Eleni Piccard arrived, she wasn't accompanied by drug dogs.

"Oh, they are finished and have gone. There was no reason for them to visit this part of the ship," Eleni said dismissively, as she hurried Caitlyn back off the vessel.

"We've gotten an early harbor clearance, so the *Arsinoe* is going to sail early. And I know you need to get to Larnaca for dinner."

* * * *

The late afternoon sun was beating down on the Larnaca marina. Caitlyn had been bustled out of Limassol so fast she had arrived at the Larnaca seafront entirely too early to be meeting

196

Jacques Piccard for dinner yet, but she decided to walk down to the marina anyway to see where the restaurant boat was berthed and to watch the activity in the marina for a while. As she was approaching the gate to the marina, however, she was grabbed from behind and dragged into a clump of palms.

"Shh, Caitlyn. Don't struggle so, and don't do any screaming. It's me, Paul."

Caitlyn rounded on what seemed to be becoming her nemesis. "What in the . . .?"

"C'mon, hold it in Caitlyn. I'm working here, and I don't want you to get in the way—or get hurt. Hunch down and look over there."

As Caitlyn looked out over the marina in the direction Paul was pointing, she saw a man in Arab dress step off a fairly large yacht. As he reached the dock, he whipped off the Arab garb, under which he sported a natty suit. As he strode down the pier toward the gate, several other people, mostly women, bubbled out of the yacht onto the dock, repeated the transformation from fundamental Muslim to party time, and followed in the wake of their leader.

As they got closer to the marina's gate, Paul pulled Caitlyn deeper into the shadows of the palms. She started to stand after the group had climbed into several stretch Mercedes taxis and roared off, but Paul pulled her back down, with the whispered comment: "Stay down. The real show is just about to begin. Those were Lebanese Mediterranean crawlers. They party from one country to the next all over the region. They stop in some very interesting ports. My guess is they're off to the nightclubs of Ayia Napa and will be gone for a while. But just stay put." With that he lifted binoculars to his face and started scanning the marina.

"Ah, ha," he whispered at length. "Look over there."

Caitlyn saw a tall, bulky man in worker's coveralls toss a small dolly out onto the wooden dock from a sailboat about midpoint in the marina and hoist a wooden crate over the side. He looked familiar, but, by the time she had managed to talk Paul out of the binoculars by threatening to scream, the man on the pier had turned his back to her. Three crates had been hoisted out onto the dock by now. Caitlyn could see that two of the crates had pictures of fish on them and the other had some sort of logo and the word "Mumms" on the side. The only Mumms Caitlyn knew about was a brand of champagne. The man started to turn toward her as he lifted the first crate onto the dolly. But, just as he was turning his head around, Paul grabbed at the binoculars and Caitlyn fell from her crouching position onto her rear end with a muffled "umph."

The man looked around, but, seeing nothing, proceeded to saunter down the dock between the two boats with the first "fish" crate on the dolly. He was also scanning every horizon he could get into view without attracting attention. Paul and Caitlyn saw him haul the crate on board the yacht the Arab and his entourage had just vacated and then go below. When he returned to the deck, the crate on the dolly had been replaced by what appeared to be a big plastic bag full of rubbish. The man returned to the sailboat and threw the plastic bag onto the open deck. He subsequently made two more uneventful trips to the yacht with the dolly and the remaining crates over the next half hour, leaving several minutes between the trips. It appeared he wanted to ensure no one was taking notice of the transfers.

After returning to his own sailboat following the last trip, he popped a beer and sprawled on deck for some time. At length, he stood, stretched, and surreptitiously eyeballed the activity in the marina. He went over to the bag of rubbish, opened it, and pulled out several beer cans. These were stowed somewhere out of Paul's and Caitlyn's view and the plastic bag and the remainder of the rubbish was unceremoniously dumped over the side of the sailboat and into the water. After this, he appeared to have a sudden inspiration, cast off, and leisurely sailed out to sea.

Caitlyn stood, brushed herself off, and strode through the marina gate, with Paul groping at her and hissing from the fringe of the palms. As she reached the pier, the sailboat nearly turned over as the man lurched up on his knees. He struggled for control, scrunched down in the boat, and continued his sail out of the marina.

* * * *

Having been admonished by Paul not to mention what she had seen in the marina to anyone, including Ambassador Piccard, Caitlyn was waiting demurely on a bench near the gate of the marina when Jacques arrived just minutes later. It was twilight when the two boarded the *Thisbe*, a floating restaurant that was named after one of the local tragic goddesses. They would enjoy drinks on the upper deck, and the restaurant would leave the marina and float up and down the Larnaca seafront for three hours while dinner was being served. Thus far they were nearly the only guests on board. They stood at the rail, drank white wine, conversed, and watched a small sailboat clear the marina and tack off in a westerly direction toward Limassol.

Jacques appeared a bit nervous and his eyes made several intensive sweeps of inspection across the marina.

"What's the matter, Jacques?" asked Caitlyn when this behavior had gone on at length. "You appear to be tense and preoccupied this evening."

"I'm sorry, Caitlyn," the ambassador replied. "Occupational hazard, I guess. It's been a busy weekend, and we just got another terrorist alert in the cables right before I left Nicosia. I guess whenever I am reminded of how dangerous this job can be, my initial response is to scrutinize my surroundings."

"And what do you see here in the marina?"

"A beautiful young woman and what promises to be a magnificent sunset," Piccard answered, leaving no doubt that the discussion of his public life was being ended for now.

"I haven't seen you since our chance encounter at the handicraft workshop last week, and I've been counting the minutes until we could be alone again." Piccard moved closer to Caitlyn at the rail.

Caitlyn moved away a bit, saying, "But, about Nora and . . ."

Piccard overrode her attempt to voice a concern and stuck to the topic of the handicraft workshop. "You know, when I last saw you at the handicraft center, you were pulling pottery out of shipping containers and looking very curious. What did you see that concerned you?"

"I don't think I'd say I was concerned—or even that I can think why I left the impression I was curious—but I was wondering . . ."

"Yes, wondering?" Piccard asked, as he brought his arm around her shoulder and leaned the two more closely into the rail.

"Those pottery cruciform figures. Are they all made to one pattern?"

"Well, certainly everything in one lot is made to the same pattern, and those figures are a new item. So, yes, they were all more or less identical," Jacques responded quietly.

"But there seemed to be something dif—" Caitlyn didn't have a chance to finish her sentence. She had lost her balance at the rail and was floundering and very much in danger of going over the side and down three decks and into the water. The large yacht at the side of the floating restaurant was bobbing back and forth, dangerously close to the side of the restaurant. Its engines were producing quite a wake as its crew was preparing to move the vessel away from the dock.

Suddenly a yell of "Cait!" cut through the air from the far end of the dock, from whence Paul Conte was returning following his jaunt to the local police station.

Conte's yell seemed to have steadied Piccard's own footing, as he was now able to gather Caitlyn back from her precarious perch, without any more harm having been done than the spilling of white wine on the neighboring yacht.

Piccard started to yell back to Conte—most probably to ask what he was doing there—when his cellular telephone buzzed. He turned away from the rail, as Caitlyn sank into a deck chair and Conte leaped onto the gangplank one of the restaurant's waiters had been about to pull up in preparation for the vessel's move out to sea.

"Sorry, Caitlyn," the ambassador carefully intoned. "Something has come up at the embassy, and I must return to Nicosia. You did say you had transportation, did you not? Good. I am so sorry our dinner here did not work out. We must try it again sometime soon." And, as quickly as that, he was gone, his big black Citroen roaring out of the parking lot.

"More white wine?" Paul queried Caitlyn, the relief evident in his eyes.

"No, I think I've had enough—enough of everything—this evening," Caitlyn responded, as she gathered up her wrap and headed for the gangplank.

"Hey, you still haven't eaten, you know. How about a dinner under the stars at one of the cafés on the promenade?"

Caitlyn had to grant Paul the point, and she, in fact enjoyed the meal overlooking the Larnaca seafront immensely. It was quite late when Paul walked her back to the marina to retrieve her car. They were saying their good-nights when two seven-seat taxis pulled up into the parking lot, and Paul pulled her into the palm grove once more. This time she didn't need to told to be quiet; she had been through the drill once already this day.

At length, the revelers who had arrived on the Arab's yacht earlier in the day had managed to struggle out of the vehicles. They were discoursing at the top of their voices about the high prices of the taxis and of the Ayia Napa clubs.

The Arab, his all-girl crew, and his assorted guests floated into the marina and down the dock amoebae style and onto their yacht. All of the lights on the vessel flickered on, the disco-beat music commenced its deadly rhythm, the engine came to life, and the girls started to cast off.

Then, in apparent revenge, all hell broke loose from the surrounding dock area. The coastal patrol boats lit up, their whirling blue lights providing a 1920s-movie-style backdrop to the entire action, and their wailing sirens demanding the attention of everyone in the marina who had not already been disturbed by the return of the Arab and his jolly band. The commotion also caught the notice of all the late-night coffee sippers in the seafront cafes. Customs police poured out from everywhere and descended on the yacht.

There was no question of having had time to destroy any incriminating evidence even if the partiers had had the presence of mind to start working at it at the first sign of trouble. In no time, the police had pulled three crates out onto the docks and had opened them with an ax. What was lifted out of the crates could clearly be seen by both Paul and Caitlyn to be Kalashnikov assault rifles and hand grenades.

Suddenly, the Arab surged up from where he had been sprawled in a deck chair, gave a blood curdling scream, and collapsed on deck.

"Quickly, over here," rang out a voice that Caitlyn recognized as belonging to the police official Takis Koniotis. "He's foaming at the mouth. I think he's poisoned himself."

As Paul was being hailed to join Koniotis on the yacht and Caitlyn was turning to go to her car in the parking lot, not wanting to be directly involved in the drama at the marina, they both were jostled by a man dressed in black, whose most prominent feature was the apoplectic look on his face. He gave Paul and Caitlyn a malevolent look and faded into the darkness. But he had been there long enough for Caitlyn to have recognized the mysterious watcher who had been following her during both her Kyrenia and Paphos excursions.

* * * *

As she tiptoed up the front steps to the Gladstone mansion in the wee hours of the morning, Caitlyn could hear the raised voices through the thick walls. She let herself into the front door as quietly as she could and crept up the stairs, not wishing to become any part of this family fight. But she couldn't help overhearing enough to curl her ears.

Both Nora Petrou and Vassos Petrou were on the offensive, but Nora was getting in more than her share of offensive language. In the few brief moments it took Caitlyn to climb the stairs and make her way to her room, Nora had managed to accuse Vassos of trying to take over both the NDK party and its presidency and had insinuated that he might be implicated in the assassination of his father as a means to achieving these goals.

If Vassos had initially been calm and collected, he was now very close to being out of control himself. He was making impassioned statements of his love for his father and his shock and disgust that Nora would be making such charges concerning the assassination. Caitlyn had no idea why Vassos would even be here and attempting to talk with Nora alone and on her turf. It was quite true that the two were pleasant to each other in public, but that was explained by the fact that they were both national-level politicians trying to maintain and promote a family political dynasty. But, surely

Vassos knew that, although she did run hot and cold, Nora was unlikely ever to be civil to him in private and in her own home.

Until Caitlyn had shut her door and turned on her air conditioner to cushion herself from shocking family laundry airing she did *not* want to listen to or know about, she could clearly hear Nora shouting.

"Yes, that's precisely what I want to hear about. Just what *were* you doing looking into the books at the bank and the travel . . .?"

The door was shut, the air conditioner was humming, the radio was on, and the shower water had been started. Caitlyn was once more in her safe little world, far away from other people's troubles.

Or so she thought.

Chapter Sixteen

"Well, I wasn't *planning* to fall over the rail, you know." Caitlyn was somewhat testy because Paul's telephone call had awakened her entirely too early on Tuesday morning. Since he had been with her in Larnaca much earlier the same morning, he should have known she still would be asleep at this hour.

"I know you weren't intent on throwing yourself from the boat. That's why I had to get to you when your head had cleared from all the events of yesterday. You weren't paying a bit of attention to me when I tried to warn you last night. You must watch yourself with Piccard," Paul admonished. "In fact, I don't know why you keep seeing him."

"Well, I'm not exactly stalking him," Caitlyn retorted, with a nervous little laugh. "In fact, I'm pumping like mad to keep myself from getting placed between Nora and the ambassador. I do recognize he's a lecher, I can assure you—although I have no idea why who I choose to see should concern you."

"I agree Piccard is a dirty old man, but that's not exactly what I meant. Where have you been all weekend, by the way? I tried to get in touch with you earlier."

"Since you couldn't take me to Salamis, I went to Paphos with Vassos Petrou." For some reason Caitlyn didn't feel like telling Paul she had also gone to Platres with Petrou and had spent the night, no matter how innocent the trip had turned out to have been.

"Vassos Petrou!" Paul fairly exploded. "Vassos is downright dangerous to know and be near. You need to stay away from him."

Caitlyn was getting more than a little put out at the number of men Paul wanted her to stay away from.

"I know Vassos and his stepmother don't get along and that this is another of Nora's relationships I need to try not to get involved in. But we had a wonderful time, and he was a perfect gentleman. I also realize that a member of parliament and newspaper publisher lives with a certain amount of personal danger. But I see no reason to be worried about going out with him."

"Now, *that's* a big fat lie," Caitlyn immediately admonished herself, as visions of her trip ran through her memory. "The man's stepmother tries to melt him at twenty paces both going and returning. An unsavory character is following either Vassos or me around the country. Somebody—maybe even Vassos—tried to bury me alive in Paphos. And I'm just a hair's breath from jumping into his bed. Truth be known, it would probably be safer to handle a cobra than to go out on another date with Vassos. But, damned if I'm going to admit that to Paul."

Meanwhile, Paul was in the process of telling her why he had tried to call her during the weekend.

"There is an annual performance of a Shakespearean play at Curium this weekend, and I wondered if you would like to go with me," Paul asked hopefully.

"Oh, I'm sorry, Paul, Viktor Gorodov has already asked me and I've said I would go with him."

Now Paul *did* explode. "Viktor Gorodov!? Surely you wouldn't go out with that gorilla. Come on, Cait, you wouldn't be safe for ten minutes with that man. He's *really* bad news."

"Well, Paul, you've pretty much reduced the men I would be safe with to one," Caitlyn said sweetly. "Don't worry, I won't go to Ayia Napa with him. Bye now. Hope to see you around."

The telephone clicked on Paul's plaintive, "That wasn't the sort of safe I meant," a comment that was completely lost on Caitlyn.

"You are *not* my father," Caitlyn muttered nastily, after she had hung up on Paul. Her subsequent thoughts were less impulsive, however. "Still, I'm sorry I was so quick to accept Viktor's invitation. I do agree he's a handful, and Paul's invitation was just the most recent of several I've had to turn down, all of them preferable to going with Viktor." Piccard had asked her to the Curium play as they were boarding the dinner boat the previous night, and even Andriko Visiliou had asked her if she was interested in going with him and his wife.

"By Paul's standards and by all rights, Dr. Visiliou's invitation was surely the safest one," Caitlyn chuckled to herself. "Although I'm not sure what Eleni Piccard's reaction would be, since she seemed concerned that I had come to Cyprus to snatch away her prize archaeologist." This time she laughed out loud—which momentarily brought Nora, wearing an inquisitive face, to her doorway.

"Sorry, my dear, I was just passing and heard you laugh. It's good to see you so happy this morning. I missed you at breakfast. Shall I tell the cook to prepare something for you?"

"Good morning, Nora. No breakfast, thanks. I'm late. I'll pick up something at the café across from the museum on my way to work." With a cheery "Have a good day," Nora breezed on down the hall, leaving Caitlyn wondering just how long her hostess had been lurking outside her door.

Caitlyn received a phone call soon after she arrived at the museum. When she put the receiver down, her list of rejections had stretched even further. Upon arriving at his office and checking his calendar, Vassos had found he could manage to attend the play and had called Caitlyn to invite her to go with him. For some reason, the rejection she had to give him hurt Caitlyn more than any of the others.

Before getting started with her carbon dating work, Caitlyn called Dr. Visiliou at Kaliana. He excitedly reported that they had managed to get the electronic detectors out on the new hillside site the previous afternoon and had picked up traces of circular walls not far below the surface. It was looking more sure that Caitlyn's educated hunch had been right on target. They had gotten permission to open up another excavation and were getting more diggers out to the valley this morning.

Caitlyn was in a state of euphoria that lasted her for the rest of the day.

* * * *

In contrast, a stressed Takis Koniotis had stormed into his office at police headquarters at the start of the day and was just reaching for the telephone when Maria Solonos caught up with him.

"Something you might want to know before you get involved in anything else," she panted. She had chased him all the way from the front entrance.

"OK, shoot." Koniotis never second guessed Maria concerning what he might want to know.

"Two more identifications from Interpol on the murder weapon." Maria explained.

Koniotis, full of interest, gestured for her to continue.

"First case. Last year. That celebrated case of the close aide to PLO Chief Yasir 'Arafat. The aide, his wife, and a bodyguard gunned down at his home in Tunis. The guard was killed with the same gun that was used on Nicos Petrou and Jill Murray."

Koniotis whistled.

"Second case. Shortly thereafter. An Israeli intelligence agent of the Mossad hit with the same gun in London. He was working on tracing the travel movements of international terrorists."

"Interpol have any favorite perpetrators?" Koniotis asked.

"Nothing specific, but everyone—simply everyone—in the business says it was the Abu Haddad Palestinian faction. Part of the ongoing internecine warfare in the first case; to protect its travel enablers in the second case."

"Enter the possibility of a Palestinian connection," whispered Koniotis. "Thank you, Maria. Please switch to trying to trace the background and connections of last night's dead Arab yachtsman. Paul Conte, who very conveniently just happened to be on the scene, indicated that the crates of Kalashnikovs seemed to have been traded for something—something that was kept in used soda cans. My bet is that it was drugs. And I'm betting that both the American embassy and the British high commission know more about what is going on than they have revealed."

When he was alone, Koniotis took out two more note cards, scrawled the words "Palestinian/Abu Haddad" on both of them, flipped one card onto the growing Assassination stack, and, after contemplating it for a few minutes, carefully added the other card to the Drugs pile.

He stood up, stretched, moved to the window to admire the view of the homicide unit across the dreary air shaft, returned to his desk, and raised Maria on the telephone once again. "Also, please try to get us an early appointment with the minister. We need his permission to formally seek the full cooperation of the American embassy in the person of one Paul Conte."

He returned to his note cards. "What was it about what Maria had just said that had struck a chord? Ah, yes. Protection of travel enablers. Now, where have I seen that thread before?" And he started leafing through his piles of note cards once more.

* * * *

Although Caitlyn was nearly asleep late that night, after having worn out several flocks of sheep in an effort to stem her excited anticipation of a discovery of a Neolithic site across the valley from the Kaliana excavations, the roaring bang and flash of light at the front window to her room rocked her awake. She rushed down the hall just as Nora was emerging from her own bedroom. Nora didn't appear to be nearly as confused or frightened as Caitlyn felt, but, then, that's because she seemed to have a good explanation for the loud noise.

"Tut, tut," she murmured, as the two women bustled down to the kitchen, "The Turks on the other side have a lot of religious festivities. And, of course, they never warn us when they are planning on letting off fireworks near the Green Line. It amuses them to disturb our sleep."

Caitlyn had commented that she had had considerable trouble getting to sleep before the loud noise had jangled her nerves and now had no idea when or whether she would be able to sleep. Nora had suggested that they brew some tea and chat until Caitlyn grew drowsy.

The tea had been a good idea, and Caitlyn had just about reached a state of weariness that might permit her to sleep when her nerves were snapped once more by the jangling of the telephone.

"Now who could *that* be so late at night?" sighed Nora. "I'm not sure I have a single person between the political party, the bank, and the travel agency who can take care of problems themselves."

But it was obvious from the expression on Nora's face when she responded to the telephone caller that this was no minor office problem.

"Yes, yes, she's here. Yes, of course she's safe. Why wouldn't she be?"

Agonizing minutes while Nora was receiving an explanation, increasing concern etched on her face.

"Oh, how terrible. Yes, we heard it. But what does that have to do with . . ."

"I see. No, I didn't know about that. Yes, of course we'll ensure we're locked up, and we'd be quite pleased to have your men come over to keep an eye on the house."

212

After she had slowly replaced the telephone to its cradle, Nora turned to Caitlyn. Caitlyn had trouble reading the meaning on Nora's face; she seemed to be mulling what she was going to say and was struggling to maintain control over some other emotion. Fear? Anger? Caitlyn couldn't tell.

"What is it, Nora? What's happened?"

"You didn't tell me you were involved in a police seizure at the Larnaca marina last evening when you went to dinner with Jacques."

"I haven't really seen you since then. Besides, I was told not to talk about it with anyone."

"I'm not just anyone." Nora's barely controlled ire lashed out like a whip.

"I don't understand, Nora. What has happened? Who called?"

"That was Takis Koniotis of the police. He wanted to be assured that you were all right—because of last night."

Caitlyn was thoroughly confused. "Nora, *what* is going on? What does what I saw at the marina have to do with whether I'm safe."

"Takis was just making sure. That loud noise we just heard. That was a large explosion at Paul Conte's house. The police are afraid there is a connection with what happened at the marina and that what happened to that American diplomat might happen to you as well."

Chapter Seventeen

It had not been a good week for Caitlyn. She had planned to work the entire week at the Cyprus Museum and to have her research there reasonably caught up before succumbing to the call of the Kaliana excavations. There now were two separate digs in operation as a result of her realized theory of a second ancient site in the area. However, the firebombing of Paul Conte's house Tuesday night had completely unnerved her.

The bombing had caused all of the ominous happenings of the last couple of weeks, all of the frightening events that she was still trying to process in her mind, to rush forth and demand her attention. More important, it brought home the reality to her for the first time that there were events happening around her, events that were well beyond her understanding, that were personally threatening in ways she also could not understand. In addition, she had not realized until he had almost been killed how deeply Paul had crept into her life. She had thought he was someone she was trying to avoid and drop by the wayside, but she had come to realize that he meant a great deal to her. Otherwise, she would not have reacted as strongly as she had to his brush with violent death.

Paul had not helped her jumbled nerves one bit. When he had finally called her to tell her he was all right—several hours after she had heard about the bombing—all she could think about was the terror she had felt during the time of Kurt's kidnapping by the German terrorists. She had found it impossible to separate her feelings at the time concerning the perceived loss of Kurt from an almost identical feeling of the perceived loss of Paul. In her emotional response to the situation, it was as if Paul were gone, even though, intellectually, she knew that he was talking to her on the telephone.

"Paul, just let me process this. I've been getting entirely too much practice dealing with loss. Why was it so hard to find out you were OK?"

"I wasn't home at the time. And there really wasn't enough left of the house's bedrooms for anyone to have been able to tell that for hours."

"But . . ."

"No buts. The police are throwing questions at me, and I only was able to beg a few minutes for this telephone call. I had to call you, because I had to dissuade you from going on your date Friday night."

"Listen Paul," Caitlyn snapped. She was unable to connect the two different wavelengths they were on and just ended up being abrasive again. "Here I am almost destroyed over grief for something that hasn't happened, and you're still obsessed with who I go out with."

"No, that's not it at all," Paul pleaded. Then it became obvious that he was being pushed to ring off. "No, I'm not finished yet," Paul was saying. "Hell. Oh, all right. Cait—Caity, I've gotta go now. They're interrogating me down here as if I had bombed my own house."

"Good-bye, Paul." Caitlyn delivered the statement with finality, as she was the first to break the connection. And at this moment she intended this as a final good-bye. She couldn't take getting attached again only to be overwhelmed by loss—again.

* * * *

Eleni Piccard had called Caitlyn at the museum on Wednesday morning to see how she was getting along and had immediately sensed Caitlyn's frustration.

"I feel so badly about how I reacted to Paul on the telephone when he had been nice enough to make the police let him call me himself to tell me he had not been hurt," Caitlyn had said. "I just can't concentrate on my work now, and there's so much to do. Always before, If nothing else, I've had my work. It frightens me that I can't concentrate."

"It sounds to me as if you need a break in the pattern," Eleni had counseled. "I suggest you get back out on the Kaliana hillside tomorrow morning and lose yourself in the dig for a while. The carbon dating can always wait, and I'm sure you've already processed a representative sample of the various levels that have been excavated."

"Perhaps you are right," Caitlyn had answered. "I certainly couldn't be doing any less good at the excavation than I am doing here at the museum just now."

"Good girl," Eleni had responded. "Go out and find me some new designs for my handicrafts. In fact, I'll be going up to

216

Kakopetria again tonight. Perhaps, if you haven't been there yet, I can come back to Kaliana and take you on up to the village for lunch."

And so, here it was Thursday, and here Caitlyn stood in the middle of the original Kaliana dig in the coolness of the early morning. She gazed longingly over at the other hillside. However, although the archaeologists had, through soundings, found a promising location for buried, circular, human-made structures and were digging directly for these structures, the care required for archaeological excavation forced them to work at what now appeared to Caitlyn to be a glacial pace. She knew she couldn't trust herself to go over to that area just yet for fear she would become an impatient nuisance in what was, in fact, a very well-organized and properly paced operation.

She knew she had to be content with helping with the original dig, which, she had to admit, was probably about to achieve another—and possibly the last, if her theory about the pattern settlement of the valley had been correct—new level of discovery. And, indeed, this was exactly what was happening right before her eyes as she stood and dreamed of having found a Neolithic site.

Just at that moment, the team working around her broke through the Early Bronze Age level and found the remnants of a round house.

"Could I have been wrong?" thought Caitlyn. "Could this be evidence that there had been a Neolithic site here?"

But, after several hours of careful clearing away in this area, it appeared that they had found evidence of the properly sequenced Chalcolithic period, rather than the older Neolithic period. The first round houses cleared away did not contain burial chambers beneath them as they should have if they were dated to the Neolithic Age, and, indeed, another team working downhill and to the north of the current area Caitlyn's group was focusing on had found what appeared to be a cemetery. If Caitlyn was able to carbon date these two areas as being of the same age, then the archaeologists were now at the level of the Chalcolithic period.

At nearly noon, the group that had been working what might have been the cemetery area called Caitlyn's group over. They had found artifacts among what might have been grave goods in a burial vault. One of the first things Caitlyn saw was a soapstone talisman in a cruciform shape that had been clearly identified with the Chalcolithic period at other excavations around the island. The talisman, an obvious symbol of female fertility, was in the form of a human figure, with short arms perpendicular to the body, legs pressed together, and a long neck rising to an oblong head. Around the neck of the idol, carved in the soapstone as if suspended from a necklace, was the image of an infant.

Upon seeing the artifact, Caitlyn's mind flashed back to the very similar pottery figurine she had seen being crated in the Ledra Handicraft Center. She began to ruminate on what it was about those pottery figurines that had disturbed her at the time.

And that's where Eleni found Caitlyn when she came to fetch her for the afternoon's trip up the mountain. Caitlyn was standing, holding the soapstone idol, turning it over and over in her hand. She seemed lost in another world and was mumbling almost incoherently. "Pottery idol. Something different. Heavier."

"Caitlyn!" Eleni was trying to break the spell, the command in her voice unmistakable.

Caitlyn snapped back to the current world. Eleni was looking at her with somewhat of a perturbed, almost angry expression on her face.

"Here," Eleni said, guiding Caitlyn toward the car. "You are in even worse shape than I thought from our telephone conversation yesterday. You must just forget about everything that concerns you now. For this afternoon, you need just to relax and concentrate totally on new sights and experiences."

She bustled Caitlyn into the Jaguar—chattering away all the time and not permitting Caitlyn to speak at all—whipped the car into gear, and roared up the hill for the five-minute drive to Kakopetria.

* * * *

The mountain resorts of the Solea Valley, first Galata and then Kakopetria, strung along the Klarios River—really not much more than a stream—up into the Troodos toward Mt. Olympus, whose crowning radar dome could easily be discerned at the top of the mountain. The new road rose ever higher on the eastern hillside; the old road ran through the towns and beside the river. Just before turning off the mountain road and down into Kakopetria, Eleni Piccard pulled the Jaguar over to the shoulder and the two women got out to take in the panorama of the village stretching below them.

"Where is your hotel?" queried Caitlyn. "Can we see it from here?"

"But of course," answered Eleni proudly. "In fact it dominates the village. Look down into the center of the village."

Eleni was right; the Old Mill Restaurant and Inn was a huge stone warehouse of a building, rising some five or six floors and built into the slope of the western side of the valley. The slopes enveloping

219

the village were set at a very steep incline, and the top floor but one of the inn was directly accessible from the mountainside. The building rose up out of a grove of trees near the town square. This line of trees, Caitlyn was to discover, marked the path of the river through the village. The floors of the base of the structure were constructed entirely of large, rounded brown type of stone, and the facades of two of the floors were broken by wooden balconies, with wood and glass French doors. The upper two floors featured deep, wrap-around verandahs that were suspended out over the stone walls below. All of the wood trim was in a reddish brown color.

"It's beautiful and overpowering all at once," Caitlyn gasped. "Did you build that structure especially as a hotel?"

"Oh, no," Eleni smiled. "It is explained by its name. It was constructed in the early nineteenth century as the storage section for the flour mill that had been on that site since at least the seventeenth century. Its location gives you some indication of the importance of this mill to the region in those days. It eventually fell into disuse and just hovered there, brooding over the village for nearly a hundred years, waiting for the day that Guy and I took it over and began to rebuild it as part of the effort to make this a summer tourist retreat." Eleni's eyes had misted over as the name of her long-lost husband had been introduced into the conversation.

"The restaurant came first." Gathering breath, she steamed on. "The restaurant takes up the entire level of the bottom verandah of those two floors at the top of the building. In the summer the premium tables are those out on the balcony. From there the vista out over the village is gorgeous, especially at night. In the winter the favorite tables are the ones inside, beside the fireplace. The restaurant is reached by a winding stone staircase on the southern end of the building or by a very small and slow elevator. The Old Mill Restaurant has become quite popular with the residents of Nicosia, who like to come up here in the summer to escape the heat and to enjoy our specialty, mountain trout grilled in a butter sauce."

"Well, there's no question what *I'll* order for lunch," laughed Caitlyn. "I love trout."

"I've added the hotel rooms since I lost Guy, although it has all been constructed and decorated to plans he had already laid out. The two floors below the restaurant constitute the inn. There are six large suites per floor. Everything you could possibly need for a luxury hotel. Happily, I have a regular and appreciative clientele, and nearly all of the rooms are booked a year in advance. Below the hotel levels are the storage rooms, which are still pretty much in their rough state. I don't want to add more accommodations, but perhaps someday I'll fulfill Guy's dream for that space."

"And what was that?" Caitlyn asked gently.

"Kakopetria was once uniquely famous in Cyprus for its saddle making and silk extraction and weaving industries. Guy wanted to revive those as folk arts in the old mill building. That's really where my interest in handicraft industries started, you know."

"And what is the floor at the top used for?" Caitlyn asked.

"That's my home. That's my family's real home," Eleni responded. "Everything that I could not part with from the period of Guy and Pierre's presence is housed there. That's my retreat from the world whenever I'm not sure I can go on another day without my husband and son. This project has been my salvation. That's probably why I come up here so often."

The two quietly got back into the car and drove down through the narrow streets of the village, through the town square with its earthen floored and tree-canopied central coffee and gossip gathering point. After clearing the square, they turned left onto a dirt and stone road running alongside the river, which cascaded over the rocks a good ten feet below the level of the road. At the end of this road, they entered a stone-bedded parking area at the foot of the old mill.

While driving through the town, Eleni had provided a further note: "Kakopetria is also responsible for my interest in archaeology. Although Andriko Visiliou's research crew is finding the remains of very early civilizations at the bottom of the valley, as a girl I was engaged in finding the remains of historical sites in this area, further up the valley, that dated, in one case, from Roman times and, in another, from the sixth or seventh century BC. In both cases, this area was apparently used for some sort of religious rites."

"As a young girl?" Caitlyn asked with surprise. "You were here as a young girl?"

"Certainly. I thought I had told you. This is my home village, and this is my family's mill. It has been connected with my family as long as the mill has been there. For all I know, I am a direct descendent of those whose settlements you are now discovering down in Kaliana. That's why your project has been so special to me."

A shudder went through Caitlyn's body. That was exactly what she herself had been thinking upon learning that Eleni was a native of this area. That explained why Eleni had been so insistent that the human remains Caitlyn had discovered not be disturbed. Suddenly it clicked, even though it made no natural sense. Caitlyn's visions of the last couple of weeks. Eleni's presence had been associated with all of the visions Caitlyn had experienced since arriving in Cyprus. Somehow Eleni, who Caitlyn had only met once before these particular visions had started, had made such a strong impression on Caitlyn that her visage was intruding into Caitlyn's spells. But Caitlyn herself, in her visions, had felt a close relationship with all of the Eleni-like presences in her recent spells—much closer connections than Caitlyn enjoyed in such a short time with Eleni in real life. But was that true? Caitlyn acknowledged that she had felt very close to Eleni upon first sight, and she sensed that Eleni had felt the same. The questions Vassos had challenged her with at Curium concerning one's ancestors and connections with the afterlife were starting to form. But these thoughts evaporated with the click of the car door. Eleni had gotten out of the Jaguar, and Caitlyn snapped out of the spell and followed her purely by habit.

"Stop. Listen. What do you hear?"

Caitlyn closed her eyes and concentrated on her surroundings. "Well, the dominant sound I hear is the running water."

"Yes," Eleni said. "That's it. This is the only stream of any size in Cyprus that has running water year round. Cypriots will come from all over the island just to be able to hear the sound of running water. Just over there, by that stone bridge, you will find that two streams have converged. If you walk up into the upper village, you will find that the villagers have diverted parts of various streams running into this river to cascade down drains at the edge of their houses. The sound of running water means everything to them. Let's take a quick walk through the upper village before we have lunch."

From the parking area in front of the mill, they crossed the stream on the stone bridge, which was covered by shady tress and overlooked, on one side, the mill's old water wheel and, on the other, a small mill pond with geese. After crossing the stream, they turned up the old town's "high street" to the right and traversed what is probably the most photographed example of a mountain village street in the country. All of the buildings were quaint in a way that planned communities can't possibly achieve. Some had been restored; some were unobtrusively in the process of being restored; and some were beyond any hope of restoration and were being left as interesting ruins rather than being replaced with new construction.

"It is hard to believe," said Eleni, "But this was once the highway to Mt. Olympus."

Caitlyn laughed. She could almost stretch out and simultaneously touch the buildings on both sides of the narrow, stone path.

"Come look at this house over here," Eleni called from several paces up the hill. The small house she was pointing to was quite charming and was very well maintained. It was made completely of stone, and the woodwork was in a highly polished dark wood, which was carved in a diamond pattern that Eleni had said was authentic Cypriot folk-art style. A solid door and one window, its shutters tightly closed, took up most of the ground floor. There was a balcony and another door and window on the upper floor.

"This is the Petrous' village house," Eleni announced.

Caitlyn registered surprise. "I didn't realize they had a home in Kakopetria," she exclaimed.

"Well, it was really Nicos Petrou's house," Eleni explained. "Nora rarely comes up here anymore. This was a favorite retreat of Nicos. You see, just like me, Nicos was born and raised in Kakopetria."

Caitlyn showed her astonishment.

"Yes," Eleni continued, her eyes clouding up a bit, "Nicos and I grew up together. At one time we were quite close. But then our lives went in separate directions. You know, we were very much on opposite ends of the political spectrum during his later years. Well, enough of that," she said, as she moved on. "I want you to see the other, more modern street, on the other side of the river before we return to the restaurant."

After the tour of the resort village, Eleni and Caitlyn rode up to the restaurant level in the tiny elevator that was supposedly licensed to carry four but was very much filled with just the two women. After having ordered their meal, with both selecting the trout, Eleni led Caitlyn up a winding staircase in the corner of the restaurant to see her large apartment above while they waited for the meal to appear.

Although Caitlyn could see Eleni was very much in her element in the apartment, which floated high above Kakopetria and boasted breathtaking views, she could tell that Eleni's personality didn't dominate here. Everything had been arranged just as if time had stood still and was waiting for the Piccard father and son to arrive from their long-ago flight from Bellapais. Sheet music was in readiness at the piano, the keyboard cover was up, and the stool was pulled slightly back. Eleni had already told Caitlyn that it was Guy, rather than she, who played the piano. Architectural drawings of the Old Mill Inn were strewn out on a desk along with fabric and wood samples. Three glasses were arranged on a tray on the coffee table— all in readiness for a family refreshment break. A wooden model airplane and a soccer ball were carelessly placed in the middle of the lounge floor. It was all very sad—and a bit eerie. And Eleni looked very fragile and vulnerable in this setting.

While lunching in the restaurant, Eleni seemed pensive for a while and, finally, as if having come to a difficult decision, asked Caitlyn: "The other day, when we were at the handicraft center, you seemed to be rather disturbed about something when looking at the pottery that was being prepared for export to Marseilles. What did you see that bothered you?"

Eleni was looking so seriously and intently at Caitlyn that Caitlyn was immediately put on her guard. But, she still could not have fully explained, if asked, why she was so evasive in her answer. She also could not explain why the image that came to mind when Eleni asked the question was not the shipping room at the handicraft center, but the concealed compartment in the secret room aboard the *Arsinoe*.

"Nothing. It was nothing, really. I just had seen similar figurines in a museum in New York and was comparing the two examples in my mind."

She could not look Eleni directly in the eye. And Eleni was studying her so closely that this reaction did not escape her notice and obviously did not please her.

Perhaps changing the topic, Eleni said: "I hope you are not being taken in by my nephew Jacques, my child. He is to be avoided—and I don't mean because Nora Petrou is smitten with him, although she is another one who should not be challenged too openly.

I mean because he is a very dangerous man to know; in his own way, a very evil man. A man who . . ."

But she cut off the indictment at this point. Her face had been strained and all of the color had drained out of it. She covered her agitated state by calling the manager over and complimenting him on the service and food and giving him instructions to close up the apartment above.

"I don't think I can face those memories again this afternoon," she said in a decisive voice and with a slight shudder.

"Come, my dear, we shall use the stairs. I think I need some exercise after that delicious meal, and I also cannot face that close elevator again." This last comment was delivered with a flourish and a large portion of bravado, and she headed for the back of the verandah without waiting to receive Caitlyn's opinion on whether she wanted to huff down five flights of stairs.

Caitlyn was a little off balance, because she had been irritated by Eleni's unexpected "Jacques is a dangerous man" comment, and she was musing to herself about how this was beginning to be everyone's theme song to her concerning nearly every man she had met thus far in Cyprus.

But Caitlyn should have stopped to consider her options, especially as they pertained to maintaining her balance. At the third-floor landing—she was in front and Eleni was very close behind—Caitlyn slipped and pitched out into the void.

Chapter Eighteen

She may not have made the most graceful entrance into the Curium amphitheater on the following night. She also might not have arrived with the date of her dreams, and she might have had to lean more heavily on Viktor's arm than she wanted. But Caitlyn was determined to see the annual Curium Shakespearean production. Once she had been painfully guided to her seat, she was pleased that she had come.

The steps down the staircase on the side of the Old Mill Inn on the previous day had been much more slippery than either she or Eleni had anticipated. Eleni had noted with much consternation that it had been she who had slipped and who had jarred Caitlyn off balance. Caitlyn had subsequently plummeted a good four steps before her fall had been arrested at the next landing. As a result, she had a slightly twisted ankle and a couple of bruises. These, thankfully, were hidden from general observation. She had primarily been upset that the accident had precluded her return to the Kaliana dig for the remainder of the afternoon.

Caitlyn and Viktor had very good seats—if hard, centuries-old stone could be considered good—at the top of the amphitheater and in the center section. Vassos had been right. Everyone—at least nearly everyone she had met in her three short weeks in Cyprus—was in attendance by the time the play started.

Ambassador Piccard and Nora Petrou had seats of honor in the center section, several rows below Viktor and Caitlyn. They were sitting together, although Caitlyn knew they had arrived separately, as the ambassador had had an official function to attend in Paphos earlier in the day. Looking off to the right, Caitlyn could see that Vassos Petrou had indeed come to the play. She was somewhat amused to see that his "date" appeared to be Alec Stuart of the British high commission. Vassos kept looking up at where she and Viktor were sitting, and his gazes had a distinct air of disapproval about them.

Eleni Piccard had arrived with Dr. Visiliou and his wife, who was very heavily and quite apparently very happily pregnant. Caitlyn couldn't help but think once again that Paul probably would only have been happy with her own choice of date for this occasion if she had come with the Visilious and if Mrs. Visiliou had sat in the middle. Little did he know that Caitlyn and Andriko had once been "an item" at the university.

Eleni stopped by to console Caitlyn concerning her twisted ankle and to once again apologize for the accident. Although Eleni was being sweet to her, Caitlyn couldn't avoid seeing an icy stare pass between Eleni and Viktor.

"Now, What's *that* all about?" Caitlyn wondered. "There are more hostile attitudes in the audience here than a Greek tragedy could muster down there on the stage. All we need now is the visage of Paul

Conte glowering over everyone. Well," she caught herself short. "Speaking of Paul . . ."

And there he was, just as she had just been imagining to herself, pacing around the aisle at the top of the theater. By the way his glance kept coming back to Viktor and her, Caitlyn had no doubt he had not become reconciled to her appearance at the play with the Russian. Then she noticed that the police official, Takis Koniotis, was there at the top of the theater as well. And, although she could see that he was spending a good deal of time watching either Viktor or her, she discerned that he was spreading his observations in other directions as well.

"The intensity of his sweep of the crowd is quite similar to his scrutiny of essentially the same people at the Eleon when Jill Murray was heading for the wings with Alec Stuart," Caitlyn mused. "It must be professional habit. Or maybe he just can't remember where his seat is."

She did her best to ignore the attention she and Viktor were getting from both Paul and Koniotis—and Jacques Piccard, now that she considered it, having caught his eye for the dozenth time. The scrutiny she was receiving from Jacques seemed difficult for him to manage, as he had to turn all the way around and look straight up to see the couple. He also had to be careful that Nora didn't catch him in the act. This time when he looked up, it was difficult for Caitlyn not to laugh. She didn't laugh, however, because his stare indicated that he wasn't amused. But, then, she wasn't sure he was reflecting anger at her reaction to his attentions, because it didn't quite seem now that he had been looking directly at her at all.

Caitlyn instinctively turned to see who else might have caught Jacques's attention, when she quite unexpectedly made eye contact with an apparition that made her heart leap to her throat. She blinked and looked again, but if it had been Kurt, he was gone now. She rose as if to follow him. She needed to be sure. Not because she loved him anymore, but, having recovered from the shock of his telephone call, she now needed to be sure he was, indeed, alive. And if he was alive, she thought she was due an explanation on why he had just disappeared and abandoned the life he previously had—and the people who had loved him.

"Mind the cheese," Viktor roared. And, as Caitlyn stood there, alternating between confusion and amusement, Viktor continued to produce food from the knapsack he had brought. Resigned to the fate of a lavish meal, Caitlyn sank back down on the stone steps.

Caitlyn and Viktor had barely finished their meal and settled under the blanket Viktor had brought to ward off the sea breezes, when the lights had begun to dim. The play that had been selected for this year's Shakespearean production had turned out to be delightfully appropriate for Cyprus. It was *Othello*, various aspects of which were reputed to have been associated with the island. The "Moor of Venice" was thought to have been modeled after an actual historical character, a dark-skinned Venetian, who had come to Cyprus with his wife to serve as a governor but who had inexplicably returned to Venice without her. Even Othello's castle had long been identified with the harbor fortress in the port of Famagusta, which was now popularly referred to as Othello's Tower.

The play was very well acted and fully convincing, and Caitlyn was in a total state of absorption as the last scene was coming to an end and as Viktor abruptly whispered in her ear, "Let us leave now. We can get out before there is crowd."

Caitlyn was a little piqued, as Victor nearly manhandled her toward the parking area. But she couldn't quite get a word in edgewise to indicate she thought they should be able to take a more leisurely pace, especially in view of her injured ankle. She became even more irked when they had reached the car, because Viktor said he had forgotten the blanket and left her all alone in the darkness. At length—after the departing crowd had already begun to surge into the parking area—Viktor returned to the car, embarrassed because he had not forgotten the blanket after all.

As they quickly drove toward the exit road, still a bit ahead of the crowds loading up their automobiles for the trip home, Viktor was emphasizing his dislike of traffic and of waiting in long lines of cars. He was talking so fast—and with such fractured English—that Caitlyn didn't quite catch up with the statement he had slipped in that he "just thought" they might drive up to the basilica ruins complex to enjoy the view from the cliff while the departing cars were thinning out. But she certainly did try to object when, upon clearing the parking area, he actually turned up to the right toward the darkened basilica ruins rather than down to the left to the exit gate.

"That is all right," he said. "There is back gate up this way."

When they got up to the basilica and discovered that, although there was indeed a back gate in this area, it had big boulders in front of it and obviously hadn't been used in years, Caitlyn wasn't fully convinced by his "Oh damn! I know road was open the last time was here."

"Oh, well," Viktor concluded, "As long as here, we might as well look at view."

Caitlyn tried to remain as calm as possible. In doing what she could to keep Viktor from just maneuvering her around at will, she found she was getting out of the car on her own. She hobbled delicately across the mosaic floor of the fourth-century basilica ruins to the edge of the cliff, which dropped off fairly closely to the back of the basilica complex. She did have to admit that the vista from the heights out toward the sea was beautiful. The cliff they were standing on dropped almost straight down for about forty feet and then immediately leveled out to a very flat, rocky margin of a couple of hundred feet that stretched to the sea. A wide beach, composed more of dirt than of sand, gently ran down to the sea. Back from the beach perched several shack-like restaurants strung along a coastal road— more of a dirt track. The full moon lit up the area almost as if it were day. Several cars were driving the beach road, all of the restaurants were going full bore, and people, even at this late hour, were running in and out of the surf. Immediately to the east of the Curium cliff, the seaside flattened out to a good mile from the coast before the hills began to rise toward the central Troodos peaks. The lights of Limassol could clearly be seen in that direction. To the west, the cliffs that started at Curium undulated off in a curve that reached toward Paphos. Several ships, sporting multicolored party lights, were running just off the coast, and the sky was clear and packed with bright stars.

Caitlyn had to admit that this was quite a sight. She didn't have long to enjoy it, however. Viktor, who had been standing much too closely behind her for comfort, picked just that minute, when her defenses were down and she was beginning to appreciate the view, to wrap his arms around her and bury his face in the crook of her neck. As she struggled, he seemed to pick her up and to sway back and forth precariously close to the edge of the cliff. Having been caught almost completely off guard, she was initially preoccupied with the thought that this was a very strange, rough, and clumsy sort of a sexual pass. She was incongruously on the verge of breaking out in giggles at the vision of multiple Russian couples—all in this same strange sandwich-like pose—waddling around a small park in aimless, never-intersecting patterns. In other words, she was getting pretty hysterical.

Emitting animalistic sounds, he was ripping at her blouse sleeves now, still with his arms wrapped around her and still swaying toward the cliff edge in his silly dance. His dance of passion or his dance of death? Or both?

However, Caitlyn hadn't been raised to be a victim. She got an arm free enough to be able to punch back an elbow up under Viktor's rib cage with enough force to cause him to drop one of his arms. She simultaneously brought the heel of her good foot down hard onto the top of his foot and twisted toward the side where he had dropped his hold. Despite the bad ankle—and helped by Viktor having lost his balance and fallen off to the side—Caitlyn darted behind a column that had once helped define the altar area of his pagan temple that had been displaced by the later Christian basilica. Not having any idea how long she had before Viktor recovered his balance and started in pursuit, Caitlyn slid off toward a complex of stone foundations ranging from four to six feet in height that were located to the west of the main basilica area.

She was breathing heavily and was moving about so wildly that she couldn't be completely sure whether or not she had just heard an eerie cry from the direction of the cliff side. All she could think of was that she needed to move back through the basilica toward the area where the car was parked but that she couldn't actually go to the car itself. Viktor would, of course, go to the car to cut off her escape and may already have started in that direction. She could not assume that he would not get there before she did. Also, she didn't have the key to the car. Viktor had the key to the car. In fact, Viktor seemed to be holding most of the keys to the situation at the moment. "Gorilla," Paul had called him. Gorilla was right! No, she had to move toward the parking area, but she had to reach some high place. Some high place where she could see out over the basilica but could not be seen from inside the ruins. Some place . . .

But, suddenly there was no place to go; no place to hide. Suddenly he was rising in front of her. Suddenly he was wrapping his arms around her again. Strong arms. And he was pulling her toward the wall and deeper into his clutches. She was weakening and she was screaming, but she couldn't seem to even hear herself screaming. She was blackening out, still beating at his chest with her fists.

* * * *

"Cait. Cait. It's all right. You're all right. It's all right. It's Paul."

The words were beginning to get through to her. She was stopping her struggle. But the adrenaline that had fueled her

235

resistance was also ebbing away, to be replaced with soft, nearly hysterical sobs and loud gasps for air.

Paul was guiding her toward the parking area. She was shuffling along, supported by his arm, as quickly as she could. But now her ankle was hurting like blazes, the recent focusing on her animal instincts for survival having been gradually replaced with Paul's assurances of protection. She could see two cars ahead. She struggled a bit in apprehension as they approached Viktor's car but relaxed as they moved beyond it to the other vehicle. Takis Koniotis was standing by the open door to the car. She didn't have the presence of mind to even wonder what Koniotis was doing there. He just added to her relief and to her strengthening feeling that everything was getting better.

Paul gently helped Caitlyn into the back seat of the car. She could hear the two engaging a concerned conversation in subdued tones, but she was still in enough shock that what they were saying didn't completely register at first. Gradually her world began to straighten out.

Koniotis was saying. "I've been through the basilica with a flashlight, and I can't find him. He must be hiding. But, with the fencing, he has no place to run to but here."

"I guess we both have to go back in there and search," Paul was saying, as he looked down at Caitlyn, the concern and strain quite evident on his face.

Caitlyn certainly understood *this* statement clearly. She grabbed Paul's sleeve and moaned, "No, you can't leave me alone here."

Then the possibilities hit her squarely in the face, and she began to sob "He's dead. He went off the cliff. I pushed him off the cliff. I've killed Viktor."

"There, there," Paul said soothingly, stroking her hair. "You haven't killed anyone. It's not your fault. Hush, hush. Everything will be all right."

The two men stood there for a few minutes, alternately staring into the ruins and comforting Caitlyn. As she was pulling herself together, Caitlyn remembered the strange cry she had heard, and she falteringly passed that observation on to Koniotis and Paul. Koniotis became even more serious and contemplative.

"Where were you when you heard this cry? How far away from the cliff side were you?"

As she was getting calmer, the sequence of events was getting clearer. "I can't tell for sure, but I was already well into the side chamber area next to the basilica, well away from the cliff."

"If you were that far along, even if Viktor has gone off the cliff," Koniotis responded, "it could not have been as a result of your struggle. You were too far away to have been associated in any way with that cry. We heard the cry as well as we were entering the basilica, so we know it wasn't your imagination. We left the theater in time to see Viktor pull up in this direction. At the end of the play, he had come up to Paul and told him that you and he had gotten separated in the crowd. He claimed to be worried about where you had gone. He said you and he had had a little spat and he was afraid you'd decided to get a ride back to Nicosia with someone else or, worse, that you might have tried to walk out of the ruins by yourself."

"But that's crazy," Caitlyn interjected. "There was no spat. When I got to his car, he said he'd left the blanket and had to go back for it."

Paul looked hard at Koniotis and remarked in a whisper. "I told you I didn't believe what he had said."

"Obviously for good reason," Koniotis answered. And then to Caitlyn: "It looked very suspicious when we saw Viktor driving off without having spent longer looking for you in the crowd at the theater. So we followed him up here. By the time we got to my car, though, a lot of other cars were on the move too, so Viktor had a big head start. We didn't see that you were in the car as well. Don't worry. Whatever has happened, we know it wasn't your fault."

Koniotis's calm, professional approach was doing wonders for Caitlyn's nerves. Very soon thereafter Koniotis squatted beside the door and said, in a very reassuring voice: "Now, Ms. Spencer, I'm sorry, but Paul and I do have to check the basilica again, and we must try to track Viktor Gorodov down. I am going to lock all of the doors to this car, and I am going to have the only key. We will not be far away. You will be safe in the car, and, if anything happens to scare you, all you need do is sound the horn and we will come back immediately. Now, can you do that for us?"

Caitlyn nodded. "Yes, I understand. I've got to know where Viktor is as well and that he isn't hurt badly."

The two men moved off and silence prevailed—but only for about ten minutes. Caitlyn heard the roar of a car's engine at the back corner of the graveled parking area, behind some bushes. A large, dark car pulled out of the darkness and bore down on Caitlyn, its lights off. Caitlyn instinctively dove for the floor, losing any chance of reaching the car's horn. But there was no impact and the other car raced past, stones splattering and its lights flashing on after it passed Caitlyn. It sped back down toward the theater and the exit gate and was quickly gone in a cloud of dust and gravel. Caitlyn reached over the seat and pushed hard on the horn with both fists.

Paul and Koniotis returned on the run, as promised. Caitlyn told them about the car, and Koniotis cursed himself for not having checked the fringe of the parking area earlier. He also told her, the worry evident in his voice, that the signs of her struggle with Viktor were quite evident on the edge of the cliff and that there were scuffle marks leading right up to the brink.

Without further comment, the two men got in the car, and Koniotis drove rapidly and expertly out of the basilica parking area, through the Curium exit gates, and back to the main Limassol-Paphos road. He made a right turn onto this road. He then took his first right turn at what was identified on the road sign as the Curium Beach road and sped off toward the sea. In short order, they were on the beach road below the Curium cliff. Koniotis veered off the marked track just below where the basilica was located on the heights above and drove—a bit more carefully now that he was on rockier terrain—toward the cliff wall.

Near the cliff base, the car's headlights picked up a bulky form. Koniotis slammed on the brakes. He left the lights on, as both men jumped out of the car. They spent several minutes hovering over the object at the foot of the cliff. They returned to the car at a slower pace, both with grim and pensive looks on their faces. Koniotis reached into the front seat for his mobile telephone and started to make his call.

"Is it Viktor?" Caitlyn asked Paul with a halting voice.

"Yes, Viktor is there," Paul answered flatly.

"And is he dead?" Caitlyn asked in a hushed tone.

"Yes, he's dead." was the reply.

"Then . . . Then, I *have* killed him," Caitlyn moaned.

"Not unless your fingerprints are on the knife that's sticking out of his side, and I suspect those fingerprints belong to someone else."

"What do you mean?" Caitlyn asked dully.

Koniotis returned to the car. "I'm sorry to do this, Ms. Spencer, but neither Paul nor I recognize him. We need to know if you do."

"Don't recognize him?" Caitlyn asked in confused disbelief, although she was permitting herself to be drawn from the car and toward the base of the cliff, "You both know what Viktor looks like."

"Not Viktor Gorodov," Koniotis explained as they arrived at Viktor's body. "Not Viktor, but the guy lying over there," and the flashlight's beam revealed a second body near that of Gorodov's.

"Oh, no, not again," Caitlyn moaned, as she knelt by the body and lifted the head on her lap. As she stroked his blond hair away from his face and Paul and Koniotis stood by incredulously, she muttered, "What have you done, Kurt? How many times do you have to die?"

Chapter Nineteen

Caitlyn was on the verge of going into shock over her dual grisly discovery. Viktor Gorodov had not simply fallen off the Curium cliff but had been stabbed and his killer was probably Kurt, who was now most certainly dead as well. Takis Koniotis could readily see the signs of shock in her vacant stare, her pallor, and the way she was clinging to Paul Conte. Immediately after the first police unit arrived on the scene, Koniotis briefly directed the officers in setting up the crime scene and then drove over to a nearby beach-side restaurant. When he returned, he produced a carafe of hot coffee and mugs, which he forced on both Caitlyn and Paul.

When Caitlyn appeared to be more aware of and interactive with her surroundings and when the color had begun to return to her cheeks, Koniotis took Conte aside.

"I don't know who this other man is or why Ms. Spencer knows him, but all of this can be cleared up tomorrow," Koniotis said. "Until this situation is clearer, I believe we need to keep her and her possible involvement separated from this. We don't even know the extent of her relationship with Viktor, but she could be in danger simply on the basis that she was at the scene and was in the parking area when that other vehicle left. It's also quite clear that Ms. Spencer is in no condition to be driven all the way back to Nicosia and simply dropped on Nora Petrou's front doorstep."

"Yes, I quite agree with that," Paul quickly assented.

"While I was at the restaurant," Koniotis continued, "I phoned in a reservation for two rooms at the Bunch of Grapes Inn in Pissouri. If Ms. Spencer is in danger—if there is someone who considers her a threat and is looking for her—Pissouri will be one of the last places they are likely to look. Do you think you could take her there for the night and give her a chance to regain her bearings before she returns to Nicosia? You can take Gorodov's car. We need to get it away from the scene anyway, and he certainly won't be needing it anymore."

Paul readily consented.

"Oh, and one last thing, Paul. We both know what Gorodov was. But we don't know what Gorodov's interest in Ms. Spencer was. Was he just clumsily trying to satisfy his sex drive or did he have other interests in the woman, interests that might have intersected with our own interest in Gorodov's activities? And then there's the unidentified man. Please try to find out if Ms. Spencer is or has a piece to either of these puzzles. At this point—especially since she was somehow involved with both of these men—her innocence in these deaths is largely only supported by her own statements and her demeanor. We still know as little as we ever did concerning Gorodov's criminal associates. It could be this man she called Kurt is one of them. As much as we both would like to do so, we cannot rule out the possibility that Ms. Spencer is also one of these associates and is merely a superb actress as well."

"Of course, I very much want an opportunity to pin these issues down as well," agreed Paul. However, in his own mind he had already totted Caitlyn up as an innocent. At the same time, he could not disagree that she unwittingly held one or more of the pieces of the puzzle of Gorodov's racket. In fact, he was more convinced than Koniotis was that she did so. He also didn't want to get into a conversation with Koniotis just now about the other man. Paul distinctly remembered who Kurt was. Caitlyn had told him about her kidnapped boyfriend. And, now that he had seen Kurt in the flesh, he knew what the man had been doing on the Curium cliff. From what Caitlyn had told Paul about Kurt's kidnapping and the authorities' suspicions about that at the time, it was quite possible that Kurt had long been involved with international terrorists, which made for a very interesting linkup with Gorodov. This may be one of the real keys to Jill Murray's assignment, and the embassy would fully expect him to try to beat Koniotis to the punch on unlocking that particular door.

As the police officers brought Gorodov's car down from the basilica, Paul returned to Caitlyn's side to explain the plans for the night and to obtain her assent.

* * * *

Caitlyn was even more numbed by events than it had appeared to Koniotis and Paul. She readily consented to the overnight on the southern coast. Everything was happening in such a rush and it gave her some comfort to know that she wasn't just going to be thrust back into her Nicosia life until she could gain complete control over her emotions. Under those circumstances, she wasn't sure she could bear the burden of relating and reliving the events of the last hour to

Nora Petrou and to any and all of her other acquaintances and colleagues who awaited her in the city.

And the knowledge that there were Kurt's parents—and her own—to notify of Kurt's death had rushed in on her while Paul and the police official were conversing. "Oh, no," she had agonized. "How can I explain to them what Kurt was doing here and how he had died, when I can't even explain it to myself?"

The coffee helped give her strength. The strong, concerned presence of both Paul and Koniotis—and especially of Paul for whom she was gaining a deeper appreciation—also helped. Not that she hid in their strength, but, rather, that their strength helped bring out her own.

Strangely enough, the shock of Viktor's attack and having seen his and Kurt's shattered bodies at the base of the cliff, although initially horrifying, were also helping her. She could now come to grips and closure with the kidnapping and disappearance of Kurt. There would be no more wondering about that. And the possibility that Kurt had died for her—saving her from Viktor's clutches— allowed her to see him in a better light. By the time Viktor's car had arrived and, although she still appeared fragile to both Paul and Koniotis, she had, in fact, become stronger than she had been over the past four years since the disappearance of Kurt.

As she and Paul made the twenty-minute drive to the hillside village of Pissouri along the coast to the west, Caitlyn became increasingly alert and alive to her inner emotions and to the aimless, dulling drift her life had been taking despite her highly successful and complex career as an archaeologist. She also began to look on her relationship with Paul over the past two weeks with new insight. She had been devastated when she thought he had been killed in the bombing. She now remembered that that had made her begin to acknowledge to herself that she had deeper feelings for him than she had previously thought.

"What made me forget those new feelings?" Caitlyn thought to herself. "Ah, yes. Paul called just then and irritated me about going out with Viktor. But, then, Paul did prove to have been right about Viktor. And Paul *had* thought enough of me to call himself to let me know he had not been killed. Hmmm."

When they arrived at the small, quaint Bunch of Grapes Inn, perched high on Pissouri's hill and overlooking the island's primary grape-plantation valley, it was not out of either shock or vulnerability, therefore, that she asked that Paul not leave her alone. She requested instead that he sit with her on the balcony and drink in the vista of the moonlit valley below. It *was* the result of the perception of and consideration of Caitlyn's fragile condition that Paul had consented to remain with her until she had gotten settled into her surroundings. But he had no intention of further discussing either Gorodov or Kurt—or their possible activities—with Caitlyn this evening. That could wait until the morning when she had regained her bearings.

Little did Paul know, however, that Caitlyn had already more than fully regained her balance and that she had already formulated some long-term decisions about the quality and direction of her personal life and had made one significant short-term decision on setting off in this new direction. He did start to understand the situation, however, when, as they left the balcony, Caitlyn drew him toward the bed rather than toward the door. And he increasingly understood the circumstances, as her steady, controlled reasonings and pronouncements of conviction melding into endearments and expressions of need began to erase his fears of her momentary vulnerability.

Later, as sleep crept up on Caitlyn and she molded her body more comfortably to the side of the already-sleeping Paul, she thought to herself: "Life has begun again. No matter how this relationship with Paul works out, I am now fully alive again. I do not regret my time with Kurt, but that relationship was fundamentally flawed. He could not have loved me deeply and then left me to worry about him and mourn for him. The time to let loose of mourning has come and gone. It's time to live now."

* * * *

His telephone call early the next morning woke Eleni Piccard in her Makedonitissa home from a long night of deep, yet restless sleep. She had only reached a state of peace and blissful calm for what seemed like seconds before the ringing of the telephone had jarred her awake. The images of her loved ones had kept rising out of the darkness, their eyes wide with fear, their lungs fighting for breath, their mouths open in perpetual but unheard screams.

"Soon, my loves, soon," she kept murmuring to herself in her sleep. "Revenge. Soon."

And intruding on this nightmare that often clutched at her was the image of Eleni, herself, being pursued by some unknown terror through a maze of crumbling rock. But at least this nightmare had suddenly turned into a pleasurable tranquillity that had, at last, permitted her to sleep. She thought she had some idea what this new dream meant, but the intruder had not allowed her time to think about that.

246

"We must talk," he whispered almost breathlessly into the telephone.

"We were going to stay away from each other," Eleni answered, instantly awake and on guard. "You yourself said they were getting too close for comfort."

"Yes, Yes, I know," Vassos Petrou answered. "But everything has changed. Did you know that the mercenary is dead?"

There was a long silence on Eleni's end of the line before she spoke.

"And the girl? What of the girl? They were together last night at Curium."

"She's apparently all right, but I don't know for sure. No one answers at Nora's house, and none of the reporters who are working the case had heard about Caitlyn Spencer's whereabouts. They scoured the hotels in Limassol, but without luck."

"It's still too dangerous to meet here in Nicosia," Eleni reasoned. "I'll go on up to the inn at Kakopetria. See if you can find out what is going on, how much he knows, and what sort of danger we are in. Come up to Kakopetria Monday night, and we will rework our plans. I must know what he is going to do now. And find the Spencer girl if you can and find out where she fits in all this—and what she knows about the drugs and arms movements, if anything."

Both rang off, and Eleni Piccard started closing up the house for her drive up to Kakopetria, the expression on her face grim, calculating, and determined.

* * * *

Even though he had been up half the night sorting out the Viktor Gorodov killing and putting into motion an identification of

247

the other man found at the bottom of the Curium cliff, Takis Koniotis was back in his Nicosia office early on Saturday morning. It was much too early for leads on the unidentified man—unless Conte was quick at getting information from Caitlyn Spencer. But all hell had broken loose over Gorodov's death, as was to be expected, considering his sensitive international position as the deputy coordinator of the UN peacekeeping effort on the island. The reaction and questions were bad enough now that they were still billing the death as a probable accidental fall off the Curium cliff. Takis knew he would never get any peace or have time to pursue the case once the press and diplomatic corps heard that the Russian had been fatally stabbed before he went over the cliff.

"Paul Conte and the American embassy had been right," Koniotis thought bitterly. "Until we were able to find out who, if anyone, was behind Gorodov's gun running activities, it would only have seriously impeded our investigations to arrest Gorodov in the act. And now we only have a few days—maybe only a few hours— that we can keep the nature of Gorodov's death and of his illegal activities under wraps. Only a few days to solve this case."

With a hopeless look on his face, Koniotis returned to the five piles of note cards on his desk.

"Illegal Arms. Money Laundering. Drugs. Assassination. And the biggest pile: Unassigned. I'm no further along with this case than I was a month ago. Only now my sole physical lead has been silenced. I don't even know if I have one case or more here. Well, I've been treating it as one case with four or more facets for too long. I need to start looking at this from different angles."

He wrote out another note card reflecting the words "Viktor Gorodov/murdered. ?Caitlyn Spencer" and placed it on the Illegal Arms pile. He then picked this deck up and began reviewing the cards. After a while, he put the pile down and rubbed his eyes.

"I've got to think this through. We know that Viktor Gorodov has been delivering small shipments of hand arms, which have borne markings of Russian or East European origin, to vessels at various places on the southern coast. Paul Conte alerted us to two of these shipments in the past two weeks. The people we picked up in these two raids were Arabs, and they all were associated with Lebanon, only a short distance across the Mediterranean. We can also surmise that Gorodov has been picking these arms up in the Turkish zone and transporting them across the buffer zone in his own UN-licensed vehicles. No one would have dared to stop and search a vehicle being driven by the deputy UN coordinator."

Koniotis picked up one of the note cards and looked at it.

"This also accounts for the suspicious diversion into that area of the Bulgarian vessel two weeks ago. Paul Conte says he saw a vessel that was flying a flag other than the Turkish or Turkish Cypriot flags at the new Kyrenia harbor the same Saturday the Bulgarian vessel was in the Kyrenia area. He also says he saw Gorodov speeding from the Kyrenia area toward the south in a small UN-licensed van on the same afternoon. We had always thought that the arms that were being rumored to be shipped through Cyprus were coming into Famagusta port and were being shipped under Turkey's direction. It seems Gorodov and crew outfoxed us on this one—although they must have an understanding with Turkey as evidenced by the

Bulgarian vessel's cryptic radio message about calling on help from the Turkish port.

"The arms movement part is now quite clear, although it's still unclear whether this is part of a larger operation or if Gorodov has been operating alone. No, my guess is that Gorodov was not operating alone. Gorodov did not simply fall off the Curium cliff. He was knifed. I see no reason to believe that he was killed because he was assaulting Caitlyn Spencer. My hunch is that his own people killed him because they knew or sensed that we were on to him. They obviously knew we were closing in on them because we had intercepted two of their shipments this week. Their clients could not be happy, and they would have to stop up their leak of information fast. That's why they tried to have Conte killed. He was observing the arms deliveries. But it certainly must have occurred to Gorodov's partners or superiors that he had been hopelessly compromised and that it was only a matter of time before he would lead us back to them.

"And what was he doing on the cliff with Caitlyn Spencer, and where does she fit into all of this? *If* she fits into this." Koniotis broke off his thoughts and rubbed his eyes again. These late nights and frustrating days were taking their toll.

Changing tack, Koniotis resumed his thoughts. "But, what did Gorodov get in exchange for the arms?" In recalling the small briefcase reported from the Zygi exchange and the soda cans from the Larnaca marina raid, the answer was obvious. "Drugs. Drugs from Lebanon." And then to himself: "The arms were destined for Lebanon, where there are endless numbers of independent radical groups that would be ideal recipients for AK-47s, and they were exchanging drugs from the Al-Biqa' Valley."

Koniotis proceeded to sweep the Illegal Arms and Drugs piles together. He was tidying up the new deck with the intention of going through the now-combined stack one more time, when Maria Solonos fairly flew into the room.

"Look at *this*!" Maria commanded, slapping a piece of paper down on Koniotis's desk.

"And what is *this*?" Koniotis responded with a laugh.

"*This* is the Interpol report on those fingerprints you sent in."

Koniotis leafed through the fax pages.

"My, my. Look at who's been playing with guns," he whistled. "This adds a whole new dimension and just might be the missing link we've been looking for to Gorodov's partner or partners."

"*And*, look at this last paragraph," Maria trumpeted.

"Under the wheels of a subway car," Koniotis read back phrases. "Listed as a suspicious death. Not more than a week ago. Left a large amount of money, recently deposited in the bank."

Koniotis returned to his piles of note cards, tapped the combined Illegal Arms and Drugs piles more uniformly into one deck and reached for the phone.

No answer at the house. The response from her office: "I'm sorry sir, she has gone to her home in Kakopetria for a few days. Would you care to leave a message?"

But Takis already had hung up and was asking Maria to contact the interior minister. "It's time for more clout," he said, as he started flipping note cards out of his new, enlarged deck.

251

As Maria was leaving the office, Koniotis called her back. "Also, I need another hunch checked out, please."

He furiously wrote several names on one of his note cards and handed it to Maria. "Please try to find out where and when these people were living during their adult lives—and what jobs they had."

Maria smiled. "Of course," she answered. "I see where this might be leading."

Chapter Twenty

At the same time Takis Koniotis was narrowing his investigation, Paul Conte was following an entirely different line of reasoning in his discussion with Caitlyn. He had started off at a disadvantage, as he had commenced the day still wondering whether Caitlyn had just been in shock the previous night and was even now preparing to have him hauled into court as a mad rapist.

When he had awakened, Caitlyn was already up and on the balcony. He had slept right through the ordering and delivery of an elaborate room service breakfast, which Caitlyn had positioned where she could indulge both in the food and in the view down into the Pissouri Valley.

After Caitlyn had managed to assure Paul that she had not resented or regretted the previous night, he began to question her about Kurt Schwin's unexpected reappearance. He also sought to learn about her relationship with Gorodov and her understanding of the nature of his assault on her at Curium. Caitlyn was having nothing to do with such a one-sided grilling, however, and refused to discuss the issue at all until their discussion became a mutual exchange of information.

"Why," she asked, "were you so adamant about me not going to Curium with Viktor? What did you know that you wouldn't tell me? And what do you know now that you aren't telling me?"

"These are sensitive diplomatic matters," Paul responded uncomfortably. "My God, Gorodov was an international official."

"But to me he was just a gorilla," Caitlyn retorted. "You called him that yourself. I have been violated by that man. I sense that I am somehow involved in something that is outside my realm of understanding and that is a personal danger to me. I am a big girl. I can take care of myself if I can just get the measure of the playing field. And I can take care of you, too, Mr. Paul Conte, if necessary."

"Yes, I dare say you can," Paul said with a grin, despite his discomfort. "OK. Equal information. Where do we start?"

"We start with who *you* are, Paul. You aren't just a normal embassy political affairs officer, are you?"

"No," Paul admitted. "And here I find I must trust you fully—because I have little real evidence you are just a normal private archaeologist either."

"And what is *that* supposed to mean?"

"This old boyfriend of yours, Kurt Schwin. He's just conveniently turned up from the presumed dead on Cyprus to save you from an assault by one of his chums?"

"I have no idea why Kurt was here. I admit I thought I saw him a couple of times in crowds, and he called me one night. But I was too upset to talk with him. You know as much as I do about why he was here, how he turned up at Curium, and what his part in all of this is. Wait a minute. Maybe you know more than I do. Why did you say he was a chum of Viktor's?"

"Because I've seen him before last night—probably twice. He was in Zygi one night last week with Viktor and a woman. They were loading crates of assault rifles—probably some of the same ones Viktor was smuggling in from the Turkish side the day he passed us on the Kyrenia pass after he and someone who looked very much like Kurt unloaded them from a Bulgarian freighter. Some would say that some of the associates you've acquired in the brief time you've been in Cyprus are a bit too much of a coincidence."

Caitlyn threw a small breakfast roll across the balcony at Paul. "Nonsense. I am not and I have never been anything other than a normal private archaeologist. You of all people should know that. You're on the Fulbright Commission Board that pulled up my application for this project and that accepted it. You're just trying to distract me. Reveal!"

"Fair enough," answered Paul. There was nothing to be gained by continuing to bait Caitlyn on her associations. It was obvious that he was on her side. "No, I'm not just a political officer, but I don't have any super secret mission either. I'm a U.S. Treasury agent, and it's normal for officers in my job category to be assigned to embassies as political officers. In my case, however, I've been specializing in trying to track down rumors that Cyprus is being used as a drugs or arms shipment conduit—or maybe both. Both of these issues are well within the legitimate concerns of the Treasury Department."

"And where does—excuse me—did Viktor fit into this assignment?"

"He was the muscle for an arms shipment racket," Paul said and went on to detail what he and Takis Koniotis had managed to piece together on the Russian's activities.

"What put you on to Viktor in the first place?" Caitlyn asked.

"Strangely enough, it can be traced back nearly a year to something Eleni Piccard said at a diplomatic party," Paul replied. "She seemed to be a bit in her cups that evening. I think it was the anniversary of the disappearance of her husband and son or something. But she sidled up to me and we found ourselves talking about arms and drugs smuggling. She asked if I realized how easy it would be for a diplomat to take advantage of his ability to move back and forth from the Greek to the Turkish zones in such a smuggling scheme. She asked in such an intense way that she almost seemed purposefully trying to convey a message. I put it up to drunk fantasizing at the time, but, when I saw Viktor passing us in the UN van the other day, it all sort of clicked into place. Interesting that Eleni would have thought of that though."

"Yes, unless, of course, she knew all too well how such an operation could be set up," said Caitlyn with contemplation. The vision of the hidden crate in the secret stateroom on the *Arsinoe* was running through her mind.

"And why do you describe Viktor only as the muscle?" Caitlyn went on to ask. "He was no dummy. He was a senior UN official. Why do I get the feeling that you aren't celebrating the closing of this case with Viktor's death?"

"Partly because of the manner of Viktor's death," Paul replied. "The 'good guys' didn't put that knife in his side."

"But, if it turns out Kurt's fingerprints are on the knife, it could be . . ." Caitlyn could not finish the thought aloud.

"Yes, of course it could be that Kurt killed Viktor to save you and was, himself, pulled off the cliff in the struggle. But, what of the other car that was up there? And there have been rumors floating around of a more complex hand in all of this than Viktor's. For all his smarts, he was a pretty straightforward hoodlum. Maybe Kurt came into the picture to save you. But, maybe both you and Viktor were supposed to die up there—whether or not Kurt knew that."

"Yes, of course, there's that." Caitlyn meekly responded. Paul didn't even know of some of the strange and suspicious events she had encountered since arriving in Cyprus.

Using this as an opening, Paul went on: "We know why Viktor's friends are after me. I've been spoiling their expensive game of late. But we do need to find out if you are in such danger as well. Beyond that first Saturday we were together in the north, there is no reason that I know of why they might be after you as well."

"After me?" Caitlyn asked, the possibilities and the fear of the possibilities creeping into her voice.

"I know it will be painful, but think back on Viktor's attack on you last evening. Did it seem like a sexual pass or something more personally threatening?"

Caitlyn wrinkled her brow, frowned, and tried to dredge up the experience. "I do remember at the time that it seemed to be awfully clumsy for a sexual pass. I remember almost feeling like laughing—thinking that picking me up bodily in a bear hug and shuffling around seemed like a pretty stupid way to make love. While

257

we were struggling, what I remember most is the sense of laughter echoing all around us."

"By all reports Viktor was not a clumsy romancer, Caitlyn," Paul said softly. "He was popular with the women, and he was considered enough of a charmer to have satisfied his women and to have kept them from complaining or deriding him after they had parted company. It just doesn't seem in character for him to have sexually assaulted a woman who had become well known in diplomatic circles and who was connected to prominent people the likes of Nora Petrou and Eleni and Jacques Piccard—a woman who doubtless would accuse him later if she were able to do so. The lies he told Takis and me at the amphitheater seemed intended to establish that something really bad was going to happen to you. When he had you in this bear hug and was shuffling around, did he seem to be moving in any particular direction?"

"Toward the cliff," Caitlyn replied weakly after some length.

"Can you think of any reason these arms dealers might have to want to get rid of you?"

"No, I'm sorry. Paul, I can't think of anything." But then she remembered something, something she had intended to tell him days previously. "But there *is* that man."

"What man?" Paul asked sharply.

"I'll tell you about him, Paul," Caitlyn said quietly, "but first let me ask another question. I think it might relate. Does any of this have anything to do with Jill Murray's death?"

"It shouldn't have," Paul sighed, "But I just don't know. Jill was not working the same cases I was. She was a genuine economic affairs officer, and she and Alec Stuart were trying to pin down the possibility that Cyprus was being used as a major money laundering center. Alec is still working the case, but Jill apparently was following some new leads in her last couple of days that Alec either didn't know about or isn't ready to tell us about at this point. Why do you ask about Jill?"

"You remember when we were at the castle in Kyrenia and I asked you about those rude men at the harbor café?"

Paul looked confused, but then he remembered and nodded his assent.

"Well, that day I saw one of those men follow Jill Murray out of the harbor, and the other man was watching that British diplomat when we went to the castle—and then was tinkering with your car. And that's not the last time I saw him."

"What do you mean? Where did you see him again?"

"Well, first I'm sure he was following Vassos Petrou and me when we went to Paphos. I saw him at the restaurant at Aphrodite's Rock and later the same day in Paphos. And the next day he was staring at us from a Forest Park Hotel balcony in Platres while we were having our breakfast."

"Having your breakfast with Vassos Petrou at the Forest Park?" Paul bellowed, as he lifted out of his chair.

"Yes," Caitlyn answered hotly. "We had separate rooms, we didn't do anything the least bit questionable—*and*, it's none of your business or concern if we did."

Choosing not to be drawn off on that particular tangent, Paul returned to his chair and to the original purpose of her explanation. "Vassos Petrou. I know you like him, but he keeps coming up in these investigations. He certainly seemed central to Jill's work. I'm going to have to talk to Vassos. With all the other leads going cold, he may be the only key available to unlock this mystery. And the connection with our mystery man might make sense. Any chance he could have been Vassos Petrou's bodyguard? Vassos writes some explosive articles in his paper, and he's been known to hire protection."

"Yes, I thought of that possibility as well," Caitlyn replied. "But then I saw the man again—and so did you, but you obviously didn't recognize him. I sort of thought you would recognize him as the man who followed us from Bellapais back into the Greek sector."

"I thought you hadn't seen the man I saw in Bellapais."

"No, I didn't. But I keep seeing this man, and it makes sense he was the man in Bellapais, although it's still a mystery how he was able to follow us across the Green Line. And we've both seen him since my trip with Vassos."

"Where and when was that?"

"The night of the raid on the yacht at the Larnaca marina. The man passed by us after the police had arrived, and he gave us both a very dirty look—just like he did in Kyrenia harbor."

"Why didn't you tell me this that night?" Paul exploded with exasperation.

"Well, I tried to at the marina, but the police pulled you away when I attempted to talk to you and it was so late I had to get back to Nicosia. I was going to tell you the next time we spoke, but then we had that fight on the telephone about who I should date and, following that, your house got bombed, and then we fought again. I guess it just slipped my mind in the middle of all of that."

"Well, this is something we'll need to tell Koniotis right away. It makes sense that you would be a target for this gang, as well, if they

260

think you had a hand in rolling up their operation at the Larnaca marina. Incidentally, that was Viktor who put the crates on the yacht. I didn't want you to know that at the time."

They sat in silence for a few minutes, both trying to bring more clarity to the muddle.

"I do like Vassos," Caitlyn finally broke the silence. "But I too have suspected he might be involved more deeply in questionable activities than I would like. And now that we're talking about such things, I must admit that last night may not have been the first attempt on my life—if that's what last night proves to have been."

"What do you mean?"

Caitlyn told Paul about her near entombment under the Paphos acropolis and of her fleeting suspicion of Vassos at the time.

She went on to say, "I agree that our next move—*our* next move," Caitlyn said firmly, as a shadow of stubbornness was cast over Paul's face, "is to talk with Vassos. And, since he will be far less suspicious of making a date with me than with you, I propose that I call him when we return to Nicosia and set up a meeting—say in the Garden Café next to the parliament building sometime next Monday?"

"I suppose that makes sense," Paul answered with resignation. "I'll see if we can get Alec there too. He's part of this, and I'd like to corner him into revealing more about what he and Jill were doing."

"I hope," Paul said, as he rose to get ready for the return trip to Nicosia, "you won't have trouble facing the Nora squad for having stayed out all night."

"I seriously doubt she will ever know," Caitlyn answered, as she followed Paul into the room and gave him an affectionate hug when she caught up to him. "I tried calling her early this morning. No one answered at home. When I called her office, I was told she had moved up to her village house for a while. She must have gone straight to the mountains from the play last night. She and Jacques Piccard drove to the play separately, you know."

"No, I didn't know," Paul responded thoughtfully. He seemed to mull this information for a while before putting his shirt on.

Upon leaving the room, the two paused at the door in a lingering embrace and a kiss.

"No regrets?" Paul asked, somewhat apprehensively.

"Truly no regrets," Caitlyn answered promptly and firmly, a twinkle in her eye that Paul had never seen there before.

Chapter Twenty-One

When they had returned to Nicosia, Caitlyn telephoned Vassos Petrou and arranged a meeting for mid-Monday afternoon at the Garden Café, directly across the street from the Cyprus Museum. Paul, in turn, called Alec Stuart and, after a fair amount of arm twisting, got the British diplomat to agree to join them a half an hour before Vassos was to arrive at the café. Paul also informed Takis Koniotis of their plans after he had filled him in on what he had learned in his discussion with Caitlyn. The police inspector approved of the meeting, but he seemed strangely unenthusiastic about the intent to focus on Vassos as the next step in Paul's investigation of Gorodov's activities.

The couple had made their calls from Nora's Gladstone Street mansion. The house was deserted, and Caitlyn was very happy Nora wasn't there. Nora had proved to be much too curious about Caitlyn's affairs for the latter's comfort, and Caitlyn still was not fully prepared to talk about her harrowing experience following the Curium play. In truth, at this point she didn't even know what to tell people about the events surrounding the deaths of Viktor Gorodov and Kurt. When Paul talked to Koniotis, the inspector had said the police were trying to keep the fact that Gorodov had been murdered quiet for as long as possible. Consequently, no one, Caitlyn included, had bothered to devise a story for where she had been and what she had been doing during and since this "accident."

When Paul's conversation with Koniotis was completed, he turned the telephone over to Caitlyn, who told the police official what she could about Kurt Schwin. Koniotis didn't seem all that surprised about her information, and he admitted that he had already learned a few things about the German's background through Interpol. It had, indeed, been Kurt's fingerprints that had been found on the knife that killed Viktor. Caitlyn couldn't decide whether—and how much— Koniotis believed her about her connection with Kurt and the wild coincidence, because coincidence it was, that had reconnected their lives in Cyprus. Caitlyn was disturbed by Koniotis; she found him to be inscrutable most of the time—which she found mildly irritating.

Despite the natural nervousness engendered by being alone with the nocturnal noises in the big, old mansion, that night Caitlyn slept more peacefully than she had for years. She did, at one point, have the old familiar dream of Kurt drifting in and out of her presence—although his features were no longer just beyond recognition in the dream. But she was sure now that this dream would slowly fade away. As gruesome as it was, the knowledge that it had been his fingerprints on the knife that killed Viktor helped to bring closure on her confused emotions over their relationship. No matter what anyone else told her, she would choose to believe that, in the end, Kurt had maintained his love for her and had sacrificed his life for hers. That went a long way toward healing the hurt he had inflicted by choosing to drop out of her life and making her suffer in false mourning.

* * * *

Following a fretful Sunday of unsuccessful attempts to sleep away her exhaustion, Caitlyn awoke early Monday morning fully refreshed. Recent events did not scream out at her from her memory for several minutes. She still had not devised a story to tell her friends about her whereabouts and activities on Friday night, and now it had been absolutely necessary that she do so. Although Takis Koniotis had somehow managed to keep Viktor's death out of the Saturday and Sunday newspapers, the story was prominently displayed on the front page of all of the many Monday papers that had been delivered to the Petrou mansion. Unfortunately for Caitlyn, the English-language papers didn't publish on Monday, so the papers that had arrived were not able to give her much of a clue as to what line they were taking on the death. This, in turn, prevented her from making up a plausible story to match what was being reported. She did note with relief, however, that her name wasn't carried in any of the articles.

"That apparently gives me some respite from the press for now," Caitlyn gratefully reflected. "But some of my friends are bound to start trying to get in touch with me. Nearly everyone I know here was at the Curium play on Friday night—just before Viktor and Kurt died—and all of them saw me with Viktor."

She contemplated her situation while she ate a light breakfast. Checking her wrist watch, she saw that she was doing well on time.

"If I hurry, I can make the first personnel relay from the museum to the Kaliana dig. At least there I will only have Andriko to answer to about Friday night, and I can count on him being more interested in talking about the dig than about Viktor, especially if I just indicate that I left the play with someone else."

Caitlyn was in luck when she arrived at Kaliana. Andriko Visiliou's wife had conveniently gone into labor the night before, so there wasn't anyone at the excavation site who seemed to have any interest in what Caitlyn had done that weekend.

She stopped at the original excavation first, but work there had more or less been suspended and all effort was being furiously applied to the dig she had caused to be started on the other side of the valley. Caitlyn joined the rest of the crew and was just in time to participate in the initial entry into a large, circular, nearly intact structure that had shown up prominently on the electronic soundings the previous week and thus that had become the initial focus of the excavation. As she approached the site, Caitlyn could see one fairly large beehive-like structure, the roof of which was largely in place. Beside and at the back of that structure was a somewhat smaller circular house, the roof of which had caved in entirely. A few workers were busy carrying out the last of the dirt that had been inside the larger structure. Most of the workers, however, were intent on the last stages of lifting the debris off the top of the smaller circular house.

Caitlyn entered the larger structure and was immediately struck with and exhilarated by a fairly distinct wall painting on the opposite wall. The simple, yet elegant schematic of a human figure, its arms raised to the sun, was nearly identical to the figure from the Khirokitia Neolithic area that was on display in the Cyprus Museum.

"Yes," Caitlyn thought in triumph. "I will certainly carbon date what we find here, but now I know I've done it. I've found a new Neolithic site in Cyprus in an entirely new area."

For several hours Caitlyn helped dig out the smaller structure. She once more was in her element, and she was viscerally in touch with a meaningful life's work that blotted away all of the mystery, danger, and pain that had assaulted her life away from this excavation in recent weeks.

When the diggers had broken through the rubble of the smaller of the buildings, they were met with a somewhat grizzly sight. The floor of the structure supported literally piles of human remains, the evidence of which had not been entirely obliterated thanks to the collapse of the roof into a tomblike room and the dry climate of the lower valley. Prominently in evidence were stone weapons that clearly indicated that, at some long-ago point in time, people—probably the village's inhabitants—had been herded into this circular house and slaughtered. In keeping with the Neolithic pattern, the structure had the usual opening in the floor to be used as the tombs of the ancestors. Therefore, the remains found within the main room itself were very unlikely to have been purposefully entombed here by the surviving villagers themselves after some sort of natural calamity.

"Perhaps we've found out why these two excavations are separate and we haven't achieved a Neolithic level at the main Kaliana excavation," said a senior researcher, as he placed a comforting hand on Caitlyn's arm. "We've always believed that other Neolithic sites we found on the island were abandoned during some sort of natural calamity that cleared the entire island of human habitation. But it looks like this site didn't last even that long. Look at the white-coated pottery shards and the stone implements lying around. These are associated with the early Neolithic period of around 7000 BC, not with the later Neolithic, when red ware became prominent. It looks like

267

this particular village was attacked, wiped out, and then abandoned for all time. When habitation returned to this area of the valley, an entirely different site was established."

Caitlyn wasn't really listening. The sound of battle and of women and children screaming had already poured over and enveloped her.

She was watching from the fringe of the pine forest. She had been returning from the upper reaches of the valley, from the shrine itself, when she came upon the carnage in her village. They had had considerable warning, of course, of the growing enmity and suspicion of the foreigners settling on the plain below. Perhaps the clash of the two cultures had been inevitable. The gentle, mountain folk, with their connection with the true spirits of nature and their advanced knowledge of herbal cures and spiritual incantations had somehow raised the ire of the ignorant folk pouring into the plains below from who knows where.

The specific breaking point had been her own fault. When she had come upon the woman at the fringe of the hills who had left her village on the plains to give birth, she should have known that her efforts would be to no avail. She should have spent more effort in communicating to the mother that she was trying to help her and to save the baby. The birthing had already gone on too long. It was a breech birth, and both mother and son were near death when she had come upon them. But what else could she have done? She was devoted to the goddess of healing, the goddess whose shrine overlooking the confluence of the rivers up the mountain valley her villagers had dedicated themselves to maintain. She had built a fire, hauled water from a nearby stream, and delved into her herb pouch. The mother had lived, but no amount of herbal and incantation care had managed to save the baby. But it still was her fault. The mother had no idea she was trying to help; she had not taken the time to try to communicate. She had treated the frightened woman like a dumb animal. She had been guilty of asserting the superiority of her own knowledge and beliefs.

She and the mother had made no connection of understanding, and she had no means of alleviating the fear and horror with which the weakened mother had met the ministrations offered to her and the baby. While she was tidying up her herbs, the mother had gained enough strength and determination to rise, snatch up the dead child, and melt into the trees.

In succeeding days, the village had been attacked twice already. The villagers were totally confused by what was happening. They could not understand why the people of the plains were suddenly attacking them. But she knew why. She was ashamed. And she was doubly ashamed, because the goddess had chosen not to include her in the death of the village below. That could only mean the goddess wanted her due. She turned her back on the carnage to return to the shrine. She would stay there, caring for the shrine, and she would never come back to the profaned ground of her village. But she would return to the lower end of the valley someday. Someday the goddess would release her, so that she could return and help to rebuild the idyllic life her people had lived—until the plains folk had started to settle the land between the marshy mountains.

As Caitlyn snapped out of her vision, she felt slightly nauseous. And so she backed out of the excavation and found a convenient rock that she could sit on and gaze out over the plain toward Morphou Bay.

"The more time passes, the more things stay the same," Caitlyn reflected bitterly. "Some nine thousand years ago here, humans killed humans—all through greed and ignorance. They had the whole island open to them; there surely were so few of them that they could easily have shared this paradise without killing each other.

269

And they showed no effort to understand each other, to learn from each other.

"It happened then, and it is happening now on this beautiful island. There is a long-standing ethnic division that has resulted in physical political division—all based on the apparent basic human inability to get along with each other, on a failure to try to understand, and on greed. That's probably what the deaths of Jill Murray, Viktor Gorodov, and Kurt are based on too. Alienation and greed."

Caitlyn sighed and sadly stared off at the beautiful vista opened out below her to the sea—a vista that incongruously, but almost unobtrusively, included Greek outposts, a UN buffer zone, and Turkish outposts stretched out between her and Morphou Bay. It was here that Paul found her when he arrived to take her down into Nicosia for the afternoon's meeting with Alec and Vassos.

* * * *

The day was glorious, as Caitlyn, Paul, and Alec Stuart met at the entrance to the open-air Garden Café. They had found a somewhat secluded table placed under a grape vine and removed from the street noise of the many buses jockeying for illegal—and obstructing—places to park while their passengers visited the Cyprus Museum across the street. It had been a hot day, but it was late afternoon, and the evening breezes were already beginning to flow into the cultural center of the new city outside the old Nicosia walls.

Although he was pleasant enough, Alec was not being particularly helpful concerning what he and Jill had been working on that very probably had resulted in her death. He did acknowledge that they had been working on a general money laundering problem, but that much Paul had already known from his embassy relationship with Jill.

"As you know," Alec explained, primarily for Caitlyn's benefit, "Cyprus is both economically developed and strategically placed between Europe and the Middle East. Thus it is ripe for being used as a clearing house for tainted money. It's natural that the Americans and British would cooperate in combating this problem. Our resources are thin in Cyprus, so Jill Murray and I were cooperating closely on some of these money laundering issues. We weren't romantically involved; we were just working together on the same problems."

"And how long were you working together?" Paul queried.

"Since Jill arrived on the island. A bit more than a year, I suppose."

"And you only recently seemed to be encountering opposition. Would you say that's a true statement?" Stuart nodded his assent. "Then maybe you only recently hit on activity that caused reaction. Were you and Jill into anything new recently?"

"Well, we had been focusing on East Europe until just of late. And then Jill got some other ideas. I really can't get into that further."

Undeterred, Paul pressed in. "The question of money laundering and the East Europe connection is at the foundation of our current interest in Vassos Petrou," he said. "He is a well-known and vocal supporter of East European banking interests on the island. You know that's why we are trying to pin him down today—to look for his involvement in this whole affair with Jill's murder and possibly with the bombing attempt on me. We're also trying to figure out

271

whether there is a connection to Viktor Gorodov's activities and death. And now you are saying your interest had drifted away from Vassos?"

Stuart gave Paul a meaningful look and then turned to look in Caitlyn's direction. But Paul would have nothing of the evasion. "I believe you know that my ambassador has talked to your high commissioner about this, Alec, and that you know you are supposed to cooperate with me now. We indeed are partners in this. Jill's been murdered and both of our principals are interested in getting to the bottom of her death and of any cases that might have caused her death. Caitlyn has been thrust into the middle of this, too. It's time for us to get on with it. You're saying you have lost interest in Vassos Petrou?"

Stuart sighed and hesitated, but he did now respond to the question: "Yes, that's exactly what I'm saying. I'm saying too much to tell you even this, but I don't want you lighting into Vassos on issues that no longer are relevant to us. And as for the attempt on your life—"

Alec's revelation was interrupted by a succession of loud popping noises and the sound of crashing metal from the street. Alec was under the table in a flash, closely followed by Paul, who dragged a completely bewildered Caitlyn down with him and who covered her body as best he could.

There was a silent pause that seemed to last an age and then pandemonium broke out. People were screaming and whistles were blowing and car horns were honking.

With a curt "Stay here" to Caitlyn, Paul headed for the street, Alec closely in his wake. A shaken, but determined Caitlyn was not far behind.

The block in front of the Cyprus Museum looked like a battleground, a sight that was not helped by the buses that were scattered haphazardly about even on a calm day. Other cars and buses that had been on the move on the street now were stopped, some smashed into others. Their occupants were either struggling out into the open or frozen in shock where they sat. Many people were on the ground and a few of these were bleeding. An unusually large number of policemen were in evidence. Several were gathered around one prone figure near the entrance to the café, and several more were running off toward the municipal theater end of the block. Most had their guns drawn.

"Oh, my God, Paul!" Caitlyn screamed. "Look. It's Vassos."

And so it was. The parliamentarian lay on the sidewalk in the midst of the gathered policemen. He looked like a heap of old rags; a heap of rags with blood oozing from it. He no longer looked like the god that Caitlyn remembered. And from the lack of life-support attention being accorded to the prominent politician and newspaper publisher by the group of policemen, he clearly was already dead.

Paul and Alec had registered the sight, but their attention was being drawn further up the block, toward the municipal theater, and in the direction in which most of the policemen were running. Paul and Alec—and eventually Caitlyn—followed the retreating policemen.

As Paul and Alec approached the imposing theater building, with its column-adorned facade, they saw the black Mercedes. It had left the roadway—a miracle in itself considering the concentration of parked buses along the path—and had careened up the steps of the theater and onto the portico, where it had tried to push its way into the lobby through the main doors.

When they reached the car, they were amazed to see that Takis Koniotis was already there and was trying to retrieve something from the back seat.

Two men were in the car, both obviously beyond repair. One was in the front seat, behind the wheel. The other was in the back seat. Both car and bodies displayed a few too many bullet holes to be functional still. Koniotis fished around in the pockets of the two men and came up with passports, among other paraphernalia. He flipped one of them open so that the other three could see them.

"Diplomatic passports. From Syria," Paul whistled. "No wonder."

"No wonder what?" snapped Koniotis.

"No wonder that one in the back seat was able to follow Caitlyn and me over from the Turkish side. He had a diplomatic passport. I'm going to love hearing how the Syrian embassy is going to explain this."

Koniotis returned to his fishing expedition in the back seat and came up with a pistol. Turning to the two men, he held up the gun by its barrel with a handkerchief, carefully avoiding the handle, and said:

"A Markarov. Any bets against this being 'like father, like son'—that both Nicos and Vassos Petrou were killed by the same gun?"

Paul and Alec did not have a chance to respond, as Caitlyn, having now joined the group, was interjecting, in a small, strangled voice: "It's them. It's them. Oh, Paul, it's them."

"It's who, Ms. Spencer?" Koniotis spun around and asked in a voice that cut through all of the hubbub.

"The two who were following Jill and Alec the Saturday we went to Kyrenia. The one in the back seat there is the same man who was following Vassos and me in Paphos and Platres the following weekend. Oh, Paul, it's them. What does this mean?"

"Yes, that's exactly what I want to know," said Koniotis in an angry but controlled voice, as he turned on Alec, who had been standing there quietly but in a state of sheer horror.

"I want to know what you and Jill Murray were working on and I want to know now," Koniotis demanded. "If this proves to be the same gun that killed Mrs. Murray, and I quite definitely believe it is, it has killed before—not just here but across the world. This particular gun may not kill again, but I seriously doubt the related killing has stopped. I want to know what you and Mrs. Murray were working on. Now, not later, after there are more deaths. I can get this information through the high commission or the American embassy—you know I can now. But I don't have the time. *We* don't have the time. You may be next, Alec. Tell me."

"Money laundering," Alec responded in a small voice.

"Yes, we *all* know that much," replied Koniotis, his tone starting to take on a very sharp edge.

"Palestinian," Alec croaked. "The use of Cyprus by Palestinian splinter terrorist groups for money laundering and international travel accommodation."

Chapter Twenty-Two

Takis Koniotis was stopped dead in his tracks by Maria Solonos as he burst through the front doors of police headquarters the following morning.

"You're going to have to stop leaving the office," Maria quipped. "Every time you come back someone else connected with our cases has died."

"Very funny, Maria," Koniotis retorted in mock anger. "Do you have something for me, or were you just leaving for the day?"

"Here's your list of where these people have lived before. Notice any interesting overlaps?"

"I most certainly do," Koniotis responded, with the first happy note of the day surfacing in his voice. He studied the list further. "In fact, take a look at that as well."

"Istanbul, 1973 to 1975," Maria read over his shoulder. "So?"

"So, that's close enough proximity to the time of the 1974 Turkish invasion to help clear up another one of our mysteries. And look at those other countries as well. And compare those countries and times with these."

"Yes, it's beginning to get a lot clearer now," Maria admitted.

"Do we have an appointment set up with the interior minister yet?" Koniotis asked.

"No, I'm sorry, he's in Athens. Tomorrow afternoon was the first slot I could get."

"Damn. Every minute counts. Well, at least we can get some surveillance out on the street even if we can't get too close."

"Right away," Maria answered, as she swayed off down the corridor.

* * * *

Later, in his office, Koniotis had concluded he wasn't likely to get anywhere further today on the Gorodov case, so he decided to turn back to the newly acquired Petrou case. Luckily, he hadn't had any trouble asserting jurisdiction. If he hadn't been on the scene establishing surveillance on Petrou at the time of the shooting—having known from Conte when and where Petrou was scheduled to appear—it might have been another story altogether. Even then, he might have had trouble maintaining the lead on the murder of a Cypriot parliamentarian if he hadn't found those Syrian passports on the bodies of the assassins. The hit men hadn't been identified as foreigners yet, but they certainly hadn't looked like Cypriots to him.

The inspector turned to his decks of cards. In one sweep, he combined the Money Laundering and Assassination piles. He hovered briefly over the combined Drugs and Arms deck as well with half of a notion of just shuffling all of the note cards into one deck. But, on a hunch, he wavered and finally decided to keep the two current piles separate.

"Vassos Petrou. Yet another lead cut off before we could figure out his role and connection. Why was Petrou hit? We know he was the target. He died before our eyes, and, although a few more were wounded, the hitters were obviously aiming for Petrou alone. We, in turn, got the assassins. Too bad they're both dead, though—although they didn't look like the type who would talk to us a lot even if we had captured them alive. Did they take him out because he was on to them and getting in the way, or did they do it because he was one of them and getting to be too exposed—presumably like Gorodov? Either way, he had been asking a lot of questions. And a lot of those questions were the same ones I've been asking. As a parliamentarian and a newspaperman, it was natural for him to be asking questions. But his questions were becoming quite pointed. And I didn't see him using any of the information he was getting either on the parliament floor or in his newspaper."

"Palestinians. Radical Palestinian factions. Alec Stuart may have given us the key," he mumbled, as he began looking through the new, combined Money Laundering/Assassination deck.

Maria was on the scene once more. "The ballistics check," she was saying. "It is indeed the same gun that killed Jill Murray and Nicos Petrou—and probably countless others."

"Ah, yes," Koniotis replied. "I was sure it was the same gun. And we seem to have a common denominator, which Alec Stuart has reluctantly provided us—the fringe Palestinian terrorists, and most likely the Abu Haddad faction. But that links only to Jill Murray at the moment. What's the link to the two Petrous, I wonder? And to Paul Conte or Caitlyn Spencer, who said one of these assassins has been following them?"

Maria didn't answer the questions—directly—but she did introduce a new element. "While you are wondering, we have been

278

working. Your hit men were a little negligent. There was a hotel key for the Europa Hotel in their car."

"Great," Koniotis's face lit up. "Has anyone followed up yet?"

"Naturally, and I think we can do something for your wondering. Look at what we found in the room."

It was a folder jacket for a boat ticket.

"OK, that gets us closer. It doesn't prove her personal involvement, but it *is* her company. Go get us the necessary search orders."

Maria was off in a flash.

Koniotis twirled his telephone number Rolodex, grabbed at his telephone, and punched in a number. This being unsuccessful, he referred once again to the listing and entered another number. After a short, unsatisfactory conversation, he slammed the receiver down.

"Damn. Not at the house. Her office said she'd gone to the village. The village? Double damn. Why didn't I ask which one? Maria!"

* * * *

Caitlyn hadn't balked at Paul's invitation to spend the night at his apartment. There was no question of going back to the Petrou mansion. Besides not having any idea what to say to or do for Nora Petrou when she heard about Vassos's death, Caitlyn was frightened by all this mayhem about her and about how closely she seemed to have become unwittingly involved in it all. She also couldn't bear the thought of being at the Petrou home when the press arrived there. Any time now they would be ferreting out the true story of Viktor's death, and she was no more ready today to face questions on this issue than she had been the previous day.

She had, of course, been crushed by Vassos's death. As soon as the shock of having recognized the assassins had worn off, the murder of Vassos had swept back into her consciousness and she had almost collapsed on the street. Almost, but not quite. Paul was able, with Koniotis's permission, to get her back to the car and to his apartment.

"Good old Paul. He certainly seems to be there when needed," Caitlyn thought. She had not forgotten his effort to shield her body with his own while the shooting was going on.

To try to help take her mind off Vassos and to keep her beyond the reach of the press, her own friends, and any villains who might still be lurking in the shrubbery, Paul suggested that they go to Laiki Yitonia, the tourist area of Old Nicosia, for lunch on Tuesday. Not having seen the area yet, and agreeing that the best place to hide was out in the open in the tourist section, Caitlyn quickly consented.

Paul parked in the large municipal parking lot that was located in the dry moat across the wall and below the Laiki Yitonia area, and the two walked into the picturesque village within the city, with its narrow walking streets and abundance of cafés and shops. As they moved toward the restaurant Paul had picked out, Caitlyn drank in the splendid chaos of the sidewalk shops. To her surprise and delight she encountered several of her acquaintances from the Kaliana dig, where work had been so successful of late that a day of rest had been mandated. She was thus in a very good mood when they reached the government's own Arhondiko Restaurant in the heart of the district, and she was only mildly surprised to see Jacques Piccard approaching the restaurant at the same time. Not only was Paul surprised—it being unusual for permanent residents, let alone ambassadors, to spend much time in Laiki Yitonia—but he was also visibly irritated at the encounter. Piccard was all charm, however, and insisted that the three eat together. The day being unseasonably pleasant, they opted for the outside tables rather than the air conditioned inside rooms of what had once been a charming old Cypriot traditional house.

Paul's surprise was doubled when no less than Inspector Takis Koniotis also joined the group within minutes of their arrival.

"I was just passing by and thought I'd stop into the Arhondiko for a bite to eat," Koniotis smiled. "What a surprise to find all of you here as well. I hope you don't mind if I join you."

"Likely story," Paul thought to himself, as he said "By all means, do join us." He couldn't resist, however, adding under his breath while Ambassador Piccard was engaged in a discussion with the restaurant's proprietor: "My, you *do* get around. I would think you would have better things to do other than tailing Caitlyn and me." Paul's chief pleasure at the moment was that Piccard was looking a little uncomfortable at the arrival of the police official.

Mercifully, the ambassador did not mention Gorodov's death and Caitlyn's date with him on Friday night at all, but, rather, spent a good deal of time talking about Vassos Petrou's assassination, the latter topic apparently having completely displaced the first in his mind. As they were finishing up their various selections of Cypriot dishes, Koniotis revealed—strictly confidentially—that Nicos and Vassos Petrou had been killed with the same gun.

"How extraordinary," the ambassador intoned. "Assassination with the same gun and virtually in the same spot, but several years apart. I don't know what one can make of that. The two men could not have been further apart in their political views. The father was a far rightist and the son was a far leftist."

"Well, they may have met on one mutual interest," Caitlyn said innocently.

"What do you mean, Caitlyn?" asked Paul.

"Well, I discovered in a discussion with Nora Petrou that she had close ties in the Middle East—even to such countries as Libya. These associations dated back to when she and Nicos were dating in France. Nicos probably had the same associations, and some of these people certainly can be categorized as far leftists."

"Well, thank you for the company," Takis Koniotis suddenly said. And he rose, dropped a Cypriot five-pound note on the table, and was gone—leaving three surprised expressions in his wake.

Paul seemed both perplexed and disgruntled that Jacques Piccard continued to stroll around the area with them rather than breaking off and leaving following lunch. The three entered the small Cyprus Handicrafts Center store that was also just across the narrow roadway from the restaurant, and Caitlyn moved from shelf to shelf, examining the motifs that were being used.

"Oh, look, Paul," she said as she picked up a pottery cruciform statuette. "These are just like the ones at Eleni's handicraft center. Or at least like some of those at the center," she corrected herself, as she turned the figurine over and over in her hand. She contemplated the figurine for a while and then turned to the two men.

"Now I remember what has been bothering me all this time. The figurines at Eleni's workshop. Eleni said that they were all alike, but the ones that were being packed for shipping were slightly heavier and their backs were round and smooth. The ones out on the shop floor were hollow and their backs were open. There also was a bit of powdery white residue on the figurines that were being shipped. I remember at the time that it seemed strange that such a few, inexpensive figurines were being packed so carefully for shipment in a crate. Oh, well, I'm sure it doesn't mean anything. It just bothered me at the time. You remember, don't you, Jacques? You were there."

"Yes," Piccard replied. "Yes, now that you mention it, I remember that shipment. It was just a small order going to Marseilles."

"To where?" Paul asked.

"To Marseilles, France."

"On a Ledra corporation vessel?" Paul asked.

"Certainly. Why do you ask?" responded the ambassador.

"Just a few loose ends may be coming together," Paul answered. he had already learned to take Caitlyn's observations quite seriously. "Both Marseilles and the Ledra corporation vessels have been flagged for watch in our narcotics trafficking cables. I'm sure you are aware of that, Ambassador. The French embassy gets this reporting and you yourself are connected with the Ledra Consolidated companies."

"Indeed I am," answered Jacques. "And I have been volunteering to work with the shipping end of the business expressly in an attempt to help track down and dispel these rumors. You don't think the handicraft center could be involved, do you?"

"Anything is possible, Ambassador. Do you know if Eleni was on friendly terms with Viktor Gorodov?"

"Yes, I think they were very good friends. They saw each other often," Piccard answered.

With a flashback of the venomous stares Eleni and Viktor had shared at the Curium play, this assertion of close ties sounded strange to Caitlyn, and she was just about to interject a question into the conversation, when Paul continued. "We haven't released the information yet, but I'm afraid Viktor Gorodov was heavily involved in an illegal trade racket here in Cyprus. We knew he was receiving small-caliber arms in the north. We now suspect that he was trading those guns in the south for drugs from Lebanon's Al-Biqa' Valley to be shipped elsewhere. France certainly seems a likely destination."

The ambassador looked shocked.

Paul concluded: "We've heard strong rumors that drugs are entering France at Marseilles by way of Cyprus. But until now we had no inkling how these drugs were getting out of Cyprus. We hadn't observed Gorodov's involvement at this end of the transaction."

"And you think my aunt might be involved in smuggling drugs? You think she's shipping out the drugs inside handicrafts?" Piccard asked these questions with considerable disbelief in his voice. And then, after he had contemplated the situation for a while, "Yes, it's just possible. She's an ambitious, driven woman, and she has not been at all pleased by my efforts to participate in the business operations of the handicraft center. You saw a glimmer of that yourself, Caitlyn, when you visited the handicraft center. Eleni was quite snappish with me when she found me near the shipping room.

Well, there's one good way to find out. She's up at Kakopetria. let's go up there and find out what she has to say."

"What? Right now?" Paul asked with dismay.

"Yes, immediately," Piccard answered. "It will be a great embarrassment to me if my own family business is implicated in drug trafficking, and I cannot rest now until I have gotten to the bottom of this. If you don't want to go, I'll go alone. If you do go, we can use my car, and I'll bring you back to pick yours up later."

Paul was caught. It didn't meet with his instructions or investigation schedule to be running off and confronting Eleni Piccard directly on this business. But, if the ambassador was going to break open the case and reveal to his aunt that she was under suspicion—as he was clearly intent on doing—then Paul had to be there as well. But then, what about Caitlyn? He turned and gave her a quizzical look.

She read his mind implicitly. "Oh no, you don't," Caitlyn responded firmly. "If you are going, so am I."

With no further discussion, they started for the mountains.

* * * *

Immediately after having checked in at his office, Koniotis had his car keys back out of his pocket and was setting out to track Maria down. She found him first, however.

"Did you manage to find out about the village?" he asked, as he kept moving down the hall.

"Yes. It's Kakopetria."

"They're *both* at Kakopetria? How convenient."

"Yes, isn't it?" Maria said to his retreating back.

Koniotis called back over his shoulder: "Call Alec Stuart at the high commission. He said he'd stay put until I called. Tell him I'm on my way over to pick him up for a little out-of-town trip."

Chapter Twenty-Three

When Jacques, Paul, and Caitlyn arrived in the forecourt of the Old Mill Inn in Kakopetria, Jacques told Paul and Caitlyn to go on up in the building's small elevator and that he would follow after he had parked the car and when the elevator had come back down.

As the elevator wheezed slowly up the building, Paul and Caitlyn could hear loud quarreling above them. And then, as the elevator had finally achieved the restaurant level and doors were contemplating whether they wanted to open, the couple heard a woman's terrified scream.

The doors parted to the scene of two women struggling mightily against the restaurant's balcony railing. It was clear that one of them was about to go over the side, but it was unclear who, if not both, was trying to push the other over the railing.

Paul and Caitlyn stood transfixed in the elevator door. In what appeared to be slow motion, two figures appeared from the top of the open stairway at the other end of the balcony and separated the wrestling women, each dragging one of the women back from the brink and firmly holding her in a bear hug. Both women continued to struggle, their eyes electric and still shooting shards of lightning at each other. Alec Stuart held Eleni Piccard and Takes Koniotis held Nora Petrou. Both Paul and Caitlyn turned their eyes on Eleni, beseeching her for an explanation.

"Eleni, what is going on here? What have you done?" Paul asked searchingly.

Eleni turned wild eyes on the source of this outburst, but it was Alec who answered. "I'm afraid this particular party is Nora's, isn't it Nora? What do you have to say for yourself, Nora?"

Nora didn't have anything to say for herself, so Alec continued for her. "Nora was trying to help Eleni off the balcony. Weren't you, Nora?"

This time Nora gushed out with vehemence: "I hate her! I have always hated her. She kept my husband from me. He was always telling me that he should have married her rather than me and that he would have if I had not trapped him into marriage while we were in France. They were lovers; they continued to be lovers. Everyone says it was Kakopetria he loved. But I knew it was Eleni that he loved— what he loved was to make love to Eleni in Kakopetria!"

Eleni gave a sharp little cry: "It's not true. Nicos and I were never lovers. We were old childhood sweethearts, but we were never lovers. I loved only my own husband."

Nora became sullen but subdued.

Alec continued. "Yes, yes, Nora, I'm sure your compulsion about Nicos and Eleni was connected with it all in your mind. But that isn't the primary reason you tried to kill Eleni today, is it?"

Nora went rigid and looked away, but she didn't speak.

"Oh, no. You tried to kill Eleni today for the same reason you had Jill Murray and your own stepson murdered. Isn't that right?"

288

Nora went white and screamed at Alec: "Why are you doing this to me?" Then she collapsed in Koniotis's arms. Almost simultaneously, Caitlyn slumped against Paul, and he walked her past the others and settled her at a table.

"And your reason for trying to kill her was probably the same," Alec went on, "as your reason for having had your own husband murdered."

"Yes, I'm afraid your little game is up, Mrs. Petrou," Koniotis took over the conversation from Alec. "You see, we know now that you have been using your bank to launder money for some of the radical Mideast terrorist organizations and your travel agency to provide them with untraceable travel tickets and hotel reservations. You had your terrorist friends kill both Jill Murray and Vassos. And there is every reason to believe you had your own husband killed by the same people. Had he also discovered your involvement with terrorists and that your ultraconservative views were just a pose? And did he threaten to expose you, as well?"

No response—which might have been the only response that was necessary.

Koniotis continued. "The shooting of Vassos the other day—as poignantly as it paralleled the death of his father—wasn't the first attempt on his life, was it? From what Ms. Spencer tells us about her trip to Paphos with Vassos, your friends tried to drop the acropolis onto their heads. But the final shooting was a desperate act, wasn't it? Vassos had told you he knew what you were up to and that he would expose you. It was just your luck that you cut him off just before he was to meet with Paul Conte and Alec Stuart, a meeting at which he likely would have revealed everything he knew about your operations. And Eleni. I'm sure you know, just as we knew, that Vassos and Eleni were in close contact over the past few weeks. You knew for the same reason we knew. Like us, you were having Vassos tailed to see what he was up to. No, Nora, you haven't picked today to assault Eleni because of some possible old love affair between her and your husband. You tried to kill Eleni today to tidy up loose ends in your operation with the terrorists."

"Rubbish, all rubbish," Nora spat back. "It's all wild lies."

"No, I'm afraid not, Nora," Alec interjected sadly. "Jill and I had already zeroed in on you."

Nora shot Stuart a strange, shocked look, but the British Intelligence officer continued: "The night Jill was killed we had you under surveillance in Larnaca. We had already seen you meet up with known agents of the Abu Haddad terrorist organization at the Four Lanterns Hotel. My mistake was in breaking off that surveillance to tail Vassos when he passed by. For all we knew at the time, he was part of your scheme. Jill stayed to follow you. But Jill never got home alive."

Koniotis immediately picked up the thread of accusations. "And just earlier today, thanks to your careless hit men friends, we got the last linkup we needed."

Nora looked up at Koniotis, hatred still in her eyes, but with a new sharpness of attention.

"Your friends apparently were overly confident they would get away at the museum square. They should have cased the area better, and then they would have realized that people can't just speed past the Cyprus Museum during the tourist season because of all the parked buses. They might also have noticed the extra police present in the square, called there to keep tabs for us on Vassos. The assassins had a key to their room at the Europa Hotel in their car. And they were careless at the hotel too. Although we couldn't find their outbound boat tickets, they hadn't destroyed the travel agency's folder jacket in which the tickets had been delivered. And I must say, Nora, that someone at your travel agency was quite negligent—or wholly unsuspecting of the nature of your covert business—as well. Otherwise they would not have put the tickets in a Petrou Travel Agency jacket, now would they? Our people have obtained a warrant and are searching your company and personal records even now. Any bets they won't find some interesting discrepancies?"

All eyes had turned to Nora. But Nora wasn't paying any attention to any of them anymore. Her eyes were wide in fright and concern and were directed to a point beyond the seated figure of Caitlyn. Her mouth opened wide, and she let out a shriek: "No, no, don't do it," she cried, as she lurched toward Caitlyn and fell to the floor at the bark of three loud pistol shots.

* * * *

In the ensuing chaos, Alec also went down with a groan, Koniotis leaped at Eleni and dragged her behind a table. Paul reached for Caitlyn with the same intent—but only came up with empty air, lost his balance, and fell to the floor.

Caitlyn wasn't where Paul had expected her to be, because Jacques Piccard, his pistol still blazing at a point across the balcony—a point that had been blocked from his line of fire by the advancing Nora Petrou, had grabbed Caitlyn himself and was using her as a shield. He backed toward the outer staircase that he had been quietly ascending during the last few minutes while the attention above had been riveted on Nora and while Paul and Caitlyn had assumed he was waiting for the elevator to return to the parking lot level.

As they reached the top of the stairs, however, Caitlyn adroitly lurched to the right and hit Piccard in the midsection with a mighty backswing of her rump. Then she artfully fell forward. *She wasn't in the mood to fall down these particular stairs again if she could avoid it.* Piccard's gun skittered across the tile floor and over the side of the balcony, as the ambassador himself undiplomatically tumbled backward down the staircase.

Both Koniotis and Paul raced past Caitlyn and down the stairs.

Caitlyn struggled to her feet and hobbled over to Nora Petrou. The woman was dead. Her facial expression was frozen in an incongruous mixture of fright and devotion, her murderer and imagined lover having been the last object her eyes had seen in life.

Koniotis and Paul returned with Jacques Piccard, who looked no worse for wear for his tumble down the stairs than Caitlyn had looked after her last visit to Kakopetria and stumble down the same stairs.

"Where in the hell did Piccard come from?" queried Koniotis. "If I'd known he was lurking anywhere around, I'd have had the place crawling with policemen."

"He came with us," Caitlyn mumbled. "Or, more correctly, we came with him. We came up here to talk with Eleni."

Eleni had been ministering to Alec. "He's all right," she announced. "It was just a graze. He just fainted a bit and is coming around already. My God," she interjected, "It seemed like Jacques was firing at Alec and me, not at Nora."

"You're half right, Mrs. Piccard," Koniotis said, hands with a firm grip on the ambassador. "I think he was shooting at you, not at either Nora or Alec. And you know why."

Eleni gave a short cry and plunked down in a chair.

"You mean Jacques is involved in Eleni's arms and drugs shipment scheme?" Caitlyn asked.

Eleni gave Caitlyn a withering look.

"No, Caitlyn," Koniotis answered. "Only Jacques can take credit for masterminding the arms and drugs operation. Isn't that right, Mr. Ambassador?"

Piccard was too busy contemplating his fingernails to respond.

Koniotis continued. "But he thought Mrs. Piccard was the last person alive to have enough pieces to put this puzzle of his guilt together. And she was the last person alive he wanted to have the power of this knowledge over him. You yourself, Ms. Spencer, seemed to be unknowingly holding some of the puzzle pieces as well. I would not have been surprised if you had suffered some sort of unfortunate 'accident' while in his presence."

Both Caitlyn and Paul reacted with surprise and consternation. Both remembered at the same time the near 'accident' Caitlyn had had at the Larnaca marina.

"He's already tried to kill Mr. Conte," the police inspector went on relentlessly. "He probably lured you both into coming up here with him today to Mrs. Piccard's place so that he could deal with all three of you at once. He didn't kill Mrs. Petrou on purpose. Of all of us here today, she was the least threat to him. She merely got in the way as he was trying to silence the rest of us. What do you say, Ambassador Piccard? Am I wrong?"

No answer.

"Piccard and Gorodov were in this together. We've been putting some background material together. The two met in Russia when Piccard was assigned there and probably instantly recognized in each other the mutual values of greed and ruthlessness. Gorodov undoubtedly maintained good connections with the Russian and East European arms suppliers as that area of the world broke up and privatized. He eventually conveniently wound up here in a UN job, which enabled him to travel freely between the two zones. For his part, Piccard had the necessary family connections with useful businesses—the export company and the shipping company. He had worked for the French defense ministries, where he also apparently learned a lot about small arms. He also served in Lebanon, where he could—and apparently did—make friends with groups that had access to drugs and that were happy to exchange these drugs for illegally acquired and untraceable small arms. Is that perhaps where you met up with Kurt Schwin?"

Caitlyn felt her heart stop, but there was no response or reaction from Piccard, and Koniotis continued: "Both Piccard and Gorodov were diplomats and thus enjoyed legal protections and had access to official information on efforts to counter arms and drugs smuggling. Both also had far better access across this island than do the authorities of either zone.

"But you should not have trusted your own office secretary to help with the arms deliveries," Koniotis lectured Piccard. "And, if you were going to trust her to help with your dirty work, you should have trained her to keep her gloves on throughout the transfer. There were prints from one of her hands all over the crates we seized from the Zygi shipments. And, if you were going to use someone so close to yourself, you should not have changed your mind and had her thrown under a Paris subway car by your terrorist friends in France. You sent her home on an unscheduled vacation, a leave that Paris wanted to deny but that you personally insisted on."

"Not a shred of truth," muttered Piccard. "Besides, I have diplomatic immunity. I refuse to say any more, and I demand to see your foreign minister."

"I'm sure my foreign minister will be delighted to see you as well, Mr. Ambassador," Koniotis calmly replied. "Just as I am sure your own government is going to look forward to seeing you. They have been very interested in and concerned about the narcotics that have been flowing through Marseille. Perhaps your biggest mistake was in having failed to find some other country than your own in which to inject these filthy drugs."

Piccard didn't look quite so sure of himself anymore.

"I'm sure one of the questions my foreign minister will be asking you, Mr. Piccard, is where you were after the play at Curium last Friday night. I'm confident we will be able to place you at the scene of Viktor Gorodov's death. You ordered the firebombing of Paul Conte's house, hoping he was in it, because he was messing up your shipments, which inevitably would have made some very nasty clients of yours turn on you. And you ordered Schwin to kill Gorodov after Gorodov took care of Caitlyn Spencer for the same reason you ordered your secretary killed—because you believed Gorodov had been hopelessly compromised and would lead us back to you. That's true, isn't it, Mr. Piccard?"

Caitlyn held her breath. This was where her neat little rationalization of Kurt's feelings for her were going to come crashing to the ground. But, again, there was no corroborating or countering response from the ambassador.

"But the irony is that you think all of these revelations result from various lucky or brilliant deductions by the embassies and by the police authorities, don't you?"

Piccard was suddenly alert, his eyes fixed on Koniotis, as were the eyes of everyone else present, except for Eleni, whose own eyes were boring into her nephew and slitted in concentrated hatred.

"Would it interest you to know, Mr. Piccard," continued Koniotis, "that your aunt, Eleni, has probably known—not suspected or about to learn, as you were afraid, but known—about your activities for some time and has been dropping subtle hints to any and all concerned?"

"That's right," gasped Paul. "Just the other day I was telling Caitlyn that I first got an inkling about Gorodov's activities because, when Eleni was in a tipsy condition at a party nearly a year ago, she sketched out such a scheme to me involving diplomats. That's also when I started suspecting Eleni of being involved."

Koniotis smiled grimly. "I doubt that Mrs. Piccard was as tipsy as you thought, and I assure you that, although she has probably known her companies were being used by Jacques for his scheme, she was not, herself, involved in these operations. I'm sure also that you misunderstood what diplomat she was fingering. You came to believe it was Viktor Gorodov, and you were at least partially correct, because

Gorodov *was* involved. But Mrs. Piccard was probably trying to expose Jacques Piccard. Isn't that so, Mrs. Piccard? Don't you think it's time for you to tell us why you let this scheme go on so long without directly reporting it to the authorities?"

All eyes were on Eleni, no less Jacques Piccard's, whose face increasingly took on a look of desperation as she unfolded her story.

"Yes," Eleni started. "I knew what sort of man my husband's nephew was and I maneuvered to get him to Cyprus. He didn't earn his ambassadorship to Cyprus; I bought it for him—without his knowledge. I encouraged him to become involved in the shipping end of the Ledra companies, believing that it was inevitable that he would use his connections to set up some illegal activity. And he didn't disappoint me. It was Vassos Petrou who told me about the arms and narcotics scheme Jacques had devised and put into operation. Petrou had fallen onto the scheme while investigating the issue for his newspaper. Vassos also told me about Viktor Gorodov's involvement. Vassos was conscientious. He wanted to expose the activities at once. But I kept putting him off by saying we needed harder evidence to make the charges stick."

Eleni's voice was becoming harder. Her bitterness was surfacing.

"Yes, I told Paul Conte and others about the possibility of such an operation, but I didn't tell them directly. I wanted them to start figuring it out for themselves and for them to hurt Jacques and to start slowly cornering him in, strangling him until he couldn't breathe—which is exactly what happened. When Jacques started to feel suffocated, I also started working on him directly myself, making

297

him believe that he couldn't trust his own, and only, support—that mercenary—Viktor Gorodov."

Piccard had withered in his seat, but he still looked very confused, as did almost everyone else in the room.

"But to what purpose, Mrs. Piccard?" Koniotis asked quietly. "How could you hate your nephew so much as to feed on his own human weaknesses so cynically and disastrously?" And then even more quietly: "Does this have anything to do with Jacques having served in the French embassy in Istanbul from 1973 to 1975?"

Eleni looked sharply at Koniotis. A new sense of respect was in her expression. Jacques Piccard's eyes also showed a new glint of understanding and fear. Eleni closed her eyes for a moment, made her decision, and answered:

"I wanted Jacques to suffer just as my husband and son must have suffered. Yes, this has everything to do with where Jacques was on the 10th of August, 1974—the last day I saw Guy and Pierre alive. You thought I'd never find out, didn't you, Jacques?" she spat across the room.

Jacques looked horrified. He started to speak but then bit back his words and withdrew into himself, no longer closely following the indictments raining down on his head.

"Yes, a French diplomat can't just slip over to another country unnoticed in the wake of an invasion force. I had little trouble finding those who were willing to tell me that it was you who Guy and Pierre went down to Kyrenia to meet that day. And I knew you had always resented Guy and his standing in the family companies. And knowing what kind of man you are, it didn't take much imagination for me to understand what had happened. All these years, however, I

298

never knew what you did with the bodies. I only had recurring nightmares of my loved ones in pain and gasping for air. It wasn't until just last week that I figured out what probably happened. Vassos told me—his people had read the story in a Turkish Cypriot newspaper. You lured them into Kyrenia Castle, didn't you? You somehow gravely wounded them and threw them down an isolated air shaft to die in the dark, didn't you? *Didn't you?*"

Caitlyn went pale. She had already envisioned this scenario. History was repeating itself. How could this be?

Eleni was out of her seat and clawing at Piccard, who had withdrawn entirely into another world and was making no attempt to defend himself.

Paul and Koniotis gently pulled Eleni off Piccard and placed her back in her chair, where she was reduced to gasping sobs.

Taking Piccard in tow, Koniotis, Paul, Caitlyn, and a recovering Alec Stuart slowly descended the stairs to the parking lot. As they reached the mid level, they heard it—and they could still hear it even after they had reached Piccard's car and had started for the police station.

A woman's uncontrolled, hysterical—but triumphant— laughter, rolling down the mountain.

Epilogue

Caitlyn Spencer had returned to her parents' home in the Central Virginia foothills of the Blue Ridge Mountains. She had managed to serve out her five-month Fulbright Program stint in Cyprus. But the tumultuous events of her time on the Mediterranean island had worn on her emotions and nerves to the point that she gladly fled the island at the end of her contract. As always in such times, she had sought the security of her parents, who now lived in a lovely antebellum home near where her mother's ancestors had first settled when they had come to the New World, in the rolling hills of Virginia. She wasn't at all sure where she wanted to go from here, and she thought either her mother or father could help provide direction.

It was late morning of her first full day back in the States. She had slept for nearly ten hours following the long parade of flights across Europe to New York and then back down the East Coast. As she stood at the bedroom window, tracing the hazy blue crest of the mountains to the east with her eyes, she couldn't help seeing the similarity with the Troodos Mountains she had just left. What was very different about the Virginia landscape, however, was what she was able to see between the house and the mountains. Emerald-green,

300

white fence-laced hills undulated towards the mountains, with majestic trees punctuating the horizons. Cyprus, in vast contrast, had been much more arid, its greens more dusty than vibrant. As she stood at the door to the second-floor balcony, her forehead pressed against the window pane, Caitlyn debated which of the landscapes was more compelling. Certainly this one was more peaceful. But, then, perhaps she just was not able to separate the disturbing and turbulent events she had encountered in Cyprus from its majestic landscape.

Pulling herself out of her reverie, she moved toward the stairs to seek out one of her parents. She found her mother first, at the desk in her den off the living room, spectacles perched on the end of her nose, and poring over enlarged photographs of ancient Grecian urns. Caitlyn had learned the evening before as the trio were returning from the airport that her mother had been asked to bring some chronological order to a collection of Grecian artifacts. The collection had recently been donated to the nearby University of Virginia by an elderly gentleman who had been far more art enthusiast and lucky collector than researcher and historian.

Mrs. Spencer smiled somewhat absently at her daughter and started to rise to greet her. Caitlyn waved her mother back into her chair, knowing that when she was absorbed in puzzling out one of her artifact mysteries, she had great difficulty in pulling away.

As her mother sank back into the desk chair with a sigh and picked up a magnifying glass, Caitlyn began circling the walls of the den. She knew it wouldn't be more than a couple of minutes before her mother had unraveled whatever specific query she was pursuing at the moment and would be ready to visit with her daughter.

301

For the first time in her life, Caitlyn was really seeing the accumulation of her mother's busy lifetime on the shelves that lined the den. Her mother hadn't put her artifacts on display like this until she and her husband had moved to the Virginia countryside from their cramped Boston townhouse. This had occurred after Caitlyn herself had started graduate school and was preoccupied with initiating her own life.

What Caitlyn's mother had collected, mostly ancient pottery from all corners of the world, staggered Caitlyn. It truly was an impressive collection. Caitlyn had had no idea how seriously her mother had taken her interest and expertise in ancient artifacts and only now was beginning to realize the influence she must have had on Caitlyn's own decision to pursue archaeology. Until now, Caitlyn had been assuming that she had been primarily influenced by her father, a university historian.

Caitlyn looked at her mother, who was busily flipping from photo to photo and occasionally zeroing in on a minute feature with her magnifying glass. The younger woman felt a new-found love and affection welling up toward the older woman. She had reached the far corner of the den and her eyes were arrested by a framed, obviously old parchment rendering of a coat of arms hanging just beyond the reach of the light.

"What's this?" she asked reflexively.

"Um?" her mother muttered, her attention not engaged enough to look up.

"This coat of arms. Whose is it? It looks familiar." The shield was marked off in four sections. The upper right and the two bottom sections reflected fierce, crowned red lions, rising in attack. The

302

background for one section was a blue and white horizontal stripe, for another plain white, and for the third yellow. The upper left field bore a gold Jerusalem cross on a white background. The shield was backed by crossed swords and topped with a jeweled crown, the sign of royalty. Blue banners fluttered from the sword handles down each side of the shield. There was writing on the banners, but Caitlyn could not make the letters out in the dim light.

Another distant "Um?" was heard from the other side of the room. This was followed by an "Ah ha!" and a sparkling laugh, as Caitlyn's mother slapped the photographs down on the desktop. She obviously had solved her little mystery.

"Now, what was it you were asking, Caity?"

"This coat of arms. I've never seen it here before, but it looks familiar."

"Oh, I just found that in one of my boxes a couple of months ago. That came down through my family. I think it's our ancestral coat of arms or something. Something to do with the crusades and Jerusalem, or Armenia. I can't rightly remember. I think it's from our French line."

"French line," Caitlyn queried with surprise. "I thought you were Canadian, Mother."

"French-Canadian, my dear. Just like you Americans, most Canadians came from somewhere else. My family came from France—or, at least, one line of it did. The family name started with an 'L,' I think. Now what was it?"

"Lusignan," Caitlyn's voice was small and distant, almost as if she was beginning to withdraw into herself.

"Yes, that sounds like it." Caitlyn's mother gave her a sharp look. "How did you know that? I didn't know you had studied my family's history."

"You said something about Jerusalem or Armenia," Caitlyn continued.

"Yes. I think it's all written out on the back of the picture. Turn it over and look for yourself."

Caitlyn took the frame down with shaking hands and turned it over. The inscription there read, originally in French, but with a note card with English translation taped below "The arms of Charlotte, Queen of Cyprus, Jerusalem and Armenia, with the insignia of the Order of the Sword."

Caitlyn nearly dropped the coat of arms in the realization that her mother's ancestry, and therefore her own as well, traced back to the late years of the Lusignan dynasty in Cyprus. Queen Charlotte had been the next-to-last of the ruling monarchs. It had been she who had escaped back to the European mainland from Kyrenia Castle and abdicated to her half brother James in the mid-fifteenth century. And Caitlyn's Cyprus visions had predated this event. It was dawning on her that her ancestors had had a link to the island. She knew that she should understand why. Now, what was it she had envisioned from the Queen Charlotte period? And why did some of her visions of Cyprus far predate the Lusignan period?

Caitlyn stumbled a bit and steadied herself by reaching out to the edge of the shelf next to where the coat of arms had been hung. Her hand brushed against a pottery object, and she gently grasped it to keep it from falling off the shelf. Her eyes focused on the object. It was a pottery, cruciform-shaped female figure. The familiarity of the figure shot through Caitlyn like a lightning bolt. It was nearly identical to the Neolithic Cypriot figures that Eleni's handicraft center had been making, the ones that had been used to smuggle drugs.

Caitlyn's mother had moved to her side as she had stumbled. She gently took the figurine from Caitlyn's hand and rearranged it on the shelf.

"Where did you get that?" Caitlyn managed to form the words in a natural tone, although it required a great deal of effort.

"I found that with the coat of arms. It came down through my family as well. It isn't anything I've acquired myself. I've been meaning to work on dating it and discovering its origin."

"I think you'll find its Chalcolithic period from Cyprus," Caitlyn said evenly.

"Oh, my. Do you really think it's that old? Why that would make it some 3,000 years BC I don't think I have anything nearly that old. On second thought, that might make sense, however. There's a Cypriot branch of my family, as well, and it would naturally go back further than the French."

"I don't understand? Cypriot branch. I knew you traced your family back to someone who went on Crusade and who was on Cyprus with Richard the Lionhearted. But I didn't know there was a family connection with Cyprus."

"Oh my yes," Caitlyn's mother answered somewhat absentmindedly. "The ancestor who went on the Crusades with King Richard *joined* the Crusades in Cyprus. He was from an old Cypriot family. That's why I was so pleased you were going to Cyprus on that archaeological project. I knew you'd be delving into your own heritage. Didn't I discuss that with you? I know I intended to, but one

305

gets so wrapped up in their work, you know. I'm sorry, of course, that the experience didn't work out well for you."

Now it was starting to come together. It was beginning to make sense at last—if any of the mysteries of life made sense. Her flashbacks in Cyprus had not just been vivid imaginings set off by some sort of instantaneous deep connection with Eleni Piccard. It was a gift. She really did have a gift to connect with the past. And her own past connections with Cyprus and with her own ancestors and those of Eleni Piccard had brought her gift into sharp focus. She knew now that all she had gone through over the past five months had had a purpose. History did repeat itself and it was a continuum of spiraling cycles rather than a straight line of tenuously linked generations. This could be both frightening and reassuring. It did, however, emphasize the importance of her archaeological work.

Her mother's voice cut back into Caitlyn's consciousness: "Oh, but, Caity. Where are you going? I thought we'd take in a winery before lunch."

"No time, Mother, I've got to pack again."

"But," Caitlyn's mother fluttered. "Why are you leaving again so soon? I thought you wanted to discuss your future plans with your father and me."

"No need now, Mother," Caitlyn's wafted down from the stairwell. "You've been a big help. Thanks. I can clearly see my future now. It's the same as my past, and it's been staring me right in the face."

"Can't you wait for your dad to return? We were going to have a nice salad for lunch. Where are you going?"

"I'm going home. Back to Cyprus!"

Gina Drew

Gina Drew is a retired American foreign service officer who specialized in investigating and countering international crime and espionage and who still travels the world in both the imagination and in fact.

www.cyberworldpublishing.com

www.ingramcontent.com/pod-product-compliance
Lightning Source LLC
Chambersburg PA
CBHW070549260626
47161CB00002B/550